M000279439

For a frozen moment the shooter maintained his position as if he were between rounds at a firing range, and I pushed through and practically crawled over the people scrambling to find safety in the small space and I probably damn near trampled several, but I dove at the little bastard and shoved him against one of the steel serving tables.

Breathing hard, I yelled, "Take him!"

But our captive was shooting again, orange-blue flames licking out the barrel of the .22, and bystanders were falling like clay pigeons over five or six seconds that felt like forever. Finally he was clicking on an empty chamber.

Five wounded besides Kennedy were slumped on the floor here and there, in various postures of pain and shock. Bob was spread-eagled as if nailed to a cross waiting to be raised into proper crucifixion position, precious blood pooling like spilled wine and shimmering, reflecting the popping flashbulbs...

Too Many
BULLETS

by **Max Allan Collins**

A NATHAN HELLER NOVEL

A HARD CASE CRIME NOVEL

A HARD CASE CRIME BOOK
(HCC-160)
First Hard Case Crime edition: October 2023

Published by

Titan Books
A division of Titan Publishing Group Ltd
144 Southwark Street
London SE1 0UP

in collaboration with Winterfall LLC

Print edition ISBN 978-1-78909-946-1
E-book ISBN 978-1-78909-947-8

Design direction by Max Phillips
www.signalfoundry.com

Typeset by Swordsmith Productions

The name "Hard Case Crime" and the Hard Case Crime logo are trademarks of Winterfall LLC. Hard Case Crime books are selected and edited by Charles Ardai.

Printed and bound by CPI (UK) Ltd, Croydon CR0 4YY

Visit us on the web at www.HardCaseCrime.com

For DAVE THOMAS
friend and collaborator.
Today's topic…

AUTHOR'S NOTE

Although the historical incidents in this novel are portrayed more or less accurately (as much as the passage of time and contradictory source material will allow), fact, speculation and fiction are freely mixed here; historical personages exist side by side with composite characters and wholly fictional ones—all of whom act and speak at the author's whim.

"*Success was so assured and inevitable
that his death seems to have cut into
the natural order of things.*"
JOHN F. KENNEDY
ON HIS BROTHER JOE'S WARTIME PASSING

"*This could very easily happen.*"
GEORGE AXELROD, SCREENWRITER,
THE MANCHURIAN CANDIDATE

"*If they're going to shoot, they'll shoot.*"
PRESIDENTIAL CANDIDATE ROBERT F. KENNEDY,
APRIL 1968

TOO MANY BULLETS

PART ONE

The Path Through the Pantry

June 1968

ONE

At the end of this narrative, certain guilty people go free. You may even feel I'm one of them. Some will pay, while others will not, enjoying the unearned happy remainders of their lives. And any reader inclined to dismiss everything ahead as a conspiracy theory might keep in mind that conspiracy—like robbery and rape, murder and treason—is a real crime on the books. History, I'm afraid, is a mystery story without a satisfying resolution.

But know this: I did get some of the bastards.

The sullen sky seemed to know something we didn't. Fog lingered over a wind-riled sea under a gray ceiling while a mist kept spitting at us like a cobra too bored to strike. Gun-metal breakers shooting white sparks rolled in like dares or maybe warnings.

It was a lousy day at Malibu Beach, so of course Bob Kennedy was helping his ten-year-old son Michael build a sandcastle while twelve-year-old David swam against the tide—like Mr. Toad, going nowhere in particular—and nine-year-old Mary and eleven-year-old Courtney laughed and danced in the relentless surf.

U.S. presidential candidate Robert F. Kennedy wore an unlikely loud pair of Hawaiian swim trunks and a nubby short-sleeve shirt as light blue as his eyes. I had on borrowed red swim trunks and my own Navy blue polo, the patriotic complement of my pale Irish complexion undone by a tan realized lazing around the pool at the Beverly Hills Hotel on better days.

I was, and for that matter still am, Nathan Heller, president and founder of the A-1 Detective Agency out of Chicago, putting time in at our Los Angeles branch. In such instances the Pink Palace (as the Beverly Hills Hotel was known) provided me with a bungalow, a perk for the A-1 handling their security. I'd come out this afternoon to this private stretch of sand at my friend Bob's request.

None of us called him Bobby, by the way. Not even Ethel, who was in the beach house playing Scrabble with two other kids of theirs, sixteen-year-old Kathleen and fifteen-year-old Joe. Normally all of them would be frolicking in the California sun, only of course there wasn't any. The wife and older siblings had shown enough sense to come in out of the chill wind off the ocean, away from fog drifting over the water like the smoke of a distant fire.

Bob Kennedy was forty-two and I was a year younger than Cary Grant, a fit 185 pounds with my reddish brown hair graying only at the temples. Bob was fit too, five ten and slender, wiry in that way that keeps you going. But he'd been campaigning his ass off and had admitted to me he'd damn near collapsed after doing 1,200 miles in twelve hours—Los Angeles, San Francisco, Watts, San Diego and back to L.A.

"Ethel and I slept till ten today," he'd admitted.

I was here filling in. Ex-FBI man Bill Barry had come down with Montezuma's Revenge after the Cesar Chavez swing, and tonight at the Ambassador Hotel I would mostly be at Ethel's side when her husband was braving crowds. I was already wishing I hadn't said yes and the frosty breakers rolling in and the spitting wind had nothing to do with it.

Bob had called last night.

I said, "Bill was in charge of security, right?"

That familiar nasal high-pitched voice came back with, "Uh, right. That's right."

"How many people does he have working for him?"

"None."

"What does that mean, none?"

"Bill's all the security I need."

"Oh, that's crazy. I can bring half a dozen guys along and—"

"No. The hotel took on extra guards. They have something like seventeen men in uniform lined up."

"Okay. How much LAPD presence?"

"None."

"Does that mean the same thing as the other 'none'?"

"It does. Nate, police presence sends the wrong message. Anyway, I, ah, am not on the best of terms with Chief Reddin."

"Jesus Christ."

"Oh, He'll be there, pursuant to availability."

That caustic sense of humor often caught me off guard, and before I could muster a comeback, he said quickly, "Come out and have lunch with us around noon and we'll talk more."

He'd already told me he was staying at film director John Frankenheimer's. My name would be left at the guard shack where you entered the Malibu Colony. Well, at least the director of *Seven Days in May* maintained *some* security.

The two girls in their swim caps and one-piece swimsuits were splashing each other and laughing and now and then their joyful yelps would escalate into little girlish screams.

Bob tousled Michael's hair and left him in charge of castle building, then joined me on our towel-spread patch of beach.

"That's the one consolation if I lose," he said.

That famous boyish face had deep lines now and the blond-tinged brown hair had gray highlights.

"What consolation is that?"

"Spending more time with my kids."

"You really think you might lose?"

He shrugged a little. "Touch and go. And if I do win, there'll be a world of bitterness to overcome."

"McCarthy you mean."

Bob nodded. "Already a lot of resentment from Gene and, uh, his young supporters."

"Tell me about it," I said. "My son is campaigning for him."

"Good for him. How old is Sam now?"

"Twenty-two. Another year of college and he'll be draft fodder."

Bob's mouth tightened. "Not if I can help it."

Sam, my only child, was a senior taking Business Administration at USC. He still lived at home in Bel Air with my ex-wife and her film director husband, who was no John Frankenheimer but did all right. When I was in town, Sam would bunk in with me at my Pink Palace bungalow. We'd go to movies, concerts, sporting events; he'd let his old man buy him good meals. We got along well.

"Fuck you, Dad!" he'd said this morning.

I had just told him about my call from Bob. That I'd be working security for the RFK campaign tonight.

Sam was a good-looking kid, by which I mean he resembled me, excluding his shoulder-length hair and mustache (and MCCARTHY FOR PRESIDENT t-shirt and bell-bottom jeans). I suppose twenty-two wasn't really a kid, but when you're a year younger than Cary Grant, it seems like it. We rarely argued and hadn't talked politics beyond both being against the war in Vietnam, neither of us wanting him to go off and die in a rice paddy.

I hadn't discouraged his work for the McCarthy campaign. And when Bob announced his candidacy, late in the game, I didn't reveal how I felt about the two Democratic candidates... that I considered RFK way more electable than that aloof cold fish Eugene McCarthy. Richard Nixon, who had been batting away all comers in the Republican primaries, was a tough, seasoned candidate who'd be hard to beat, though his lack of charisma would be a boon to a Kennedy running against him.

We were in the living room of my pink-stucco bungalow, a modest little number with rounded beige and brown furniture, vaulted ceiling, fireplace, and sliding glass doors onto a patio. I was on the couch and my son stood ranting and raving before me.

"Haven't we had *enough* of these goddamn Kennedys? Eugene McCarthy puts his career on the line, takes on a sitting president and shows America that evil S.O.B. LBJ is vulnerable! Your *Bobby* sees what Senator McCarthy has pulled off and decides to just, just…horn right in!"

"I'm not going to argue with you, son."

"Of course not, because you know damn well that Bobby Kennedy doesn't have a single solitary idea, much less a plan, on how to get us out of the goddamn Vietnam quagmire!"

I sighed. "McCarthy can't beat Nixon, Sam. Hell, he can't beat Hubert Humphrey for the nomination. But Bob could beat 'em both."

Sam was pacing now. "How long ago was it your 'Bob' was saying he'd back Johnson, despite all the anti-Vietnam talk? He's a phony, Dad. A goddamn fucking phony. Just another politician. Another *Kennedy.*"

The last thing I wanted in the world was for my son to go to Vietnam. But sometimes I thought the military wouldn't be such a bad experience for him.

Of course, he'd have to live through it.

"This isn't worth us working ourselves into a lather," I said. "Bob is an old friend, and he's in a jam with his security guy dropping out. This is just a job, a favor really, for a friend."

His chin crinkled; he looked like a baby with a mustache.

"Are you going to vote for McCarthy if he gets the nomination?"

"Are you going to vote for Humphrey if *he* gets it?"

His eyebrows rose and hid in his hair. "Fuck no! Why even *vote* in that case?"

"Oh, I don't know. To save your spoiled ass?"

He threw his hands up in sullen surrender. "I'll get my things. You're heading back to Chicago tomorrow, right? I'm going back home now. Good fucking *bye*."

I could have told him what I believed would happen, which Bob Kennedy surely already knew. Even if Bob won delegate-rich California, that left New York, where many resented the way he'd put his presidential bid above his senatorial duties. Bob did not have a lock on the convention by any means, but even if the Kennedy magic and emotion didn't sway the delegates to him, he could almost certainly squeeze the vice presidency out of Humphrey and move that old liberal away from Johnson's war policy and onto the RFK anti-war view.

The presidency *would* be Bob's, though maybe not till 1976 —a year that had a ring to it. But what did I know about politics, except that aldermen could be bribed?

Sitting next to me on the beach with his knees up, Bob said casually, "I'm thinking of offering McCarthy secretary of state."

"Gene or Joe?"

Bob's laugh was short but explosive. "A dead secretary of state *would* be easier to handle."

Even now Bob took heat over his time as a counsel on McCarthy's infamous investigative committee; but he'd always stayed loyal to Tailgunner Joe, who was a longtime friend of the Kennedy family. Less well-known was that Bob had gathered the facts that guaranteed McCarthy's censure by the Senate.

"With everything at stake," I said, "you seem pretty cool-headed to me."

"There's a reason for that."

"Oh?"

He was looking at the sea or maybe his kids or both. "Much as I dislike campaigning, it's going well. I get a good feeling from the people—finally they're not wishing I were Jack…or imagining I *am* him. I think I'm finally out of my brother's shadow. Making it on my own."

"You are, Bob. You really are."

His eyes turned shyly my way. "Nate, I, uh…know we've had our differences. The, uh, Marilyn situation in particular. All the Castro nonsense. My judgment wasn't always…well, I appreciate you putting that behind us. Still my friend. Helping me out."

"Don't work so hard," I said. "I already stopped and voted on my way here."

That Bugs Bunny grin. "Ah. But *how* did you vote?"

I allowed him half a grin in return. "That's between me and my conscience. Of course you know what my conscience is."

A nod brought his hunk of hair in front along with it. "That gun you carry. An ancient nine millimeter Browning, isn't it?"

His look said he remembered the weapon's significance: my father killed himself with it when I disappointed him by joining the Chicago PD and dancing the Outfit's tune for a time.

"I think your father would be proud," he said, "of how you turned out."

"Not sure you're right. But your father surely must be pleased."

"Hard to tell. Hard to tell."

The old boy's ability to speak had been impaired since his stroke almost ten years before.

Bob's eyes went to the sea again. "But, uh, about that conscience of yours. The artillery I mean."

"What about it?"

"You still carry it?"

"I do."

"I don't want you doing that tonight."

My laugh was reflexive. "Well, surely Bill Barry's been packing all this time."

"No." The voice was firm, the blue eyes on me now, ice cold and unblinking. "I haven't allowed it and he's honored my request."

"Well, I'm not about to!"

His chin neared his chest. "Look, there's no way to protect a candidate on the stump. No way in hell. And if I'm lucky enough to be elected, there'll be no bubble-top bulletproof limo like Lyndon's using. What kind of country is *that* to live in? Where the President is afraid to go out among the people?"

I was shaking my head, astounded. "Jesus, Bob, what kind of morbid horseshit is that?"

He stared past me with a small ghastly smile. "Each day every man and woman lives a game of Russian roulette. Car wrecks, plane crashes, choke on a fucking fish bone. Bad X-rays, heart attacks and liver failure. I'm pretty sure there'll be an attempt on my life sooner or later, not so much for polit-ical reasons but just plain crazy madness. Plenty of that to go around."

I guess I must have been goggling at him. "If you think some-body's going to take a shot at you—"

The blue eyes tightened. "I won't have everyday people get-ting caught in my crossfire. Not for discussion, Nate. If you want out, I'll understand."

The girlish cries from the water's edge turned suddenly into screams, shrill and frightened and punctuated with Mary's "Daddy! Daddy!" while Courtney called out, frantic, "David's in trouble!"

And the boy was too far out there, floundering, much too far, and Bob sprang to his bare feet and accidentally caused a wall of the sandcastle to crumble as he flew across the beach and ran splashing into the water and dove into the crashing waves.

The undertow had the child. His sisters were dancing in the surf again, but a wholly different dance now, fists tight and shaking. I got to my feet feeling as helpless as the young girls. So much tragedy had visited this family! Dread spread through me like poison.

I staggered to the edge of the beach where surf lapped, as if there might be something I could do. There was: the two children hugged me, sobbing, and I hugged back. Terrible moments passed, the waves roiling as if digesting a meal.

Then Bob and the boy popped up, the father having hold of his son, and wearing a vast smile in the churning tide. Both were on their feet by the time they reached the edge of the surf, the child coughing up water, the man bracing him, a scarlet red smear across Bob's forehead from a cut over one eye. Both bore skinned patches here and there from where they'd gone down to the pebbly bottom in the water just deep enough to drown.

I was there to help but Bob smiled and waved me off, his arm around the boy as the little party trooped back toward the starkly modern white house, boxy shapes spread along as if spilled there, their many picture windows on the ocean like silent witnesses.

The interior of the Frankenheimer beach house was all pale yellow-painted brick walls enlivened by striking modern art, bright colors jumping. The living room and dining room were separated by framed panels of glass that added up to a wall. From the stereo came the Mamas and the Papas, Simon & Garfunkel, the Association, adding a soft-rock soundtrack. During the buffet lunch, the film director's lovely brunette wife, actress Evans Evans, circulated slowly in a hippie print dress, making all their guests feel important, which they probably were.

Bob was buttonholed by several apparent political advisors I didn't recognize as well as two Teds I did—his brother Edward Kennedy, who I'd never met, and Theodore White, the Presidential historian I'd seen on TV. The kids were on the patio with a college boy who'd been hired to look after them. The children, bored with eating, were fussing over David and his Band-Aid badges of courage.

Ethel, who I'd been told was pregnant but didn't look it in her white sleeveless almost-mini dress, approached me with a smile, bearing a small plate of appetizers that didn't seem touched. Her words didn't go with her smile: "I suppose Bob told you not to carry a gun."

"He did."

She shook her head. "I wish you wouldn't listen to him. He's getting more and more death threats. I'm getting worried."

"He's stubborn about it."

A weight of the world sigh was followed by a quick angry grimace. "He's so darn *fatalistic*. Just resigned to accept what comes. Yesterday—in Chinatown, in San Francisco, in a convertible, as usual? A string of firecrackers went off and I thought they were shots and practically jumped out of my skin. I ducked down to the floor, just frozen. Bob? He just kept smiling and shaking hands. Barely flinched."

She shook her head, laughed a little, and was gone. That may have been the worst laugh I ever heard.

A row of televisions had been brought in, and guests huddled around the screens after lunch to keep tabs on the sporadic network coverage; exit polls were coming in and the news was promising. Bob was not among the watchers.

I found him out by the circular pool, stretched between two deck chairs, napping. He looked like hell, a cut over his eye from the drowning rescue, as unshaven as a beachcomber. He was in another polo and baggy shorts and sandal-shod bare feet.

An easy mellow voice said, "Not the best image for our favorite candidate."

I glanced to my right. John Frankenheimer—in a crisp pale yellow linen shirt, sleeves rolled up, and fresh chinos—might have been one of his own leading men. He stood a good three inches taller than my six feet, his black hair only lightly touched with white at the temples, his heavy eyebrows as dark as Groucho's only not funny. We'd met but that's all. He motioned me over to a wrought-iron patio set with an umbrella. I brought along a rum and Coke; he carried a martini like an afterthought.

"At least he cleans up good," I said.

"He does. And takes direction." He took a sip. "Or anyway he does now."

"What do you mean he does now?"

His shrug was slow and expressive. "A while back, his guy Pierre Salinger flew me from California to Gary, Indiana, where Bob was speaking. To shoot a campaign spot. And I'm not cheap."

"I believe you."

"Bob said he only had ten minutes to give me, and I said then why fly me out from California? The result was awful— the camera caught his hostility. Later he called me at my hotel and asked if we could try again. I said we could if he gave me an hour and a half to show him how not to project cold arrogance. He took that on the chin, and I went over and did the spot fresh, and we've been friendly ever since."

"He'll need makeup for that cut."

He studied his slumbering subject. "I'll give it to him. Saved his son, I hear. He is one remarkable guy. Ever hear about how he taught himself to swim? Jumped off a boat in Nantucket Sound and took his chances." Chuckled to himself. "Then when Bob and Ethel honeymooned in Hawaii, he saved some guy from drowning."

"He should've been a lifeguard."

"This country could *use* saving."

I sipped. "You're following the campaign with a camera crew, I understand?"

He nodded. "Yes, for a documentary but also to grab footage for more campaign spots. He'll need both to beat Tricky Dick. You've known Bob a long time, I take it."

"We go back to the Rackets Committee. And before."

That seemed to confuse him. "You worked for the government, back then?"

"Not directly. I have a private investigation agency in Chicago. We have a branch here. The A-1."

And that seemed to amuse him. "Oh, I know who you are. 'Private Eye to the Stars.' How many stories has *Life* magazine done about you, anyway?"

"Too many and not enough."

His laugh was a single ha. "Too many, because it's like James Bond. Him being a spy is an oxymoron."

"Or just a moron. And not enough, because publicity is good for business. Do I have to tell a film director that?"

He gestured with an open hand. "Necessary evil."

I leaned in. "John…your film *The Manchurian Candidate*? Stupid question, but…do you think that could happen in real life?"

His smile came slowly and then one corner of it twitched.

"Yeah," he said. "I do."

Bob was coming around.

"Star needs makeup," Frankenheimer said, getting to his feet. "And better wardrobe."

I needed to find a bathroom to put on my Botany 500 for tonight. I'd have to leave my nine millimeter Browning at the Ambassador desk to be locked in their safe. When I emerged I found Bob looking similarly spiffy in a blue pin-striped suit and white shirt. Frankenheimer was in the process of expertly daubing stage makeup on the candidate's scraped, bruised forehead.

In the background, Ethel was giving orders to that college kid to deliver her children to the Beverly Hills Hotel, where they rated two bungalows to my measly one. We would be driven by Frankenheimer to the Ambassador and Ethel, not ready yet, would follow in another vehicle.

The film director's car turned out to be a Rolls-Royce Silver Cloud. Even though I had made *Life* a couple of times, this would be my first ride in one. Frankenheimer, who'd seemed so cool before, betrayed himself otherwise on the Santa Monica Freeway with his bat-out-of-hell driving. When he accidentally raced right by the Vermont off-ramp and got snarled up in the Harbor Freeway exchange, he swore at himself and pounded the wheel.

"Take it easy, John," Bob said from the backseat. "Life is too short."

TWO

At just after seven, Frankenheimer was tooling his silver Rolls along Wilshire, his enthusiasm behind the wheel curtailed by downtown traffic and red lights. Bob and I, a couple of his advisors opposite us in the limo seats, watched Los Angeles slide by like postcards. With the sun still up but heading down, this was what the movie people called Magic Hour, when dusk painted the City of Angels with a forgiving brush. Young people owned the sidewalks, college kids in preppie threads, hippies friend or faux in huarache sandals, boots motorcycle or cowboy, hair straight, curly, shoulder-length or longer (as the song went), Quant cut or rounded Afro. Minis on the go-go, would-be rockers in Cuban heels, heads bobbing with beaded bands, hooped earrings, rainbow colors (clothes *and* people), peace signs and raised fists, nothing quite real in a twilight where the fireflies were neon. Times they were a changing, and the man in back next to me seemed to be wondering where he fit in.

"Your people, Bob," I said.

"Some of them. McCarthy has the A and B students. I have to settle for the rest."

At left the Brown Derby's giant bowler, half-swallowed by its mission-style expansion, squatted on a corner. Our destination was at right, past a white obelisk looking like a pillar of salt left behind by God in an Art Deco mood—

A
M
B
A
S
S
A
D
O
R
HOTEL

—with a bronze statue of a scantily clad goddess at its base posed, they say, by Betty Grable.

On a city block's worth of landscaped grounds between Wilshire and West Eighth Street, at the end of an endless drive, sprawled the Ambassador, a city within the city. Its twenty-four unlikely acres in downtown L.A. included tennis courts, Olympic-size pool and golf course. Eight coral-colored stories spawning wings were home to twelve-hundred-some rooms, restaurants, movie theater, post office, beauty and barber salons, shop concourse and the palm-swept rococo Cocoanut Grove, where Rosemary Clooney was headlining.

From its Jazz Age beginnings, including half a dozen Academy Award ceremonies until well after World War II, the Ambassador had been Hollywood's favorite movie-star haunt—from Harlow, Gable and Crosby to Marilyn, Sinatra and Lemmon. But in an era where Jane, not Henry, was the reigning Fonda, the Ambassador seemed about as up to date as when Charlie Chaplin was in residence.

Still, it didn't seem like anything could kill the old girl. In these times, the Ambassador depended on tourist trade, business seminars and political events—tonight, in addition to the optimistic Kennedy campaign's planned victory celebration, were two election night parties, Democrat Alan Cranston and Republican Max Rafferty for nominations in the upcoming Senate race.

Frankenheimer drove around to a rear door off the Cocoanut Grove's kitchen, parked back there and said he needed to check on the guerrilla film crew he'd positioned in the Embassy Room. The rest of our little group went up the freight elevator to the fifth floor, where Bob and Ethel had been staying in the Royal Suite during the California campaign. Tonight two more rooms had been added, 511 across the hall, a war room for aides and advisors, and 516 for invited press, down the hall a ways.

I stayed near the candidate, either at his side or just behind him while he dropped by the press room where he smiled in his shy way, shaking hands here and there. The twenty-five or so journalists packed into the room, which had been cleared of its bed, included some of the most famous in the country—Pete Hamill of the *New York Post*, columnist Jimmy Breslin, Jack Newfield of the *Village Voice*, and that unlikely patrician sportswriter George Plimpton.

The smoke was no thicker than the fog had been over the Pacific this morning, and the rumbly murmur of voices trying to be heard might have been Jap planes making a comeback. A small open bar had been set up to accommodate the large gathering, doing a mighty business.

Breslin and Hamill somehow managed to buttonhole Bob. Both knew me a little and granted me the kind of nod a New York celebrity grants a Chicago nobody, and started in telling the candidate what he needed to do to win in New York. Youthful Hamill, with a shock of reddish red hair to rival Bob's brown mop, grinned and smoked and leaned in aggressively, like an off-duty Irish cop.

"You better score a knockout tonight, champ," Hamill said, "if you wanna make a dent in all this anti-you shit."

Bob chuckled but his eyes were already weary. "What is all this New York animosity *about*, anyway? My guys say it's going to be a bloodbath."

Hamill grinned like the Cheshire Cat. "Face it, Bob—New Yorkers are haters! They can work up an unbelievable amount of bile. They resent wakin' up in the morning."

Breslin, a fleshy-faced bulldog who always seemed half in the bag, leaned in, raving, ranting. "It's the goddamn Jews! Ya gotta get through to the Jews if you want a shot!"

Trying to conceal his distaste, Bob swept back his bangs and said, "Personally, *I'd* like to get through to the *New York Times*," and excused himself and we got out of there.

Right across the hall from the Royal Suite, 511 was almost as packed as the press room, in this case with aides in no-nonsense work mode. No bar in here but plenty of cigarette smoke, and little phone stations had been set up everywhere, with a bank of three TVs against one wall. The overall murmur was muffled out of respect to those on the phone. In this nearly all-male room, a sea of rolled-up white shirts and a few suits of campaign spokesmen, those not phoning were huddled in little groups, strategizing. Frank Mankiewicz, Bob's campaign press secretary, seemed in charge of what reminded me of a wire room.

Mank, who I'd met a few times, was a former journalist whose late father had written *Citizen Kane*, the most famous newspaper movie of all. I wasn't sure if that was ironic or just fitting.

Someone once described Mank as a rumpled little guy who might have been a used-car salesman, but his dark eyes were as shrewd as they were sad and his high forehead seemed to tell you a good-size brain resided.

"Good," Mank said to Bob, "you're here. I've got Senator McGovern on the line. He's got excellent news for you from South Dakota."

Bob went to a nearby phone and I stayed back with the press secretary. I asked him why he wasn't with the journalists.

"Half the time I am," Mank said. "But this room is even more important. We're feeding the media that *didn't* make the trip. Look, uh, Nate, make sure Bob spends time on a speech. When he wins tonight, and goddamnit he will, every network will be covering him. That victory speech needs to sing. He'll listen to you."

"You do know I'm just a bodyguard. And not even allowed a gun."

Mank touched my suitcoat sleeve. "He likes you."

"Why?"

"Two reasons. You never kiss his ass. And you never ask about his brother."

Bob came back smiling, raising a fist chest high. "More votes than McCarthy and Humphrey combined. Got both the farmers *and* the Indians. Carried some of the Indian precincts one hundred percent!"

A smile was buried somewhere in Mank's furrowed puss. "Exit polls say the same about the blacks and Mexicans."

Bob nodded and his smile faded. "If I could just shake loose of McCarthy. I shouldn't be on street corners in Manhattan begging for votes when I could be chasing Humphrey's ass all over the country."

"Ass" was unusually salty language for Bob.

"Bob," Mank said through a battle wound of a smile, "I told you this would be an uphill struggle." Then he patted his candidate on the shoulder and went back to work.

Next stop was the Royal Suite, entering into the expansive sitting room, a celebrity cocktail party where laughter rose like bubbles in a glass. The maybe one hundred supporters, stuffed in the space with its own bank of TVs and bar, were blissfully unaware of the frustration their hero was suffering on a night that seemed headed to victory.

The eclectic mix encompassed L.A. Rams tackle Rosey Grier and decathlon champion Rafer Johnson, astronaut John Glenn and Civil Rights activist John Lewis, labor leader Cesar Chavez and comedian Milton Berle. Plenty of Kennedy people, too, including Pierre Salinger and Bob's sisters Pat Lawford and Jean Smith with her husband Steve, a trusted RFK confidante. Others were familiar but I couldn't connect with names. No sign of brother Ted, though the four Kennedy kids from out at Malibu—David, Michael, Courtney and Mary—were winding through the crowd as if in a garden maze, in pursuit of waiters with trays of *hors d'oeuvres*.

This was where Frankenheimer had wound up, chatting with a guy with white curly Roman hair and black eyebrows; Bob said this was *On the Waterfront* screenwriter Budd Schulberg. Listening politely, cocktail in hand and trying not to look bored, was a slender curvy beauty about forty. For a moment I thought she was the film director's actress wife, but no. Her flipped-up, lightly sprayed brunette bob was maybe too young for her, but there were worse sins. She looked familiar to me, or was that wishful thinking?

Frankenheimer, like everybody else, had noticed Bob come in and motioned for him to come over. As his appendage, I made the trip.

We said quick hellos minus any introduction of the brunette, who was either famous enough that I should have known her or dismissed by these two chauvinists as window dressing. But she had a nod and a pink lipstick smile that encouraged me to ignore the twenty-year gap between us. My self-esteem went up.

So did Frankenheimer's eyebrows, as he gestured Nero-style with a downward thumb. "Bob, I checked out the Embassy Room—must be nearly two thousand people crammed in. Security guards and fire marshals are routing the overflow into the ballroom downstairs. I wish the fucking networks would declare a winner—the natives are getting restless."

"With these new computerized voting machines," Bob said, "you know it's going to be damn slow. Could be midnight before we know."

The director shuddered. "Hope to hell you're wrong. It's stifling down there. People may start passing out. And frantic! Chavez has a marimba band going at times. At least I'm getting good footage—lots of cute girls in straw hats, white blouses, blue skirts, red sashes. Chanting 'Sock it to me, Bobby.' "

"Well, *that's* embarrassing," he said with a shudder.

The brunette spoke for the first time. "For the record, *I* did *not* wear a straw hat for the occasion, or a sash." She did have a white blouse on, silk, and a navy skirt, short but by no means mini.

Bob gave her a half-smile. "I never dreamed you had, Miss Romaine."

Now I remembered her.

I noted that she seemed at ease in front of the candidate; being here made her somebody in the campaign.

Schulberg was saying, "If you win big tonight it'll be thanks to black and brown people. Don't forget that, Bob, if you find yourself making a victory speech. You're the only white man in this country they trust."

"If Drew Pearson hasn't changed that," Bob said glumly, referring to a column that laid the Martin Luther King wiretap at his feet.

Frankenheimer said, "Bob, what's this about me going up with you on that postage-stamp stage for your big speech? You don't want to be seen with *me*!"

Bob gave him the "What's Up Doc?" grin. "I can't be too particular, campaigning."

"A Hollywood director standing next to you on that dais is *lousy* for your man-of-the-people image. Surround yourself with Chavez and that guy from the Auto Workers, Schrade. Best I just wait back behind the stage till you finish."

Bob thought about that for a second, then said, "When I say, 'Let's go on to win it in Chicago,' or something to that effect, you go collect your Rolls. Wait for us by the kitchen, then drive us to the factory."

"What factory?" I asked.

"*The* Factory," Frankenheimer said, addressing the slow student in the classroom. "Nightclub over on North LePeer that Salinger has a piece of." To Bob he said, "I'll have a table waiting for you and Ethel with Roman Polanski, Sharon Tate, Jean Seburg, Andy Williams…"

The glittery list went on. How did Bob's man-of-the-people image fit in with jet set hobnobbing and riding around in a Rolls-Royce?

Misreading me, Bob said, "You can skip the nightclub baloney if you like."

"That," I said, "is exactly the kind of place you *need* a bodyguard."

The brunette, who'd been taking all this in, flashed me a chin-crinkly smile and said, "Who do you think you're fooling, Nate? You just want to meet Sharon Tate."

So she remembered *me*, too.

"Well," Bob said to me, almost irritated, "I don't need a bodyguard here. I'm obviously among friends. I'm going across the hall to check on Ethel and maybe get away from this madness for a while."

I fell in after him, but he turned and raised a warning forefinger, then wound through the bodies casting smiles and nods like manna to the masses, and went out.

I turned and Frankenheimer was gone. Schulberg, too.

That left the brunette, whose cocktail glass was empty.

"Let me get that freshened for you," I said, wanting to be useful to somebody.

"Sure. Ginger."

"And what, seven?"

"No. Ginger and ginger." Her very dark brown eyes flicked with amusement in their near Cher setting. "You don't remember me, do you?"

"Sure I do. You're on TV."

"Guilty. Just guest shots and bits. Never did land a series for all the pilots I shot."

"In the war?"

Her laugh was nice, throaty but feminine. "I fought a different war than you."

We were threading through the rolled-up white shirt sleeves toward the bar where a Chicano guy in a tux jacket was making drinks for a steady crowd and wishing he were anywhere else.

"*I Dream of Jeannie*," I said. "Harem girl, right? *Bewitched*. Salem-style witch, only glamorous?"

Her mouth was wide, in a nice way; it widened further in a smile no whiter than a Bing Crosby Christmas. She said, "You don't look like somebody who watches that kind of pap."

"If the pap has Barbara Eden or Elizabeth Montgomery in

it, I'll lower myself. Now, if you had a juicy role on a *McHale's Navy*, I'd never know."

We were in line at the bar.

"I've been on that and worse," she confessed. "Now, you? You look more like the *Have Gun — Will Travel* type."

I *wished* I were traveling with a gun. "*Maverick*'s more my style."

The cat eyes narrowed. "Weren't you a consultant on *Peter Gunn*? Wasn't that *based* on you?"

"That's the rumor. And I *do* remember you, Miss Romaine. Nita. But not entirely from situation comedy appearances."

It had been a good five years, and only that one evening. A very nice evening though. Ships that docked in the night.

We were at the counter now and the bartender gave Nita her ginger ale and made me a rum and Coke; and I made a friend forever stuffing a five spot in his tip jar.

The chairs and couches were long gone but we found a corner to sit in, on the floor, like kids at an after-prom party. She sat with her knees up and a lot of her pretty tanned nylon-free legs showing. Like we said in the service, nice gams. They probably still said that on *McHale's Navy*.

"I'm hoping," she said, after a sip of her ginger ale, "that you remember me for more than my TV walk-ons. Neither Barbara nor Elizabeth are big on giving other girls much airtime."

"Guess I haven't seen you turn up on the tube lately," I admitted. "But you're still acting?"

The eyes were big and brown; the Cher makeup was overkill, as naturally lovely as she was. "My agent claims I am. Calling myself a 'girl' is a little sad, don't you think? I'm at that age where casting directors say nice things that don't include, 'You've got the part.' "

"You look young to me."

"Sure. But you're, what? Sixty?"

A gut punch but I still managed to laugh. "Maybe, but then I never claimed to be a 'boy.' "

"Oh, I *know* you're a boy. I remember Vegas even if you don't."

I shrugged. "My memory is pretty good for a man of my advanced years."

It had been a JFK campaign event. She'd been heading up the Young Professionals for Kennedy. I asked her if she was doing the same thing for Bob.

"Not quite. I'm attached to the Kennedy Youth campaign. Kind of a den mother for the *actual* girls out fundraising. I help with secretarial work, too. When you're an actress in this town and don't care to wait tables, typing a hundred words a minute comes in handy."

Smoke drifted overhead forming a cloud that promised no rain, despite the room's pre-thunder murmur.

"About Vegas," she said.

"What about Vegas?"

"I was a little drunk."

"Not on ginger ale you weren't."

"Well, I wasn't drinking ginger ale. Tonight is work, so I'm not drinking. What I mean about Vegas is…uh…I'm not always that easy."

"Oh, hell, I am," I said.

That made her laugh.

"Or anyway," I said, "I used to be, before I got so elderly."

Her mouth pursed up like a kiss was coming, but it was a promise not kept. "I bet you still do all right with the 'girls'—or maybe the ladies. Are you married, Mr. Heller?"

"No. Why, don't you keep up with my press?"

She put a hand to her bosom. "No, I'm sorry, since the acting roles slowed I've had to cancel the clipping service."

I shrugged. "I can catch you up easy enough. I have one ex-wife and one son who, this morning, said 'Fuck you, Dad,' because he's for Eugene McCarthy. How about you?"

"No children. One ex-husband. I'm fussier about husbands now. I'm looking for a prospect about, oh, sixty, who is very well-fixed. What they used to call a sugar daddy."

I nodded sagely. "You know, I have certain connections at a prosperous private detective agency. I could arrange a bargain rate for locating such a rare catch."

We sat and talked that way for a while. We laughed quite a bit. I didn't recollect her being that funny back in Vegas, but then she admitted being tight that night. I said that's just how I remembered her, with a sexual tinge that got me playfully slapped on the sleeve. I did not tell her that I also recalled how beautiful she had looked naked with neon-mingled moonlight coming in the windows of my Flamingo bedroom.

Barbara Eden and Elizabeth Montgomery who?

About then I noticed the guy ordering over at the bar—about five-eight, average build, in gray slacks and a dark sweater over a button-down white shirt on this hot June night. Tan with curly bushy black hair including sideburns, his eyes striking me as both furtive and sleepy. Two PRESS badges clipped together around his neck with what I recognized even at a distance was one of the PT-109 tie clips that Bob and his people sometimes handed out.

"You need another refill?" I asked Nita as I got to my feet. She didn't, and I added, "Well, save my place. I need to freshen mine."

Other than the guy in the sweater with the double press passes, the bar was in a momentary lull. I stepped up just as the Chicano bartender announced, "Scotch and water, sir," handing a glass to his curly-haired customer.

Conversationally, I asked, "What paper?"

"Uh, pardon?" He blinked at me, hooded eyes going suddenly wide.

"What paper are you covering this for?"

"Uh…freelancer. Something this important, you know, someone will want it."

"You have any I.D. you can show me, besides those press
passes?"

"Who's asking?"

"Senator Kennedy's security chief. Let's see your I.D."

He smiled nervously. "Okay, you got me."

"Have I."

"I'm just a fan. Bluffed my way in. Snatched a couple of
passes. So sue me."

I nodded sideways toward the door. "You're on your way out.
Leave the drink."

He had a trembling look now, his voice defensive. "Oh yeah?
Let's see *your* credentials!"

I put my glass on the counter while the bartender watched
with amused interest. I plucked the Scotch and soda glass from
the guy's grasp and set it down, too. Then I took the curly-
haired interloper by an upper arm and walked him out quick
enough that he barely maintained his balance and during our
exit I only had to say "Excuse me" two or three times.

In the hall, I shoved him against the wall and patted him
down. Clean. Then I walked him down to the elevators.

"I'm just a fan!" he said.

"Then you can keep the tie-clip but give me the press passes."

Pouting, he slipped them off his neck and handed them
over. I pushed the elevator button and we waited.

He said, "You're not a very nice man."

The elevator doors opened.

"I get that sometimes," I said, and shoved him in.

The elevator doors closed on him.

Returning to the Royal Suite, I found Nita in the corner where I'd left her; she was hugging those nice legs.

I crouched and gave her an apologetic smile.

Her big brown eyes got bigger. "What was *that* about?"

"An interloper. Harmless fan. But it's indicative."

"Of what?"

"The slipshod security around here. Look, I have to get back to the Senator. He doesn't like it, but he needs somebody looking out for him. And I'm elected."

Her pink-lipstick smile was mildly mocking. "Did you have to run against anybody in the primary?"

"Yeah. Peter Gunn."

We shared a smile, then I was moving.

I found Bob in the Royal Suite's master bedroom, where some of his closest cronies were crowded around the TV sitting on pulled-over chairs or on the floor while David Brinkley on screen echoed Bob's irritation with California's new computerized voting machines. Ethel, looking young and fresh, was seated on the foot of the bed in an orange-and-white minidress with white stockings. Bob was pacing off to one side like an expectant father, though his wife was less than three months along.

He saw me enter and came over, sticking a fresh stick of Beech-Nut peppermint gum in his mouth and chewing it into submission. "What are you doing here, Nate?"

"Haven't you heard? I work here."

I told him about the curly-haired interloper but he didn't seem too concerned. Still, he didn't shoo me away. Instead, he said, "I need some space."

He went out into the hall, which was largely empty, and I kept an eye on him but gave him plenty of room. He had gone from this morning's easy grace to animal prowling his cage. He paced in thought, pausing to scribble notes about his speech on a little pad, tucking it away and then punching a fist in a hand repeatedly as he resumed his trip to nowhere.

Finally some reporters noticed him and gathered around. Bob leaned his back to the wall.

From one reporter came, "What do you think of the returns so far?"

"I can't comment on that yet." His arms were folded, his eyes on the carpet, his tone barely audible.

Another voice: "Looks like a long road ahead. How do you feel about having to deal with all the politics and politicians?"

His eyes came up and, surprisingly, brought a smile along. His voice picked up traction, too. "Oh, I like politicians. I like politics. Like to hear a favorite quote of mine and my father's? 'Politics is an honorable adventure.' Know who said that? Lord Tweedsmuir. Anybody know who that is?"

No one did, me included.

Bob said, "He was a Scottish statesman who wrote under the name John Buchan—wrote *The 39 Steps*."

They scribbled as he headed back to the Royal Suite and I fell in alongside him.

I said, "*39 Steps*. Isn't that the old Hitchcock picture?"

"It is. You ever read Buchan?"

"No. I don't read thrillers."

"Oh?"

"I live them."

He liked that. He was smiling and laughing and his hand was on my shoulder as we entered the Royal Suite.

THREE

Time had ceased to have meaning. Our corner of the fifth floor of the Ambassador Hotel was like Las Vegas only not fun and you weren't losing anything but your mind.

Bob would wander to 511 and check in with advisors and aides who clustered in intense little groups. He'd pace, chew gum and scribble in his notebook. Sit sullenly against the wall on the floor, then come to life when new information came in, all of it favorable and yet never favorable enough.

I tried not to dog his heels, keeping him in close sight but never breathing down his neck, and only getting snippets of conversations when he dealt with Mank and various advisors and aides.

The only place they could achieve privacy in this loony bin was the can, where for conferences Bob would sit on the sink counter, Mank take the lid-down toilet and whoever else was in there perch along the tub's edge. Then they'd close themselves in and I'd just watch the door like the next frustrated guy in line for the facilities.

And of course those who actually had that need found themselves scurrying for standing room or immediate seating in either the press room or Royal Suite. This would have been comical if it hadn't just added to this bizarre crawling along at a frantic pace.

Bob himself would move from 511's political whirl to the Royal Suite's festivities, only briefly nodding and bestowing a few words to the swarming celebrities before slipping into the master bedroom where he would again sit on the floor against a wall and maybe smoke a cigarillo and sporadically make more notes on his speech in progress.

On these Royal Suite visits, tagging after Bob, I'd send my eyes searching out Nita and she would smile at me and I would smile back and shrug. It was as if we were both wondering whether our brief time together was a continuation of, or the finale to, our Flamingo fling.

The two networks called the primary election for Bob at eleven. By then Bob was back in room 511, where I heard Mank say, "If L.A. County holds up, some of McCarthy's team'll be ready to jump ship. The nomination belongs to whoever can get to the undeclared delegates headed to Chicago. Time to call in Jack's markers, Bob."

Bob always looked uneasy when his brother was mentioned in terms of political capital, but he nodded. Grimaced a little, but nodded.

A crewcut bespectacled advisor said, "We need to get our guys off the media calls and onto phoning delegates. ASAP."

Everybody nodded but me, the invisible man, but when Mank said to Bob, "We need to find somebody to type up that speech," I materialized to chime in: "How about Nita Romaine?"

Mank and Bob looked at me as if Bob's dog Freckles (who was among the Royal Suite guests) had spoken. The crewcut guy explained for me: "One of our staffers."

"Hundred words per minute," I said.

"Fetch her," Mank said. Then to Bob: "Get your notes together. Be sure to thank everybody, Chavez, Schrade, Unruh, Rosey, Rafer. Hit the black vote hard. And talk about your admiration for Don Drysdale."

"Who?"

Mank's eyes flared. "Jesus, Bob! If America finds out you don't follow baseball, we're screwed. Drysdale pitched his sixth straight shutout tonight!"

Unfazed, Bob said to me, "Nate, have Miss Romaine add something to that effect. How we hope we'll have as much good fortune in our campaign as Don Drysdale did tonight."

The crewcut advisor was already on the move. "I'll rustle up a typewriter."

Mank took Bob by the arm and started gently hustling him out. "Time to do the network interviews. We've got both Mudd and Vanocur chomping at the bit."

Roger Mudd was CBS and Sander Vanocur was NBC.

In the outer Royal Suite, Nita was in the middle of a conversation with Rosey Grier when I stole her away. I explained the situation and she got on board immediately, no qualms or nerves. Took a while for that advisor to organize a little portable typewriter, but then we were in business.

We soon had to ourselves the much-envied office space that was Room 511's bathroom. Nita stood at the sink counter typing on a little electric Smith-Corona plugged into a shaving socket while I sat in a dignified manner on the lid-down stool, dictating from Bob's hurried notes as best I could. Some whole paragraphs were crossed out, words substituted and phrases rewritten, but what was left seemed fine. I made sure Drysdale got a mention, even though I had almost as little interest in baseball as Bob. I was a boxing fan.

Her work completed, Rita handed me several sheets and said, "I kind of feel like we're a part of history."

"We are," I said, "if Bob's the next president. Otherwise we won't rate a footnote."

"Oh, he'll win. I know he will."

I was less convinced, but then she was Hollywood and I was Chicago.

In the Royal Suite, the good news had launched the cocktail party into the stratosphere. Nita re-upped while I went to the master bedroom to deliver the speech pages. I cracked the door and Bob was standing right there, getting into his suitcoat. It was a little startling. Apparently his interviews hadn't taken any longer than us typing up his speech.

"You scared me, Nate," he said lightly. "That's not a body-guard's role."

I slipped inside. He'd been at the full-length mirror on the other side of the door, making himself presentable. We moved a little deeper into the room. The crowd had cleared but for his son David, a little man in a striped tie, blue blazer and gray slacks, sitting on the edge of the bed watching his dad with glowing pride. The twelve-year-old had a few small Band-Aids on his face from this morning's near tragedy.

Still at the mirror, Bob glanced over the pages. "This seems fine. Doesn't need to be the Gettysburg Address."

The door opened tentatively and it was Ethel, looking very girlish in her pink dress and white stockings.

"Even in my own bedroom," she said with mock annoyance, "I can't find a little privacy."

She closed the door and straightened her husband's tie, tugged at his coat, then adjusted his pocket hanky.

"*Now* you look like a president," she said.

"Don't let's get ahead of ourselves," he said.

His twelve-year-old son rushed over.

"You're a winner again, Dad!" the boy bubbled. "Aren't you *excited?*"

Bob knelt and ruffled his son's hair. "Over the moon," he said.

Impulsively, the boy kissed his father on the cheek as the mother looked on fondly, their springer spaniel coming out of somewhere to dance around them, and I got the hell out. I was enough of a sleuth to detect a private family moment when I saw one.

I caught up with Nita in what might have been the go-go party at the start of a *Laugh-In* episode. She was talking to Milton Berle near a pocket of dancing, giddy laughter adding grace notes to "Cry Like a Baby" on the stereo.

As I drew her away, I said, "Stick with me—unless you wanna know if the rumors about Uncle Miltie are true."

She smirked at that, looking more than a little like Stefanie Powers. "Where are we off to?"

"I'm getting you on that stage. You've earned it."

"I think you're just trying to get lucky."

"I think you're right."

In five minutes, around 11:45 P.M., the candidate's entourage of key journalists, union officials, advisors and aides assembled in the narrow hallway, like fraternity brothers stuffing a phone booth sideways. As the candidate's bodyguard, I was waiting for Bob and his wife at the master bedroom door, Nita just behind me to one side.

Big Rosey Grier and lanky Rafer Johnson approached and introduced themselves, as if that were necessary. But in fact we hadn't met. Firm handshakes were exchanged, Grier's massive hand swallowing mine like a largemouth bass gulping down a minnow.

"Mr. Heller," Grier said, "I understand you're filling in for Bill Barry tonight."

"I am."

Olympian Johnson said, "Well, we're here to back you up all the way, Mr. Heller."

"Make it Nate," I said, "and you're Rosey and you're Rafer and we're all buddies here. With luck we won't be needed. I think you know, Miss Romaine, Rosey. She just helped type up the candidate's victory speech."

Grier smiled and nodded at Nita, and told her how everybody

needed to pitch in and make this happen, when we heard, slightly muffled on the other side of the door, Ethel say, "Ready?"

The couple was no doubt checking that mirror one last time.

Bob's slightly muffled voice came: "Ready."

The crowded hallway parted like the Red Sea and the Kennedy couple made their way to the front of the pack where Mank waited. Nita and I tagged after.

At the elevators, Bob said to his press secretary, almost sighing, "Mank, it's late and I'm beat. Let's take the freight elevator again and avoid pushing through the crowd."

Bob was the boss.

We went down with the candidate and his wife, Mank, Grier and Johnson also making the trip. We came out at the edge of the bustling main kitchen.

The rumpled press secretary took me aside and pointed. "Around there's the way to the stage, through what they call the Pantry, an adjacent serving area. We'll be going through there on the way, and back again, after, to get to the temporary press room."

"I better check it out."

"Yes you should."

I entered into a long narrow passageway representing just the kind of grubby space you hope wouldn't be part of any restaurant kitchen: bare sandy-colored cement floor, dirty blanched walls, a rusty ice machine and shelves of unwashed glasses on one side opposite a row of three steel serving tables, one all but covered by trays of unwashed dishes. Beyond that was an archway onto the main kitchen where Chicano busboys and cooks wore white smocks like medics on the edge of an accident scene; they stood clustered together, obviously eager to see the famous Kennedy.

Among them, with a holstered sidearm, was a pasty-faced security guard in a brown uniform and dark cap. So there was *some* security, at least. A few network TV cameramen were posted, too. At the east end was a door that I went through into an area with restrooms and the rear doors of the Colonial Room, labeled PRESS. At the west end, where we'd be returning from the Embassy Room stage, were double doors opening onto the backstage area, an unadorned narrow corridor with a slight slope.

Not loving any of that, I returned to Mank and said, "Looks fairly clear. Lot of kitchen staff, though. I could frisk them."

"No need," Bob said, stepping forward. "Let's get out there."

The waiting crowd agreed: *"We want Bobby! We want Bobby!"*

A campaign advance man, two hotel personnel and I led the way through this so-called Pantry—an insult to diners every-where—with Bob and Mank behind me followed by Ethel, Rosey and Rafer, Nita in the next row, as our small army of key advisors and union leaders and bigtime reporters like Hamill and Breslin trooped through the unappetizing area. Some of those Chicano workers surged out from the kitchen to shake hands and get autographs. Bob accommodated them. Then from behind the wall of brown faces and white aprons came that self-professed dark-curly-haired fan I'd hustled out upstairs, a tube of some kind in his hands.

I got him by the arm and was yanking him back, but he appealed to Bob, "Please! I have a campaign poster for you to sign, Senator Kennedy!"

"It's all right, Nate," Bob said, nodding to me to let go of the guy, and scrawled an autograph on the tube itself. I hauled the fan out of Bob's path and said through my teeth, "Don't let me see you again," and he scurried away. No surprise finding a rat in this kitchen.

That security guard hadn't done a damn thing about it, and I got in his face and said, "Sharpen the hell up."

"Yes, sir," he mumbled. His face had a soft look, gray, the color of wet newspaper.

Nita clutched my arm, but her eyes were looking at me differently. "Nate, you're scaring me."

"That's not a bad thing," I said.

Bob himself was in the lead now and, in a few eye blinks, we were through the double doors and up the slight incline within that featureless corridor. Then Grier, Johnson and I went through a door into the Embassy Ballroom, followed by Bob and Ethel, and the *"We want Bobby"* chant quickly transformed into cheers.

We'd come out to the left of the stage. After a moment of getting our bearings and registering the ballroom's overwhelming heat, we went up three creaky stairs onto the spongy platform, red-white-and-blue bunting over us and gold curtains to our backs, thunderous applause and cheers engulfing us in waves rivaling the ones that had almost consumed Bob and son David a hundred years ago this morning.

I was already sweating and I wasn't alone. The TV lights at the back of the room were burning hot, blinding bright, but that only ignited an adoring explosion from a crowd trapped in this sweltering space for hours. Bodiless heads and waving arms created a surreal scene out of Dali with red and blue and white balloons bouncing up to the curved ceiling with its glittering chandeliers while below straw hats seemed to bob in the crowd, as if tossed to float in the waters of some other time and place.

The chant of *"We want Bobby!"* had resumed with an edge of hysteria, and the candidate tried for long moments to rein them in. The mood was both exhilarating and frightening—this crowd loved their man so much they might tear him to pieces. The stage beneath the feet of the twenty-or-so of us crammed there felt as if it might give way at any moment, which seemed only to add to the anxiety-edged thrill.

When Bob was finally able to begin his speech—which was frequently interrupted by cheers of *"Kennedy power!"* and *"Bobby power!"*—he thanked everybody Mankiewicz had told him to, and more. Drysdale got his mention and so did the family dog. Ethel came last, and Bob embarrassedly said to her with a fond glance, "I'm not doing this in any order of importance." She beamed of course.

"Our speech sounds pretty good," Nita whispered. She was holding my hand.

I said, "For a list."

It improved. He went on to say the showing in the cities and the suburbs and the rural areas indicated how well the campaign could do all around the country.

"We can get past the divisions, the violence, the disenchantment with our society," he said, "whether it's between blacks and whites, between the poor and the more affluent, or between age groups or over the war in Vietnam. We can start to work together again. We are a great country, an unselfish country and a compassionate country....Now my thanks to all of you, and it's on to Chicago, and let's win there."

Joyful screams again swept the room.

Bashful Bob flashed a grin and the V-for-Victory/Peace Sign, then turned to his right to go toward where that doorway into the Embassy Room had led all of us onto the stage. But a hotel staffer called out, "This way, Senator," and guided him toward the rear curtains into the corridor behind. That got me clogged up momentarily with the others on the stage, reorienting ourselves to follow Bob and the hotel man, and when I had almost caught up, Ethel was having trouble back there getting down. I jumped to the floor to help her.

When that was safely accomplished, the pregnant woman said, "Never mind me. Help the Senator."

I sensed her behind me as I slipped through the supporters, reporters and aides, Nita included, attempting to catch up with Bob, stray balloons from the ballroom popping underfoot. The candidate and my unofficial bodyguard assistants, Rosey and Rafer, were going down the gentle slope to the double doors beyond which awaited the narrow Pantry passageway.

Our group now entered an area crammed with staffers, reporters, photographers and gawkers. Bluish fluorescent lights cast an eerie glow, as a smiling Bob—up ahead—stopped to shake hands with white-coated kitchen staff between the big ice-making machine and the three lined-in-a-row service tables where a clump of people stood, some standing up on the things.

Back toward the east end of the passage that goddamn fan with the poster tube had stuck around, standing next to a cute curvy girl in a white dress with black polka dots; better company than he deserved, and no accounting for taste. A throbbing *"We want Bobby!"* seeped through the walls from the nearby Embassy Room, adding to the frenzy of an experience that seemed at once sped up and slowed down.

This halting progress was further stalled by a radio reporter. Bob glanced back, raised his eyebrows, then looked past me, no doubt at Ethel. Barely audible over the crowd's drone came a pointless question: "Senator, how are you going to counter Mr. Humphrey and his delegates?"

Bob told the man's microphone, "Just get back into the struggle," and did his best to press on.

That puffy gray-faced security guard was finally doing his job, just behind Bob, trying to help move him through the gaggle, guiding him with a hand on his right arm. The press of the burgeoning crowd, infested by teenage girls shrilling, *"We want Bobby!"* overwhelmed me in the small space for a moment, and I had all but lost sight of Bob when a young-sounding voice yelled, *"Kennedy, you son of a bitch!"*

Then came the first *pop*, and I thought at first another balloon had burst, followed by another. Then a rapid volley—*pop-pop-pop-pop-pop*—like distant gunfire or Chinatown firecrackers.

Not balloons.

Bob jerked forward, his hands flying up toward his face, then his arms went over his head as if in surrender and he fell backward onto that filthy gray concrete floor, almost as if he had slipped on it. Tall Paul Schrade, the UAW guy, went down, too, bleeding from the forehead. People were diving out of the way and onto the cement where Bob already sprawled, blood running down the side of his face, recent cheers and applause supplanted by immediate cries and shouts.

The security guard had his gun out and I yelled at him to put it away: *"Too many people in here!"* Five feet or so beyond the fallen senator stood a small swarthy man with a big gun; his dark blue jacket and dark bushy hair initially made me take him for that fan from before, but no, that guy was at the other end of the Pantry and this one right here was smaller, almost tiny.

For a frozen moment the shooter maintained his position as if he were between rounds at a firing range, and I pushed through and practically crawled over the people scrambling to find safety in the small space and I probably damn near trampled several, but I dove at the little bastard and shoved him against one of the steel serving tables and yanked the fucking gun from his grasp and slammed it onto the steel table. He looked at me with big blank almost-black eyes, buttons sewn on a doll's face, and that nothing expression was as strange as anything I'd ever seen. I punched him hard, twice, hard right-hand punches and that zero expression didn't change. But now I had him pinned and others were converging, and at the forefront were Grier and Johnson. So was that hotel man who'd guided Bob.

That should have been the end of it, but despite the blankness of his expression, he was squirming, trying to get loose, and my God he was strong, so much power in such a little bastard!

Breathing hard, I yelled, "Take him, Rosey, take him!"

As others were closing in, Grier picked the shooter up and slammed him with professional skill onto that serving table with a *whump!* Trays of unwashed dishes danced.

But that allowed the little bastard to, *damn!*, snatch back that gun, a .22 revolver!

All of us who were on top of the punk talked over ourselves: "Get the gun, get the gun!" "Get the fucking *gun!*" "Rafer, get the goddamn *gun!*"

But our captive was shooting again, orange-blue flames licking out the barrel of the .22, and bystanders were falling like clay pigeons over five or six seconds that felt like forever. The blank-eyed gunman kept firing even as Rosey Grier and several others of us struggled with him. Finally he was clicking on an empty chamber.

Then the big lineman wrested the gun away from the little man, whose squirming finally stopped as he stared blankly at the ceiling, as if those bluish fluorescent tubes above held a secret.

Five wounded besides Kennedy were slumped on the floor here and there, in various postures of pain and shock, getting help from whoever was nearest. The end of the shooting and capture of the assailant did not bring a lull of quiet. Instead pandemonium descended, screams, cries, obscenities, wails of "Not again!" and "No!"; but also a scurrying for help, medical and police.

A white-jacketed busboy—a small dark man whose agonized expression was everything the other small dark man's hadn't been—was kneeling as if in prayer, or maybe *in* prayer, by the fallen Bob on the floor, spread-eagled as if nailed to a cross waiting to be raised into proper crucifixion position, precious blood pooling like spilled wine and shimmering, reflecting the popping flashbulbs and positioning of TV lights.

For just a moment I knelt next to him, because I could see a near-hysterical Ethel being escorted up to him by Mank, and I would soon be in the way.

Then he said the last thing he ever said to me: "Is everybody okay?"

FOUR

Grier and Johnson had the gunman pinioned on the stainless steel cart, the little man no longer squirming like an unruly child but lost in a motionless daze. It took more than three of us to subdue him—Plimpton, Breslin, a Kennedy aide and the hotel man who'd guided Bob off the stage also piled on at one point. But the footballer and decathlete had taken charge and were now, in a way, protecting the assailant, as a good number of the seventy or eighty people piled into this so-called Pantry clearly wanted blood for blood.

I was wondering if the little shooter was hyped-up on something—the dilated pupils seemed to indicate that. Might help explain the superhuman strength.

With Ethel kneeling at Bob's side now, I went back over to the site of the struggle, taking my belt off. I had Grier hold the little man down as Johnson and I cinched my belt around our captive's ankles, even as an angry mini-mob bore down.

"We want him *alive*," I said, the two black faces dripping sweat looking at me curiously. "Or do you want another Oswald?"

"We don't want another Oswald!" Grier said with a forceful head shake in the midst of all this.

Somebody heard that and echoed, *"We don't want another Oswald!"* Several others repeated this new mantra.

Nonetheless a male voice shouted, *"Kill him!"* Other voices joined in: *"Kill him! Kill him now!"*

Peace-loving supporters consumed with rage pressed in trying to pummel our captive, reporter Hamill in the lead, several at a time taking looping swings around us, punching, kicking, one grabbing the shooter's leg and twisting it.

As if a mosquito had bit him, the gunman said, "Stop that—you're hurting my leg," and it understandably infuriated his attackers.

Yet we pushed them away somehow, and Breslin shamed fellow New Yorker Hamill back: "Think you're fucking Jack Ruby or somethin'?"

Bob's brother-in-law/advisor, the collegiate-looking Steve Smith, was yelling, *"Please clear the area! Please don't panic. Everything is all right."*

Of course the circumstances were anything but all right, though over the din of swearing and screaming, a woman's voice could be heard: *"Pray!"*

At least two persons were already doing that—the fallen man's wife, kneeling at his side, and the man himself, whose blood-streaked hands cradled a rosary to his chest.

Finally a quartet of uniformed cops came in and collected the shooter from us and carried him out, holding him over their heads like a football hero after the game. Poor baby had a broken finger and a sprained ankle.

I was dispatched to find a doctor. I made my way through the double doors and into the featureless corridor and up onto the platform, empty of people now, devoid of triumph. The cheers of minutes before were wails and shrieks now, hysteria spreading like a brushfire. Kennedy Youth girls in red, white and blue ribbons and jaunty straw hats hugged each other and sobbed; a few were on their knees praying. A big black guy in a dark suit that might have been a circuit-riding preacher's was pounding the wall with his fists, yelling up to a sky somewhere beyond the chandeliers, demanding, "Why, oh Lord? Why again? Why another *Kennedy?*" A college longhair with an RFK peace button was shouting, "*Fuck* this country! *Fuck* this fucking country!"

On stage, using the same microphone Bob had, I asked in that time-honored cliched way, "*Is there a doctor in the house?*" Smith came up onto the stage behind me. He leaned in to the mic and said, "*Please clear the ballroom, so we can get medical help to the Senator and other victims.*"

Soon a doctor—the husband of a Kennedy campaign worker —was bending down by Bob, who seemed awake but as dazed as his attacker had been. The doctor reached behind Bob's head, felt around. Bob's face tightened. Moments later the doctor's hand came back with a bloody forefinger.

He said, "This will remove cranial pressure."

The victim's wife had gone off to get a bag of ice for the medic and, on her return, Bob said softly, "Oh, Ethel."

Shortly thereafter two ambulance attendants rolled a gurney in. Bob protested weakly: "Don't lift me…please don't lift me." But they did anyway, gently, and then wheeled him out. The other major player in the drama had departed the stage.

Now the Pantry was again just an embarrassing display of a celebrated hotel's questionable kitchen practices, its floor littered with trash and cigarettes and a good man's blood.

In the melee I'd lost track of Nita. Not surprisingly, many had, when the shots were firing every which way, just scattered for their lives. Nita was not among the victims and that was a good goddamn start. I returned to the fifth floor, in hopes of finding her, which I quickly did.

In the living room of the Royal Suite, the victory party was now a vigil, a mix of Kennedy staffers, celebrities, activists and a few reporters who had gathered, waiting for updates.

Nita was sitting on the floor in the same corner where we'd first chatted. Legs up, she was hugging them to her, arms clasped under her knees; what remained of the Cher-like makeup was tear-streaked racoon smears, pink lipstick gone, the big brown eyes fixed in a hollow unblinking stare. She looked like hell, frankly, but just seeing her alive and unharmed was the first welcome sight since the gunfire rang out down in Pantry hell.

I joined her, taking my previous spot against the wall. Sat with my legs outstretched and one ankle over the other; got out of my suitcoat and piled it next to me. My shirt was soaked. I loosened my tie. The suite's air-conditioning helped. But I felt like I'd awoken from a terrible dream to find myself drenched in night sweats.

The TV in the background was playing the victory speech Nita had typed up, an ironic ghost haunting the place. This much smaller group than before huddled around the TV but for a few haggard souls filling the suite's Danish modern furniture, little of which I'd even noticed when the cocktail party was in full swing.

"I'm so ashamed," she said. Her voice was small. From such a self-assured woman, this was as startling as a scream.

I didn't say anything. I thought I knew what she meant by ashamed: ashamed to be an American. For killing our own, our boys in Vietnam, our leaders at home. Ashamed to be a human being. If God created Man in his image, what kind of monster must He be? If we were the top species on this ant-farm planet, we must be the work of an underachiever among Supreme Beings.

But I was wrong. That wasn't it.

"I ran," she said, barely audible. "So many gunshots all around me and I panicked and ran out of there. Right as he was being struck down like his brother."

She started to cry, but they were dry, wrenching sobs, tears long since spent, and I drew her close and held her to me. She considered herself a coward, like I thought myself a failure. Some fucking bodyguard. I should never have let Bob talk me into going into this unarmed.

But for all the self-recrimination, I knew: when somebody was willing to lay his life on the line to take yours, you were going to die.

Someone switched the channel and the speech Nita typed up started in again.

"I wish they'd quit playing that," she said into my chest. "I can't stand hearing it. I just can't stand hearing it."

As if she'd willed it, the speech was interrupted. On the TV Frank Mankiewicz was speaking outside the Hospital of the Good Samaritan, saying the operation was still underway and taking longer than anticipated.

Not a good sign.

"I can't take any more," she said.

"You have a room here?"

She nodded. Something like a smile formed. "But you're not…not getting lucky tonight, Nate."

"Nobody is. Let me take you."

She was on the third floor, where I walked her to the door. She faced me with both hands in mine. I kissed her forehead.

"Do you ever get to Chicago?" I asked.

She nodded. "A gig now and then. Dinner theater."

"Call me when you're in town."

"I will. A-1 Detective Agency, right?"

"First in the Yellow Pages."

She gave me a kiss on the mouth. Quick. Again, the start of something or the finish? Would this tragedy bind us or separate us? Who could say…?

She slipped inside with a little girl's wave.

Back on the fifth floor I almost bumped into two phone company employees in coveralls who were hauling the extra phones out of the press room. The door to 511 was open and it was empty in there, some trash on the floor but nothing like the Pantry's, the workmen pulling wires from the wall and coiling them up, routinely professional as if this night were like any other.

When they had gone, 511 was empty. I went to that bathroom where so many political confabs had gone down just hours ago and where Nita and I put the speech together from Bob's notes. A shaving kit had been left behind—electric shaver, aftershave, powder. The bath towels were fresh, only hand towels had been used.

Impulsively, I got out of my suit and piled it and underwear and socks with my shoes outside the can, where they'd be away from the moisture. My belt was lost to history. Then I took a long shower, good and hot; hand soap was still in its wrapper. This was one of those tubs with showerhead and curtains affairs. I didn't close the curtains and the mirror fogged up. I had to towel off the glass before using the electric shaver and then splashing on some Mennen's.

When I put my shirt and suit back on, they were dry. They didn't smell wonderful, but you can't have everything. Just having them not damp made all the difference. I felt close to human, which was nothing to feel proud about.

I returned to the Royal Suite. Several familiar faces were among those sitting on the floor around the TV, others in chairs and the pulled-over couch—John Lewis shaking his head, George Plimpton with golf-ball eyes, drinking in the latest news. This was nowhere I wanted to be.

Instead I walked aimlessly, almost prowling the sprawling hotel—taking the elevator down to the massive yellow lobby with its pillars and fountains and its red-and-black carpet, leather furniture, assorted ferns. Anywhere you went, it seemed, police were on hand; but not once was I asked for I.D.

The Embassy Ballroom was crawling with scavengers, gleefully gathering souvenirs, posters, banners, rejecting any straw hats with snapped brims and insisting only on the best examples, tossing the others aside. The platform had been taken down. Removed like Bob on his gurney or the gunman into custody. I walked across where we'd all stood and slipped through the golden curtains into the dark corridor and took the trip down the slight incline to those double doors.

I'd expected to see the yellow crime-scene tape common to California but fairly rare elsewhere. But none had been used. I entered, pausing to note the bullet holes in the wood framing. The slugs had, as Nita said, been flying; of course that bushy-haired shooter had been blasting haphazardly away.

I'd expected lab rats would be crawling around the Pantry while the real vermin quivered in their hidey-holes; but the forensics team was already gone, as if the importance of the crime had intimidated them away. Or maybe they were off getting an early breakfast from a more appetizing source. All those policemen around and no police work in progress. The LAPD wasn't everything Jack Webb cracked it up to be.

At any rate, the place was empty, nothing but the dirty floor, rusty ice-making machine and those steel-topped serving carts in a row. Hard to imagine all those people stuffed in here. The kitchen itself, nearby, was quiet. It was about four in the morning and room service was unavailable now and prep for breakfast not yet started.

Tape on that filthy concrete at my feet marked off where Bob and the others had fallen after the bullets took them down. But a single rose lay in the midst of Bob's taped-off position. On the wall a homemade sign—apparently predating the shooting, a welcoming for the candidate—said: THE ONCE AND FUTURE KING.

Finally I took a cab out to Frankenheimer's place in Malibu, where I'd left my car. I rode in silence and darkness and the dawn was thinking of happening when the cabbie let me out.

The director was standing on the beach in chinos, a loose shirt and bare feet, hands in his pockets, staring out at the ocean. In the middle of an irregular band of yellow along the horizon burned the bright button of the sun, starting its rise into cloud cover that would soon mute it. The water, calm as pebbled glass, its purple highlighted gold, didn't know it was day yet.

I walked out to him.

He glanced at me, tall, tan, in Ray-Bans. His body still faced the ocean. "Nate Heller."

"Yeah. The bodyguard. You oughta make a movie about me. Some very famous people died on my watch. I worked for Huey Long, you know."

That was almost a smile. "I didn't know. But don't beat your-self up. Bob wouldn't allow security to carry guns, ever."

"Tell me about it."

"...He's not going to make it."

"No. Digging a bullet out of his brain, we probably don't want him to. A vegetable doesn't make much of a president."

The Ray-Bans stared at me. "Are you that cynical, Heller?"

"I'm trying to be."

He nodded a little, getting that, shifting his eyes back to the sea.

It was six A.M. when I got to the Beverly Hills Hotel bun-galow. Lights were on, and I hadn't left them that way. For the hundredth time I wished that nine millimeter were under my arm. I told myself the A-1 agents handling security at the Pink Palace made it unlikely there was a threat.

But I went in tensed.

Someone lay stretched out on the couch opposite the fireplace, where flames danced; last night had been cold and today so far was no different. My son threw a blanket off and ran to me. He looked at me with red eyes, his face eerily like mine forty years ago. Like Frankenheimer, he was in his bare feet, but otherwise a McCarthy t-shirt and jeans.

Lower lip quivering, voice quavering, he said, "Dad, I'm so sorry."

And he hugged me, hugged me hard. My arms went around him. That was when some tears slipped out and mingled with the borrowed aftershave. But for the first time since the gunfire, I was smiling.

Bob didn't die for another day. He was 42. I was already on my way back to Chicago, taking an afternoon flight out on the fifth. If the cops wanted an interview, they knew where to find me.

FIVE

By one A.M. Friday, June 7, over a thousand mourners were already lined up along East 51st Street, waiting to get into St. Patrick's, the Gothic cathedral where Bob's body lay. Among them were college kids with hair like my son's, black folks including vets in uniform and sometimes wheelchairs, assorted Puerto Ricans and Asians and white people too, all kinds of Americans rich, poor and in between. The church would open at 5:30 and they would begin filing past the pale mahogany coffin on the black steel frame, with the TV cameras and their glaring lights intruding much as they had in the Pantry.

The press and the people were poised to witness the pomp and circumstance of a funeral mass, but I wouldn't be among them. My mother had been a Catholic but she died young and I never attended a mass in my life, and wasn't about to start now. My father, who'd been an apostate Jew running a political bookstore on the South Side, had considered my sweet gentle mother's beliefs nonsense, or else he wouldn't have committed suicide over his only son, the crooked cop.

I would mourn Bob in my own way.

That wouldn't include riding the funeral train, with its famous faces and lots of food and drink, though I caught glimpses on TV of the stir the trip caused. A million mourners lined the Penn Central tracks on the 226-mile journey, Boy and Girl Scouts, factory workers and nuns, firemen and brass bands, people hanging from water towers, Little Leaguers in uniform, men with hats off and women clutching male sleeves, citizens brandishing hand-lettered signs ("We Love You, Bobby!"), impromptu public choruses singing "The Battle Hymn of the Republic." That, I understand, is what Andy Williams sang at the mass I'd passed on. I'd been offered a seat both in church and on the train, but said no thanks to both, respectfully.

Glad I did. The twenty-one railcars took over eight hours to get from New York to Washington, D.C. I'd flown from Chicago that morning to our nation's capital, and was at Arlington for the burial, where I wound up waiting several hours in a drizzle too meager to be metaphorical. The public showing along the way meant the funeral train hadn't made it into D.C.'s Union Station till after nine P.M., the free food and booze long since run out.

I watched with bitter amusement at Arlington as cemetery officials rushed to change their plans to an evening interment. Floodlights were positioned around the open grave as members of the military handed out thousands of candles, one of which I accepted, now that the half-hearted rain had fizzled out. A nearly full moon hung discreetly over the cemetery, as if any less illumination, or any more, might be disrespectful.

When the funeral motorcade entered the cemetery around ten-thirty, the crowd lining the lane lighted their candles to guide the way. As somebody who got there early, I had a ringside seat when Steve Smith and aides I knew from the Ambassador hoisted the casket and made it somewhat clumsily up the hill to the knoll where Bob's brother Jack was buried. Bob would rest about thirty feet away.

The service was brief, conducted by the Archbishop of New Orleans, filling in for another high Catholic mucky-muck who'd got sick on the train, the Almighty apparently having a sense of humor similar to mine. John Glenn folded the American flag that had been draped over Bob's casket and presented it to brother Ted, who handed it off to Bob's eldest son, Joe, who passed it to his shell-shocked mother. It all should have moved me but only made me feel irritated. I wished that bushy-haired little bastard, Sirhan Sirhan (as we all now knew his name to be), was the one going into the ground, just nowhere near Jack Kennedy.

Leaving, I spotted Peter Lawford and Sidney Poitier and Shirley MacLaine and Lauren Bacall and others of their rarified ilk, including a stringy-haired hippie who turned out to be Bobby Darin, under bright floodlights hovering like spots focused on a dark stage. George Plimpton and John Lewis and Mrs. Martin Luther King, among newsworthy others, trudged off with all the lightness of step of the Bataan death march.

I looked for Nita but no luck. I hadn't heard from her since that night. Probably she'd had sense enough to stay in L.A. There was, as the police like to say, nothing to see here.

But I had an excuse—Bob had been a friend and I had a right to say goodbye. After all, wasn't I the trusted bodyguard who fucked up? And, hell, I was going to be in D.C. anyway. A longtime client here had left word at the Mayflower for me to come see him.

The next morning was beautiful and warm and the sun had finally banished the overcast gray, encouraging us to move on from the latest tragedy. This was 1968, after all, and we had more horrors to brace ourselves against. Like a Democratic convention where Robert Kennedy's delegates would have to choose between cold fish Gene McCarthy with his high-school principal charisma, and passé politico Hubert Humphrey, that too eager-to-please overage needy child.

And hovering over everything were the gleaming eyes, dark jowls and sly smile of a would-be president oblivious to the scream of B-52s, the whir of machine-guns, the swoop of fighter jets, and the pop-pop-pop of firefights, so far away and yet right here.

Georgetown's shade trees let enough sun through their branches to make interesting patterns of shadow on the well-worn brick sidewalk. The cab had let me out at 1313 29th Street, a Federal-style, brass-appointed, faded yellow-brick residence commanding the corner. Formed from two smallish three-story edifices joined by a central projecting wing, this was the domain of a syndicated columnist whose dozen employees surely felt at home in these onetime slave quarters.

Drew Pearson maintained a quiet dignified residence on one side and on the other a noisy sprawling newsroom where typewriters chattered, newswires tickered their tape, and phones rang and rang and rang, a dozen young men and women moving through all of it in a stop-and-start dance.

Greeting me at the door with a slight, polite smile was a fleshy but not fat man in his mid-forties, about as tall as me, with an oval head, dark hair combed over, sideburns going white. His face was pleasant with light blue eyes a teenage girl would die for, in herself or a boyfriend. His dark suit and tie might have been on loan from a funeral director. On this trip that seemed about right.

"Nate," Jack Anderson said. "Condolences on the loss of your friend."

He offered a hand to shake. I took it, thanked him, gave it back.

Legendary legman Anderson had been with Drew Pearson for decades, a real feat, since Jack was a Mormon who didn't work Sundays, deadlines and breaking news be damned. Or maybe darned.

I followed him inside to the landing separating the two halves of the house.

I said, "Normally I'm met by somebody better-looking than you."

As long as I'd known him, Pearson had enlisted one fetching young secretary after another to be his latest "fair-haired girl," traveling with him on lecture dates and out-of-town TV bookings and so on. These were not full-blown affairs (so to speak), rather father-and-daughter relationships that occasionally got incestuous. Pearson's wife Luvie looked the other way and so did the staff.

Anderson, who was no prude (even if a Mormon with only one wife), glanced back at me as we went down the few stairs into the office area.

"Margaret, I'm afraid, is long gone," the legman said, referring to the last of the fair-haired girls I'd encountered here. "She left us to get involved with Civil Rights down South."

"Good for her."

Unlike several of Pearson's other "cutie pies" over the decades, pleasantly plump Margaret of the rosy cheeks and long black hair had never succumbed to my charms.

As we cut through the bullpen of desks and file-cabinet-rowed walls where young worker bees buzzed oblivious to our presence, Anderson and I went through into an alcove off of which Pearson's office nestled. The bullpen and its offshoot small offices were air-conditioned, which the artificial-cooling averse Pearson grudgingly allowed. I slipped out of my Botany 500 jacket and draped it over an arm, anticipating a warm welcome.

Not from Pearson himself, who was pounding away on a battered Smith Corona portable on a metal stand near his desk. He didn't care if Eisenhower dropped by; if Pearson was in the middle of something at the machine, Ike could wait.

Anderson hadn't knocked or announced us. Just walked in,

pulled up a chair while I took one opposite the desk in this den of an office, slinging my jacket over the back. The dark plaster walls were arrayed with autographed celebrity photos (political and Hollywood) and some framed political cartoon originals with Pearson appearances. To the left, over a working fireplace (not lit, thankfully), a rural landscape hung slightly crooked and obviously amateur. Windowsills were piled with books, between stacks of which a cat snoozed, not bothering to wake up for the new entrants.

An electric fan on a windowsill proved itself no real substitute for air-conditioning, and Pearson was in a short-sleeved pale yellow shirt with a bow tie as crooked as the rural landscape. You could see the cheap thing clipped on. Ah how the mighty had fallen, or anyway stumbled. He was in fewer papers these days, and unless my son had heard me bitching about my sometime client's stinginess, Sam like most of his age group had no idea who this household name of yesterday was.

A jar of Oreos towered over the cluttered desk, one of the Mormon's Quaker boss's few indulgences. Light drinking was another, and fair-haired girls used to be.

But like all of us, Drew Pearson was growing older. No, old. He remained lanky if bonily so now, not the robust presence of before. His short-trimmed hair clung to the sides and in back, snow-white now, dwarfed by a chrome dome. To go with his egg-shaped head, he had a little Poirot mustache, also white, no longer waxed.

Pearson finished his page, all but ripped it from the Smith Corona and tossed it on the desk. He swiveled to me and unleashed his well-modulated, midrange voice.

"Nathan, how is that son of yours?"

I shrugged. "Healthy. Lots of hair. He was going to vote for Gene McCarthy, but I think now maybe his candidate is Bobby Kennedy."

A curt nod, pursed lips. "Not realistic, then."

"What kid in his early twenties is?"

"Tell him McCarthy votes with the gas and oil lobby. He can count on Humphrey for good old-fashioned liberal values."

"Okay."

That was it for small talk. Not his forte.

"Drew, you don't have to pretend you liked Bob Kennedy. I'm from Chicago. Politics are just another racket as far as I'm concerned."

"Cynicism makes an undignified fallback, Nathan."

"At the circus it's best you work with a net. You never trusted Bob because he worked for that other McCarthy, a hundred years ago—Joe. And Bob never liked you because you attacked his father in 1960. Now that another son's in the ground, what's the goddamn difference?"

The Quaker did not like that kind of language. His blue eyes —that same ice blue as Anderson's—widened momentarily, but he didn't comment on my profanity.

Instead he said, "Bobby might have grown into it. But he was too young to be president."

"You don't get any older than he is now."

That didn't change Pearson's dismissive attitude. "The kids only liked him for that shaggy hairstyle."

I rested my right ankle just above my left knee. "Have you seen Gene McCarthy's hairstyle? It's about as pre-Beatle as they get."

Pearson shrugged that off. It was almost a shudder.

"McCarthy's finished," Pearson said. "He said too many bad things about Bobby. It's not fair but he'll be seen as having blood on his hands."

"That's ridiculous," I said, but I knew the old boy had a better sense of where the political winds blew than most, myself certainly included.

Anderson, who'd been sitting quietly with his arms crossed over his suitcoat like an usher on break, said to his boss, "I recall what you said about Bobby, when you interviewed him after—"

"After his brother made him Attorney General, yes." The columnist looked up, as if that were where he kept his memory; he sneered a little. " 'A gimlet-eyed, cold young man who sits in his shirt sleeves with his tie undone.' "

Said the gimlet-eyed, cold old man sitting in his shirt sleeves with his clip-on askew.

"Speaking of blood on somebody's hands," I said, not putting any edge on it—that wasn't necessary, "you sure spent last month working Bob over."

Those ice-blue eyes flashed again and the little white mustache twitched. "I'm complimented, Nathan. That you're following my column even now."

"Sure. It's fun to see a knife wielded well when you're not the victim. A whole installment, free of anything approaching news, about how ruthless Bob was. All about how his old man once said, 'Bobby hates the way I hate.' "

He sniffed, a much-ingrained habit. "I've never made a secret of my preference in this race. Hubert's an old friend. How was I to know we'd have another Kennedy martyred on us?"

"Tough break for you."

Speaking of knives, I'd dug mine in deep enough. No need to say it out loud: everyone in this room knew Pearson served as Lyndon Johnson's hatchet man and Hubert Humphrey's cheerleader.

Anderson, who had a measured, reasonable style even when he was defending his boss, said, "Nate, what we ran about Bobby was absolutely accurate. Whatever, *whoever*, our sources might have been."

I grunted a laugh. "Things that happened in 1963, when Bob was Attorney General, were somehow news in May '68? Ancient history suddenly 'stop the presses,' right before the Oregon primary?"

Which RFK had lost, the first election defeat ever for a Kennedy.

Pearson sniffed again. "Your late friend *bought* a primary in Indiana last *month*…just as his brother Jack did a West Virginia primary, once upon a time—with Papa Joe's urging…and money."

"This just in—the latest from 1960."

The columnist sat forward, bristling, spewing words: "With young Kennedy pandering so *shamelessly* after the black vote, it's only *responsible* to reveal how AG Robert Kennedy authorized the wiretap of Martin Luther King's office and home!"

That juicy tidbit would have gone from J. Edgar Hoover at the FBI to LBJ in the Oval Office to this un-air-conditioned one I was sitting in while a bored cat snoozed.

Anderson raised his eyebrows, his expression otherwise cool. "Bobby's campaign saw to it that his speech in Indianapolis, the night King was assassinated, got plenty of play in the media."

Bob hadn't handled the King wiretap controversy at all well, his defense coming across as self-serving hair-splitting. He'd claimed only wanting to prove to J. Edgar that King wasn't a Commie threat, insisting he'd never approved bugging the Civil Rights leader's hotel rooms—office and home only. Gene McCarthy had pounced on that like a hungry hound tossed a T-bone.

The hotel room bugging, whoever approved it, was an obvious effort to put King in bed with a female not his wife—a supple secretary or star-struck supporter. Which you might think a public figure like Pearson, dallying with his own "fair-haired girls," would be hesitant to use. You'd be wrong. Hypocrisy was the lifeblood of D.C.

Anderson said, "You can't fault us, Nate, for telling the truth. What do you expect from journalists?"

"Is that a trick question?"

The legman ignored my dig. "When I wrote about the involvement of Jack and Bobby Kennedy in the Castro assassination plots…this 'Operation Mongoose'…there was no denial from your friend's quarters."

How could there be? It was true. And I'd been in it up to my neck.

I tossed Anderson a look and another to Pearson. "You two gents do realize Bob isn't running anymore. And that I am only here in town because he was my friend and they were burying him yesterday."

Pearson's palms patted the air and Anderson shifted in his chair uncomfortably. The cat stirred but didn't give a damn.

The columnist said, "My fair-game criticisms of your late friend, in the heat of battle, now puts me in an awkward position with my readership."

"Liberals," I said, "in the process of canonizing another slain Kennedy."

A mustache twitch. "Precisely."

"And here you sit with bloody hands."

Sniff. "Overstated, but…yes. I may have been unduly harsh, writing about him. He was not my candidate, after all. His intrusion into the race, the factionalism he created, surely would have paved the way for Richard Nixon to sail into power. And that I couldn't allow! I felt the young Kennedy *had* to be stopped."

"This just wasn't the way you had in mind."

The air seemed to go out of him. His voice returned unusually soft, minus any energy. "Where other people were concerned, I knew young Kennedy to be exceedingly thoughtful, even…

kind. His ruthlessness he brought only to his enemies."

Anderson said, quietly, "But not to you, Drew. In that debate with McCarthy, he was asked about your story of him signing off on the King hotel wiretaps. He could have called you a liar but he didn't. He appeared evasive, and it did him no favors."

Pearson seemed to have genuine regret in his expression and voice as he said, "He was for the common man—you have to give him that."

Anderson turned back to me. "We're going to publish a memorial tribute by way of an open letter from Drew to his grandson, who was a McCarthy supporter."

That resonated, of course.

Pearson said, "I'll speak of Bobby Kennedy's loyalty, his idealism, his courage. And my television broadcast this week will be devoted to the tragic loss of this true leader."

I grinned and I'm sure it wasn't pretty. "Swell. You have a plan. Won't work on everybody, but your hands will look a little cleaner. What does any of it have to do with me?"

Anderson moved his chair a little and faced me more directly. "You were Bobby's friend. And you are, let's face it, among the most famous private investigators in America."

"Which is like being the tallest midget," I said. "So what?"

Leaning forward a little, Pearson said, "Jack has been looking into the Kennedy assassination."

"Which one?"

"JFK," Anderson said, not missing a beat. "Most of what's surfaced to date has been courtesy of kooks on the one hand and wild-eyed leftists on the other. No responsible, credible journalist has taken it on. Someone should. Someone has."

"You."

"Me," Anderson said, his smile barely there yet cocky as hell. "But it's a slow go. I'm dividing my time between our regular

D.C. beat and occasional trips to Dallas, New Orleans and else-where."

I frowned at him. "What does that have to do with Bob's murder? You're not suggesting there's a connection?"

"Anything is possible," Anderson said. "Which is about the only sure bet in this game. But I can't widen my inquiry to include your friend's killing. Adding L.A. to the mix? And there's no apparent link except that two brothers, two much-loved political figures..."

"And hated."

"...and hated figures were struck down in their prime by what the likes of the Warren Commission would have us believe is a 'lone nut' assassin."

"I did some of my own investigating into the JFK kill," I said, "back in '64. And we can sit down for an interview about it, Jack, one of these days."

Though I wouldn't be sharing some of what I did, since not all of it was strictly legal. Like removing one of the likely shooters, who wasn't named Oswald.

"But dream on," I continued, "if you think this is another Dallas....Sometimes a train going into a tunnel is just a train going into a tunnel. And sometimes it really *is* a lone nut with a gun."

Anderson said, "Some of our stringers in L.A. say the official police investigation is not only incompetent, but reeks of a cover-up."

My head rocked back, almost as if I'd been slapped. "A cover-up of what?"

With a one-shoulder shrug, Pearson said, "No idea. But it would appear there are too many bullets. The assassin's gun only held eight rounds, but many of the witnesses report sub-stantially more shots."

"Eyewitness accounts are notoriously worthless."

"Even yours, Nate?" Anderson asked. "You were there."

At least he didn't say that like the announcer on that old history re-enactment TV show.

"I heard a lot of shots," I admitted. "I can't tell you how many, but enough to nail five bystanders and the target. I am not shocked to hear that the LAPD is somewhat less efficient than television would have you believe."

Then I sat forward. Any more so and I'd fallen out of the chair.

"But, yes," I went on, "I was fucking there, and I saw the shooting go down. That bushy-haired little bastard blasted away and I *saw* it, *heard* it, *smelled* it."

"Some witnesses talk of a second shooter."

I pounded his desk and the lid on the Oreo jar jiggled and the cat looked up. "I wish there *had* been a second shooter and that it was *me*, putting at least one into Sirhan Sirhan, a murderer so guilty they named him twice."

Anderson hung his head and shook it a little.

"All we're asking," Pearson said, "is that you look into it. Or even just assign one of your people to keep tabs on the LAPD."

Anderson said, "An ex-LA cop, perhaps. With lines into the department."

"I'll pay double the daily rate," Pearson said, "and start with a ten-thousand-dollar retainer. We'll keep you on as long as the inquiry generates stories. I'll give you a check here and now."

My sigh sounded like somebody opened a furnace door. "Much as I would like your money, since no famous client of mine has ever been tighter with a dollar...but no. Gentlemen. I was fucking there. I saw Sirhan shooting. I saw Bob on that dirty kitchen floor in pain in a pool of blood. Clutching a goddamn rosary. I saw five others bleeding there, too. The creep called Bob a son of a bitch and then he shot him. What more do you want?"

"The truth," Anderson said.

I stood. Got back into my jacket. "No. You're looking for cover. You smeared a good man and you want me for damage control. No thanks."

Nobody had to show me out.

I knew the way.

PART TWO

The Girl in the Polka-Dot Dress

February–April 1969

SIX

The Hall of Justice in Los Angeles dated to the mid-'20s, a fourteen-story Beaux Arts box on Temple Street between Broadway and Spring. Pollution had tinged its classically decorated white granite a dingy gray, but tourists still took pictures of the massive structure they knew from TV—*Dragnet*, *Perry Mason*, *Get Smart*.

The celebrity defendants who had passed through the grand marble-walled lobby with its towering columns and high gilded ceiling might as well have been a reservations list at Chasen's—Charlie Chaplin (paternity suit), Errol Flynn (statutory rape), Robert Mitchum (marijuana bust).

Today a current denizen of the ornate edifice's 750-cell jail was being tried for murder in one of its seventeen courts, the defendant a nobody who'd become an instant if reviled celebrity himself. And the basement had hosted the autopsy of a famous paramour of the victim, whose own post-mortem examination took place at the hospital where he died.

Tucked away with a number of others in a waiting room for witnesses, I found myself sliding in on a bench next to a lovely brunette of about forty, slender but curvy in a blue navy suit and baby-blue silk blouse. Hair tucked back in a discreet bun, big brown eyes lightly made up, Nita Romaine wore pink lipstick, the only holdover from when I'd first seen her in the Royal Suite at the Ambassador Hotel, nine months ago.

"You never write," I said, "you never call."

Her smile was warm if embarrassed. "*You* never write. *You* never call."

I played at looking hurt, but kept my near-whisper light. "You were in Chicago. Well, Chicago area, anyway. I saw the ads. Pheasant Run Playhouse in St. Charles. Opposite Captain Kirk, wasn't it?"

She shook her head, embarrassed but amused. "No—Mr. Spock. *Visit to a Small Planet.* You could have looked me up."

"You didn't look *me* up."

"You could have bought a ticket."

"Didn't have a date."

"Too bad. You might've finally got lucky."

I didn't expect to laugh here at the Hall of Justice today. But I did, a little. "Took Bob to bring us back together."

We both knew that was also what had kept us apart. It didn't need to be said: we'd met cute, like in a movie romance, but the film that followed had been a horror show.

I nodded toward the others in the several rows behind us, narrow pews on loan from a small country church. "I don't recognize anybody. Busboys from the Pantry, I think, unless they're Chavez's Mariachi band. And isn't that the hotel man, a maître d' I guess, Karl something? Who guided Bob off stage and…"

To the Pantry.

"Yes," she said. "No famous faces, though."

No Ram lineman, no Olympian, no New York columnist.

"Just ours," I said.

She pointed a gently accusing forefinger. "*You're* the famous one. 'Private Eye to the Stars.' "

I held up a palm. "A minor celebrity at best, and if you ever use that shopworn phrase again, I'll spank you."

"Promise?"

I laughed again. "That's a good sign."

"What is?"

"We're flirting again. Maybe there's hope for us yet."

She shook her head. "Wouldn't put money on it. We're just flirting 'cause we're nervous. At least *I* am. This is my first murder trial."

"Except for that *Perry Mason* episode. *Case of the Sinful Starlet*, wasn't it?"

The smile that got out of her was sweet and warm. "That wasn't what the episode was called. And I didn't play the starlet."

"Their loss." I smiled too.

But right then our conversation ran out of steam—we were sobered by the circumstances, and genuinely embarrassed we'd both sort of ducked each other since that awful night.

Finally she leaned close and asked, "Have you kept up?"

Was that Chanel Number 5?

"With what?"

"With what do you think? The case. The trial. All the ins and outs of it."

"No."

The big brown eyes got bigger. "Oh, *I* have! How could you not?"

"Just didn't."

That wasn't entirely true. I had glanced at the stories in the paper, particularly the ones about Sirhan Sirhan and his defense team, one lawyer's name jumping uncomfortably out at me; and also checked out who the chief prosecutors would be, thinking D.A. Evelle Younger himself might handle it. But he'd assigned a deputy D.A. instead. You could bet Younger would be driving from the back seat.

We sat quietly for a while.

Then she asked, "Think we'll ever put it behind us?"

"Maybe after today."

We sat quietly again, but just for a few moments.

"Next time I'm in your part of the world," she promised, "I'll call."

"Good. Same here."

"You in town this time for long, Nathan?"

I shook my head. "Heading back tonight, but I'll be back in early April—A-1's doing some hiring. You can call me at the office, or at the Beverly Hills Hotel." I got a card from my wallet and wrote a phone number on it; I already had her contact info, unused so far. "We really will get together."

Another empty promise?

"We definitely will...*oh!* This is me." A uniformed guard was summoning her from the doorway. "Watch my purse will you? This may take a while."

But it didn't. She wasn't gone longer than ten minutes, coming back with an expression that fluctuated between confusion and irritation. Now the guard was curling his finger at me—I was next. I slid out of the bench and handed her the purse as she stood there fuming.

"What a fucking crock," she said.

That jarred me a little. She'd never said that on *I Dream of Jeannie* or *Bewitched*.

"Bunch of bullshit." Her eyes were huge, white all around, and her pink-coated lips were tight. "Why didn't they ask me about the girl in the polka-dot dress?"

She had me there.

Then she rushed off, her low heels clicking like castanets, which got the busboys' attention or maybe it was her nice hip motion; in any case, the uniformed guard almost had to jump out of the way.

From the witness stand, I got my first good look at the players. The gallery was full, of course, for the hottest ticket in

town. Three middle-aged men in dark suits sat at the prosecution table and three more middle-aged men in dark suits sat at
the defense, like interchangeable parts. By way of stark contrast,
the defendant seemed at first to be wearing white pajamas, but
that was some kind of prison garb he'd been provided. He
looked very small, this swarthy bushy-haired man, with his eyes
wide like a child at the zoo and his mouth hanging open like the
monkey house was really interesting.

When I took the witness stand, Deputy D.A. David Fitts
approached me with his shaggy black eyebrows arched and the
small mouth under a pendulous nose in the grooved oval face
pinched in an O, emitting questions like Alice's caterpillar
spelling out vowels in smoke. All very measured, but the
queries covered only why after the speech I hadn't stayed at
Bob's side (I was helping Ethel down from the stage), why
catching up with the candidate was slow (the human traffic
jam), what I had heard ("something like firecrackers") and what
I had seen (the defendant shooting, Bob falling).

This interrogation seemed insufficient to me, lacking detail
in what I was asked, limiting what I could answer. At once I
understood Nita's frustration, but didn't share it, really. I knew
an open-and-shut case when I saw one. And I had seen this one
from the inside.

However.

The lead defense attorney, Grant Cooper, was a big name in
greater Los Angeles, a former president of the California Bar, a
smiling quipster to the press, an "Attorney to the Stars" (ouch),
and a criminal defense lawyer who had never lost a client to the
gas chamber.

More significantly, his non-movie-star clients included a
number of prominent gangland figures, including Johnny Roselli,
who had been a key player in Operation Mongoose, the CIA

plan to collaborate with major mobsters to assassinate Fidel Castro. John and Robert Kennedy had not initiated the scheme, but they'd signed off on it.

Cooper's was the name that had jumped out in my sketchy perusal of the Sirhan Sirhan coverage in the papers. His mob mouthpiece reputation was no secret—he'd had to come aboard Sirhan Sirhan's defense at the last minute because he was representing Roselli in a Beverly Hills Friars Club card-cheating case.

Oddly, the noted defense lawyer rather resembled the Deputy D.A.—similar long face and steel-gray hair and thick black eyebrows, but more years on him and wearing black thick-rimmed glasses snatched off the corpse of Buddy Holly. The similarity of the two lawyers, like the symmetry of the defense and prosecution tables, made it look like there was only one side to this trial.

Cooper approached the witness stand—this particular dark suit was almost certainly Sy Devore ("Tailor to the Stars")—and mellifluously asked why the plans to take candidate Kennedy through a back stairway, to a second waiting crowd of supporters, had been changed to that route through the Pantry.

His implied point: If the path through the Pantry was last-minute that would suggest the defendant had shot the Senator without premeditation. The defense had stipulated on Day One that Sirhan Sirhan indeed shot Kennedy, and were apparently attempting to prove diminished capacity to keep their client from sucking cyanide. The curly-haired punk didn't like this tactic and, if the papers were accurate, occasionally got mouthy about it in court, to the judge's gavel-hammering displeasure.

Right now, however, Sirhan Sirhan sat mute with a slight but noticeable and vaguely imbecilic smile going. So he might not have wanted to admit being nuts, but his demeanor leaned otherwise.

I said to Cooper and the court, "The change of plan came together ten or fifteen minutes before the speech, to accommodate a press conference in the Colonial Room, past the east end of the Pantry. But even so, the Senator would've had to come back up and through the Pantry to get to the press conference."

"He would have gone through the Pantry anyway?" Cooper asked, as if this were news to him. And maybe it was.

"Yes."

He chewed on that, said, "No further questions," and headed back to the defense table and resumed his seat.

Then as I passed by into the aisle, Sirhan Sirhan's defense attorney, Grant Cooper, discreetly winked at me.

Two months later, give or take, I was lounging in the living room of my bungalow at the Pink Palace with my stocking feet up on a coffee table and my eyes on the *Huntley-Brinkley Report* on the 24" TV that angled to the right of the unlighted fireplace. I swore at Huntley, who had an annoyed schoolteacher way about him, finished off the rum-and-Coke I'd made myself, pointed the remote at the set and killed NBC's nightly news.

Last week, Sirhan Sirhan had been convicted of murdering Robert F. Kennedy; this morning, six days later, the assassin got sentenced to die in the lethal gas chamber. Why, were there gas chambers that weren't lethal?

I got up and started building a fresh rum-and-Coke at the wet bar, wondering why I couldn't get no satisfaction out of that little bastard's well-deserved fate.

Admittedly, I had a complicated view of such things. I was

against the death penalty because I didn't trust the state or federal government to get my tax refund right, let alone go around killing people in my name who might be guilty. I had done away with the occasional bad person on my own initiative, but then I trusted my own judgment.

On the other hand, what fucking doubt was there about that little wild-haired prick killing my friend?

And yet.

A day had not gone by since that slick mobbed-up shyster Grant Cooper winked at me in court that I hadn't found myself grinding my teeth over it.

Somebody knocked at the bungalow door.

Here's how paranoid I was. Though a successful businessman—president and owner of a private investigation agency with offices in three major cities and relationships with smaller firms in half a dozen others, who hadn't done any field work to speak of in several years—I still kept my nine millimeter Browning automatic next to my car keys and Ray-Bans in their hard-shell case on the little table next to the front door. I did it in Chicago, and I did the same here in my home away from home.

Such paranoia at the Beverly Hills Hotel, where my own A-1 handled the security and the bungalow's front door had a peephole, might seem ludicrous. But on one occasion, LAPD cops had rousted me here, where I'd had a few other tight moments, so I was…cautious.

I wouldn't have needed to be—the beautiful woman on my doorstep was no Trojan Horse. Anyway, I had Trojans handy in the bedroom.

"Nathan," Nita said. She was the kind of woman who could look upset and great at the same time. "Can I come in?"

"*May* you come in," I said, stepping aside for her.

Her hair didn't do that Marlo Thomas flip now, the black tresses brushing her shoulders in a Jeanie Shrimpton layered look. Her turquoise knit short-sleeve shirt, corduroy pants and tan leather boots would have been boyish but for what she stored inside them. The pink lipstick had given way to a dusty rose shade, and her eye makeup was about as subtle as it got in 1969.

She froze for a moment, noticing the nine mil on the little table. "Is that…are you…*afraid* of something, someone…?"

"That's just a gift from my late father," I said.

Big dark eyes looked at me, trying to make sense of that.

"I'm a sentimental soul," I explained, taking her by the elbow and walking her to the couch. I'd left my rum-and-Coke on a coaster on the coffee table.

Looming over her a bit, I asked, "Can I get you something?"

"Ginger ale," she said numbly.

As if we were still back in the Royal Suite.

I put together a glass of Canada Dry on ice and handed it over, then sat beside her. I slipped my arm along the upper edge of the couch but respected her space.

"What's wrong, Nita?" Didn't take a master detective to deduce it must be something to do with the Sirhan death sentence.

"I've almost called you a dozen times." She was shaking her head, the layers of black hair shifting here, settling there, like tectonic plates before an earthquake. Looking at the fireplace with no fire in it, she said, "It's frustrating, isn't it? Being part of a trial like that and not hearing what the other witnesses have to say."

"You didn't miss anything where I was concerned," I said. "I didn't share anything you don't already know."

The big brown eyes flew to me. "I bet they didn't ask you much. *Either* side!"

That was true and I admitted it.

"I told them everything," she said, "and they wrote it all down, but they never asked me about any of it in court! Not really."

"What are you talking about, Nita?"

She leaned close, gripped my left hand tight. "I heard gunshots coming from someplace not far from my right, when Sirhan was already being subdued by you and those other men, several feet in *front* of me! Shots at my *right*, Nathan, with people falling all around me, a man sliding down a wall making a bloody smear like a fucking snail. Then...then Senator Kennedy lying on the floor, on his back, bleeding. And I'm screaming, 'Oh no! Oh my God, *no!*' "

She lurched into my arms and hugged tight, her lips near my left ear as she said, in a ragged whisper, "Next thing I knew, I was ducking down, in utter shock about what was happening... then...then...I passed out."

She wept into my shoulder. I held her. After maybe a minute, she slipped from my embrace and dug a hanky out of her pants pocket. Her scant eye makeup was running and she dried her eyes and wiped them off, embarrassed suddenly. She composed herself. Held the hanky in her lap in two hands, swiveled toward me on the couch.

"I passed out," she said, "but only for seconds. Still, when I woke up? My clothes were rumpled, even torn, damp in patches, and my belt was gone and one of my shoes missing. I wasn't hurt bad, really, but I seemed to ache everywhere. I could tell...could tell I'd been...*trampled.*"

I put a hand on her shoulder. Gently. Giving my eyes to hers. "It's all right," I said, as people do when it isn't.

She went on: "I...I saw Mrs. Kennedy, Ethel, kneeling by her husband. He was on his back, sort of...staring up. She was

trying to comfort him. I never saw anything so sad, but also....
nothing ever so *horrifying*. I started to...to *scream*, and I ran
out of there and back through that corridor, behind the stage.
Yelling, 'They've killed him! They've killed him! Oh my God,
he's *dead!* They've killed him!' "

She held her arms to herself, shivering.

"They?" I asked.

She nodded, nodded, nodded. "Yes, they, they, they. I said
'they' because I knew there was more than one shooter involved!"

That hit me like a punch.

Her brow was knit, her eyes finally not wide. "And, Nathan,
the police didn't want to hear it, the FBI didn't want to hear it,
and they didn't ask me about any of it in court, not really! Cut me
off if I tried to give them one more word than I was asked for."

"Who, that defense counsel—Cooper?"

"*Both* sides! And Sandy Serrano wasn't even called as a witness!"

"Who's Sandy Serrano?"

She grabbed my hand and squeezed. Indignation had given
way to desperation. "Somebody you have to talk to, Nathan.
Somebody you need to talk to *right now*. About the girl in the
polka-dot dress."

Nita met Sandra Serrano when the girl was co-chair of the
Kennedy Youth in Pasadena, where Sandra lived with her aunt
and uncle and worked at an insurance agency. Wrapping things
up for the now defunct campaign, Nita and Serrano had shared
their experiences about the night of the shooting.

We were able to meet with Sandy mid-evening at a cozy
Mexican restaurant on Fair Oaks Avenue in Pasadena. The
beckoning neon dated back a quarter of a century:

We shared a round of *horchatas* (a delicious blend of rice, milk, vanilla, and cinnamon) before ordering the meal I'd promised the two former RFK campaign workers. We were in a brown faux-leather booth under two framed prints, one depicting every US president in cameo portraits up through JFK, who was central in a bigger oval, a similar framed print of *Presidéntes de México* alongside. The lighting was low, old Mexican-style paintings adorning the pale yellow half-walls above wood paneling, with piped-in Mariachi music.

Sandy (as she insisted I call her, though calling me Mr. Heller) was attractive, zaftig, just out of her teens, her dark hair short but full, eyes large and bright. Her demeanor was serious, befitting the subject of our conversation, her navy dress on the demure side.

Nita and I were across from her in the booth.

"You remember how crowded the Embassy Ballroom was," Sandy said. "How hot. How stuffy. I went outside and sat on the landing of a stairway alongside the building...sort of like a fire escape, but not the pull-down kind, you know? Wood, painted white. Sat away from the door on the edge, above the stairs."

I nodded. "About what time was this?"

"Eleven-thirty or so. Nice and cool out there, and I'd been sitting, oh, for maybe five minutes when two guys and a girl came up the stairs and I kind of scooched over and gave them room to pass, you know? The girl seemed nice enough, excusing herself. She was maybe five foot six, dark bouffant hair, not as dark as mine, but dark. She was kind of stacked. Cute. Pretty, but with a turned-up nose."

"Two guys with her, you said."

"Yes, with long hair, kind of bushy, but it wasn't that Sirhan Sirhan, if that's what you're thinking. This was a white guy. Average height. Kind of messed-up looking, like he could use a haircut, and had maybe slept in his clothes—what we call a *borracho*."

I'd heard that word. "Drunk, you mean?"

Sandy shook her head. "No, more like…somebody who just doesn't…look *right*, somehow. Kind of…out of it."

"What about the other guy?"

"*Not* white. Mexican American, I think. I know because I am one. Gold sweater over a white shirt. Why a sweater on a hot night like this, I got no idea."

"How old were they?"

She thought about that. "Early twenties, I'd say, all of 'em. They were definitely together, definitely a group. Oh, and the girl was poured into this white dress with black polka dots."

Nita and I exchanged a glance.

"Anyway," Sandy said, "I was just sitting there relieved to be out of that hothouse ballroom and away from the crowd, enjoying the cool air. Then around midnight or a little after, that girl kind of…*burst* out of the building and I darn near jumped out of my skin. Her, and the guy in the gold sweater, sort of tumbled out on top of each other. Almost trampled me."

Trampled, like Nita in the Pantry while she was unconscious.

"Now this is the part nobody wants to believe, Mr. Heller," Sandy said, small white teeth barely visible behind tight lips, her chin crinkling. She leaned across. "The girl, when she almost stepped on me? She stopped a second and says, 'We've *shot* him! We've *shot* him!' "

Sandy let air out, shuddered, then had another sip of horchata. Raised her eyebrows and set them back down, as if she could hardly believe what she was about to share.

"So I say, not taking it seriously, 'Who did you shoot'? And she says, 'We've shot Senator Kennedy!' And I say, 'Oh, yeah, right.' Then the polka-dot-dress girl goes running down the stairs with that gold-sweater guy coming right after her, the *borracho* one not with them. Scrambled off toward the parking lot and into the dark."

Nita squeezed my hand under the table.

Incredibly, Sandy's story that night had only begun. Starting with the early morning hours of the shooting, she'd been interviewed five times by the LAPD, at both Rampart Division Station and Parker Center, had participated in a videotaped reconstruction of her account, and even watched a police-organized fashion show of potential polka-dot dresses, none of which were right.

"A few weeks after the Senator's death," she said, "I was interviewed one last time, by a police lieutenant named Manuel Hermano, who says, call me 'Manny.' At first he seemed very nice—took my aunt Maggie and me out for dinner. A steak dinner, downtown. Bought me two drinks, even though I was underage. Kind of winking about it. I'm 21 now. Then he asked me again about what I saw, and I went over it for the thousandth time. He suggested I take a lie detector test, and go on the record once and for all, so I wouldn't have to go over the same ground again and again. I said okay. Maybe it was the drinks. After that, he drove us to Parker Center."

There she was escorted by Hermano into a small interview room and strapped into a chair with a polygraph machine nearby. After some routine questions, Hermano told her aunt to wait outside, and a two-and-a-half-hour ordeal began. Designed, Sandy said, to badger her into "admitting" she had made up her story. She was just one of over a dozen girls who had made up such tales, "Manny" told her, to get publicity for themselves and money from newspapers.

"He said I owed it to the Senator's memory," Sandy said, "and to his wife, not to shame a great man's death by making up a story. He said Senator Kennedy was probably in the room there with us right now, listening to me lie. I insisted what I said I saw and heard *really* happened, that I didn't care what his stupid thingamajig machine said, but it was all *true*."

The young woman's dark eyes were unblinking as she said, "He kept trying to push me into saying I lied, even though I hadn't. In the end I just wanted to get out of there. Finally I said, well, maybe what I'd heard some other witnesses say colored my story. I wasn't the only one talking about a girl in a polka-dot dress, you know. And that was as close to a lie as I told, because that wasn't true. But it seemed to be enough for him, finally. Mr. Heller, there *was* a girl in a polka-dot dress— and I can give you the name of a policeman—a good one, an honest one—who can verify that."

At my bungalow at the Beverly Hills, Nita and I sat on the couch and this time we both had ginger ale, our shoes off and feet on the coffee table.

Like Hermano, we'd fed Sandy at the restaurant, not steak but some good Mexican food, though nobody had much of an appetite. Nita and the young woman talked about friends of theirs who'd been on the campaign and what they were up to now. Nothing about what Sandy had told us earlier.

Hardly any lights were on in the living room. We were sitting close.

"I have some money," Nita said, out of nowhere.

"What?"

"I might be able to hire you. I know you're expensive, but—"

"Your money's no good here, lady."

She got up and stretched. Not unpleasant to watch. "Would you mind if I borrowed your shower? I've had a long day."

"Be my guest. It's off the bedroom."

I could hear the needles of water dancing, not loud enough to interfere with the call I made. It would be a little late in D.C., but I didn't care. The operator connected me to a home number that not everybody had.

I didn't identify myself. I just said, "Tell your boss if he's still up for it, I'm on the Kennedy job and not to fuck me on the expenses."

"Done," Jack Anderson said.

I hung up and she was in the bedroom doorway wrapped in a towel. And then she wasn't wrapped in a towel.

Some have said I'm a randy shallow son of a bitch and that any beautiful woman can have me with a glance. That may be an exaggeration, but no woman was ever more beautiful than this. Her damp hair hung like tendrils to the shoulders of a figure tanned except where a skimpy bikini had prevented arrest for public nudity, its ghost so white it made startling decorative touches of the pert-nippled areolas and the wispy dark triangle. Her belly had a plumpness that only made her seem ripe, and Elizabeth Taylor would have wept to see a woman with a face that could wear no makeup at all and do it so well.

"You won't think less of me in the morning?" she asked.

"Maybe," I said. "But your stock is rising right now."

SEVEN

To hike Mount Hollywood Trail, most tourists and locals alike began at the rear of the parking lot at Griffith Observatory and headed up through the Berlin Forest, planted about two years before to honor Los Angeles' new sister city. At this stage of its existence, the "forest" (announced by a sign as such) was just a scattered collection of sapling pines. Most visitors to this vast, rambling park with its winding trails, rugged chaparral, and looming lush mountain vistas would pass through this clearing unimpressed and hike on to more spectacular views of the Hollywood sign, downtown L.A., and the iconic domed Observatory itself.

The view from the bench where the policeman sat wasn't half-bad, though. The day was sunny but cool, the smog burned off till tomorrow, a mild wind ruffling the shrubs and grasses, their bleakness in the sun-blanched dirt brightened by wildflowers.

The cop wore the familiar navy blue LAPD uniform, complete with regulation belt, holstered weapon, baton, and handcuffs. Rounded cap with visor held in his lap, feet firmly on the ground (ready should duty call), he stared out at an impressive view of the city he served, lorded over by the Hollywood sign, which looked tiny from here. His expression, however, was not one of wonder...unless he was wondering how he wound up a cop, and a cop meeting that dreaded breed of citizen, a private detective.

I joined him on the bench. Sturdy-looking, older than forty, this was likely a veteran of several decades on the department, light blue eyes close-set, high forehead emphasizing the squared-off oval where his pleasant features resided. His metal name tag (a new addition to the uniforms) said: SHORE.

He recognized me, from the papers I guess, and slid his hand over for me to shake as if it were a secret document he was passing. That would come later.

Griffith Park was on Shore's beat, though I doubt he covered all four-thousand-some acres of it in his L-car (one-officer patrol) out of Highland Park Division. That a veteran cop like this was working there made him a real cop—not a rookie, burnout or soon-to-be retiree marking time in a safe environment like San Fernando Valley (aka Sleepy Hollow). But it couldn't have been where he was assigned the night of the killing—that would have been Rampart Division.

Still, this was the police officer whose name Sandy Serrano had given me last night, to corroborate her story. I'd called him this morning, from my office at the A-1 in the Bradbury Building. Sergeant Peter Shore recognized my name, which meant he had a few questions.

"Sorry to bother you at home, Mr. Shore," I said. "Sandy Serrano gave me your number. She speaks highly of you."

His voice came back medium range with the self-controlled, neutral modulation that comes with the job. "Miss Serrano is a nice young woman. I assume this is about the Robert Kennedy matter?"

Anyway, I think he said "matter"—might have been "murder."

"It is," I said. "I'm looking into it for a journalist. Anything you choose to share would be strictly confidential—'source close to the case' sort of thing."

"What kind of journalist?"

"A famous one who wonders why a nice kid like Sandy Serrano got handled like a suspect, not a witness."

"...I'll talk to you, Mr. Heller. I'm on duty this afternoon, but we could meet."

The park was moderately busy but the Berlin Forest held no fascination for the hippie hikers and vacationing families strolling by, though the former picked up the pace (likely holding, and on their way to a scenic high) and the latter included fathers sometimes pointing out to the mothers and offspring the re-assuring police presence (just like *Adam-12*!).

I asked, "What were you doing at the Ambassador? You work out of Highland Division, correct? Wasn't that way off your beat?"

He'd been staring almost tranquilly out at the city spread before us, but now his face turned to mine and his eyes were intense. They were, oddly, a similar shade of light blue to Bob's.

"Not at the time," he said. "I was at Rampart Station then. I got transferred later last year—but I'll get to that."

"All right. Sorry. Tell it your way, please."

He turned back to the rugged western drop-off out of which a modern city somehow emerged.

As senior patrol sergeant at Rampart Station, about to head out on my shift, I get tagged at the last second to take over Night Watch. Before settling in at a desk for the long haul, I make a quick cigarette run to this liquor store on Eighth and Fedora. I'm about to head back when I hear an All-Unit call come in: ambulance shooting at 3400 Wilshire Boulevard—the Ambas-sador. And I'm directly across the street from the hotel's rear driveway!

All I have to do is make a U-turn and I'm in the back parking lot, upper level at the southwest quadrant of the place. I get out of the car and damn near get swallowed up by people running from the hotel like it's on fire, taking off in every direction on foot, weaving around cars trying to pull out.

I've barely stepped from my patrol car into this mass con-fusion when an older Jewish couple, in their sixties, comes rushing up.

Both at the same time they say, 'We saw something! We saw something!'

They are almost hysterical. I yell, 'Slow down, folks! What happened?'

Understand, at this point I didn't know the Senator had been shot, only that there's been a shooting at the hotel. But already the crowd chaos told me this isn't any ordinary shooting.

The man's breathing hard now and the woman does most of the talking.

She says, 'We were about to leave out that side door, near the Embassy Room, onto that little balcony…with stairs going down? When this young couple comes barreling out from the ballroom in a gleeful state, and the girl bumps right into me! Late teens, early twenties, happy as a lark, singing out, "We shot him! We shot him!"

'I yell at her, "You almost knocked me down!" Then realizing what I just heard, "Who did you say got shot?"

'And this girl says, "Kennedy! We shot him! We killed him!"'

Mr. Heller, I've been a cop for over twenty years, and not much fazes me, but you know how it's said something can make your blood run cold? Mine sure as hell did. I knew at once what the commotion was about. What the shots fired and ambulance call were about.

Another Kennedy had been killed.

So I say, 'This couple, can you describe them?'

The old gal says the girl was white, early twenties, bouffant-type light brown hair, wearing a white dress. That lady knew fashion all right—she was very detailed in her description, dress soft sheer fabric, three-quarter sleeves, small black polka dots, dark shoes. Male was Caucasian, tall, twenty to twenty-two, very thin build, blond curly hair, wearing brown pants, gold shirt.

One thing I know, Mr. Heller, from a lot of years on the police department, is that remarks made spontaneously after a crime or an accident are very seldom colored by people's imaginations. I knew these were valid descriptions, and jotted them right down word for word.

And this old gal, though still worked up, was perfectly rational, like that fashion-show laundry list indicates.

I ask the couple for their names and the man says, 'We're the Bernsteins,' and I write that down. First names, too, and contact info, but I...I'm sorry, I can't recall anything but 'Bernsteins,' and, well...you'll see. Best I give you this as it came.

So then they lurch off and just get swallowed up in the crowd, people still running and milling and bumping into each other. Hollering, screaming. Just insane.

I notice a Rampart Station juvie detective I know, who's heard the radio call and is trying to help out. I tear the sheet from my notebook and give it to him to hand over to the Chief of Detectives. At my patrol car I radio in a Code One and tell the Night Watch lieutenant I'll set up a Command Post...which the first supervisory patrol officer on scene is required to do... and put out All Points Bulletins on the two suspects, descriptions as given by the Bernsteins, adding only that the direction taken by the suspects is unknown.

I get help from a dozen sheriff's deputies who'd been counting primary ballots across the street in the IBM Building. They'd just wrapped up their work when they heard the sirens and came over to see if we needed help. A godsend. I put them on getting identifications and license numbers of everyone entering or leaving the hotel grounds.

I ask Communications Division to send some men, a min-imum of six two-men units, as fast as they can. As they show up, I give them their assignments, logistical officer on the tele-phone, a log officer, radio officer, set up a perimeter and… uh, oh, yes. Certainly, Mr. Heller. Only what pertains to the Bernsteins.

Understood.

Later I hear from Communications that the description they have is of a small male Latino in his mid-twenties with bushy hair, light build, blue jacket and jeans and tennis shoes. Do I have anything to add, I'm asked.

I say, 'That isn't the description I put out.'

The dispatcher wants to know where I came up with these suspects and I say from two reliable witnesses, an older man and his wife. That we have their name and addresses. A detec-tive from juvie has a sheet of paper I gave him, with the name and address and phone of those witnesses.

Disregard that, I'm told. 'The people that were right next to Kennedy say it was one man,' the dispatcher tells me. 'Your two witnesses might just have been getting out of the way so they wouldn't get shot. You don't want to get any talk started about some big conspiracy.'

Detective Inspector John Powers comes by and wants to know who was responsible for putting these descriptions of two suspects on the air. I say I was and brief him on my encounter with the Bernsteins.

'Cancel that description,' Powers says. 'We don't want to make a federal case out of this. We've got the suspect in custody.'

Yes, Mr. Heller, that's exactly what he said—we don't want to make a federal case out of it. You didn't generally challenge Powers, by the way. He's famous for carrying three or four guns.

I agree to cancel the APB on the male suspect, but insist we maintain the one on the girl in the polka-dot dress, who if nothing else might be a key witness. Powers doesn't like it but has no choice. It was either that or relieve me of my post and he needed me there at that moment. But he had the last laugh, anyway. I later learned he contacted Communications directly and ordered the polka-dot APB yanked.

Anyway, I wound up manning that Command Post in that parking lot for twenty-three hours.

I asked Sgt. Shore, "Did you testify about any of this at the Sirhan trial?"

Midday, the park's greens and browns and tans lolled in sunlight, and the hippies and tourists had been invaded by retiree couples, perhaps including the Bernsteins. Who knew? Not the LAPD.

"No," the officer said. "Wasn't questioned about it, either. Not by the prosecution or the defense. But I was instructed by my watch commander, last September, to prepare a follow-up report for SUS."

"For who?"

He smiled a little, a traffic cop amused by someone trying to talk their way out of a ticket. "Not 'who,' Mr. Heller—'what.' Special Unit Senator. Surprised you haven't heard of that."

"I'm playing catch up," I admitted.

He slipped on sunglasses; I'd already put mine on.

"SUS is the 'elite' task force," Shore said, "that investigated the assassination. I delivered a copy personally to their HQ. And I let them know I was available for an interview any time, at their convenience. No one ever called."

"What became of the report?"

His grin was sudden and wide and had no humor in it. "Funny you should ask. I filed copies in my personal box at the station and at the watch commander's desk and the Records section, too. A few days later a couple of things occurred to me that I'd neglected to put in, and I went back to pick up those copies and amend them. The one in my box was gone. I asked around and nobody knew anything. At SUS they claimed not to know what the hell I was talking about. But the Day Watch sergeant at Rampart said two plainclothes dicks from SUS came around and collected all the reports, including my initial one."

"I'm guessing you didn't let it stand there."

He shook his head. "No, I went back to SUS HQ, where I was told, in no uncertain terms, that nobody from SUS had been to Rampart, much less removed copies of any report. And when I made more inquiries at the station, my superiors were openly uncooperative…and irritated."

"What do you make of that?"

"Well, it's a cover-up…but why?" Shore looked right at me and held his gaze there; before, I'd gotten glances out of him and nothing more. "It made no sense to me. A sloppy investigation is one thing, a mishandled, misguided attempt to avoid another Dallas situation…but doing something *deliberately* wrong? Why the hell?"

"You said 'made' no sense. Is it making sense now?"

He raised his hands to chest level, palms out, as if a gun were trained on him. "Mr. Heller, I haven't been trying to find things out, you understand. No investigating on my own. After a while, you just try to keep your head down…not that it's done me any good."

"What things have you learned without trying?"

He sighed. Shook his head. Stopped like a man who'd dropped some things he was carrying and felt put upon, having to bend down and pick them up.

"Evidence from the case has been routinely destroyed," he

said, looking straight ahead again, "if it wasn't going to be used in the trial. Thousands of interviews were trashed, only a few hundred preserved—what might have been important testimony, gone. Two months after the killing…just two damn months…several thousand photographs from the investigation were burned up."

"What, by accident?"

A grunted chuckle. "Hardly. In a medical-waste incinerator at L.A. County General, is what I heard. On a similar note, a roll of photos from an eyewitness, who said he had shots of the shooting, were confiscated. Teenage shutterbug from Canada, seeing how things were done in these great United States. Whether *those* photos were among the burned, I couldn't tell you. But none of the kid's photos were brought forward at the trial. And a dozen witnesses at the Ambassador Hotel, not just the Bernsteins, saw the girl in the polka-dot dress, just weren't important enough to make the grade."

"And what about the Bernsteins?"

"Who knows? The note I gave that juvie detective disappeared. I asked him about it and he said he passed it along. But it's gone, and nobody ever located that old Jewish couple, let alone questioned them."

"I'm over sixty myself, you know," I said with a smile. "And with a last name like Heller, I'm not Scandinavian."

He smiled, too, slightly embarrassed. "No offense. Cops tend to size people up."

"They do. And I've got you sized up as an honest one."

"I…I appreciate that."

I cocked my head forward to make him look at me. "How credible is it, to you, that this could've been a cover-up, right out of the gate? I'm from Chicago and even I have to question that."

He shrugged. "You talked to Sandy Serrano. You know what

she was put through. That polygraph examiner should've gone to jail for that. And, by the way, do you know who that polygraph examiner was?"

"Hermano. Lt. Manny Hermano, she said."

"Right. He's the lead supervisor at SUS."

"So I guess it makes sense he questioned her."

"Mr. Heller—doesn't that name mean anything to you… Manuel Hermano?"

"No. Like I said, I'm from Chicago."

His reply seemed, at first, like a non sequitur. "It's no secret, you know, even among the rank and file, that the CIA and the LAPD are in bed together."

No secret to me, either. I knew the Company had sub rosa ties with police departments all over America, swapping special training and equipment for ignoring surveillance and certain break-ins.

"And," Shore was saying, "here's an interesting little coincidence—Manny Hermano retired from the department a year and a half ago…after a big retirement dinner, all the top brass there…to go to work for a State Department agency, A.I.D.— Agency for International Development—training police forces in Latin America. *That* got a lot of locker room laughs."

I wasn't quite following this. "Why? Hermano doesn't sound like a laugh riot to me."

"Riot, maybe. He used to be called 'Shoot 'em Up' Manny. Killed eleven men in the line of duty—an LAPD record. Joke was, he was teaching 'advanced interrogation techniques' down south when most of his perps up north never lived to talk."

"He retired, you said."

"Got asked back in April '68."

A month after Bob had announced his run for president.

Shore turned to me and my face funhouse-mirrored in his

sunglasses. "Said the State Department job wasn't what he expected. The LAPD welcomed him back with open arms. Then after Senator Kennedy was killed, he's heading up the task force to investigate the city's most important crime of the century—the man in charge of preparing the case for trial and supervising the other investigators."

A bit of a breeze kicked up and yucca and other shrubs shivered like the warmth was the cold.

"By the end of last summer," Shore said, "my proficiency ratings, which have always been high, suddenly hit rock bottom. That can happen when there's an official story some stubborn asshole won't go along with." Another shrug. "That's just the way things are done. If they can't get you to change your story, they ignore you, then discredit you, making shit up if they have to. Finally I got transferred out of Rampart to here. People around me who've cooperated with SUS got promoted. Me, I've been encouraged to seek premature retirement. Now I'm due to leave in July on a service pension."

"You're taking it better than I would."

He flipped a hand in a dismissive gesture that I didn't buy at all. "I have a sheriff's job lined up in a little town in Missouri. I'll do just fine. Why would I want to work for a department like this, after witnessing the most grotesque abuse of police power I could ever imagine?"

"Fair point."

He took the sunglasses off and looked right at me with Bob's blue eyes. "Listen, Mr. Heller, I've got a photo for you that you might like to have. They didn't *all* get burned up at County General. It's a decent shot of Robert Kennedy and you're in it, too. You look grouchy, but you're in it."

He passed me the manila envelope and I shook out the photo. A single typed page was paper-clipped to it.

Shore said, "Those are some witness names you might want to check into—polka-dot dress sightings and three witnesses in the Pantry who claim to have seen a second gunman."

"Yeeeeah," I said dryly. "I believe I would."

I lifted the paper-clipped page and had a look at the photo.

Bob was signing an autograph.

Signing it on a poster tube for that curly-haired, sleepy-eyed, party-crashing fan who had sneaked first into the Royal Suite and then into the Pantry.

EIGHT

The A-1 Detective Agency at the Bradbury Building, that venerable brownstone on the southeast corner of Third and Broadway, had in recent years expanded to five fifth-floor suites. The turn-of-the-century Bradbury's interior was an improbable collection of wrought-iron stairwells and balconies, brick-and-tile corridors with glowing globe light fixtures, caged elevators that might have been designed by Jules Verne, and an atrium bathing the central court in golden-white sunlight via an expansive skylight. No question that the building was long on baroque charm but also in the tooth, and that we could have afforded something bigger and better or at least more modern.

But this was the City of Angels, where image is all, and the Bradbury was exactly right to convince clients seeking a private detective they'd come to just the right place. Hollywood surely did, as more crime and mystery movies had been shot here than in any studio in town, from *Double Indemnity* to *D.O.A.* We'd even rented out one of our old-fashioned pebbled glass interiors to *I, the Jury*, in 3D no less.

Meanwhile, back on the fifth floor, three of our five suites were given over to cubicles utilized by a dozen operatives (including three females), all former law enforcement; another suite was occupied by my L.A. partner, Fred Rubinski and myself (side by side in separate offices), a reception area out front with a secretary at one desk and a receptionist at the other. The remaining suite was a conference room large enough to hold a press conference or meet with studio executives.

Nathan S. Heller had come a long way from a one-room office over a blind pig on Van Buren by the El. I didn't have to sleep in a Murphy bed in this one, either, although the leather couch was pretty comfy when a guy my age wanted a nap.

I still considered myself based in Chicago, though my long-time partner there, Lou Sapperstein, ran the day-to-day at the Monadnock Building; but I spent about a third of my time in L.A. now, and at least six weeks cumulative in New York at our Empire State Building office, overseen by Bob Hasty, also a partner. Lou and Fred both went back to my Pickpocket Detail days in the Loop; Bob I knew from when he'd done work for the A-1 through our D.C. affiliate, Bradford Investigations.

My extended time in L.A. had to do with exploiting the celebrity that had come with the *Life* and *Look* articles about our Hollywood clientele: *Time, Newsweek* and the wire services had also started noticing the admittedly unlikely number of newsworthy cases I'd figured in over the years. And of course it gave me an opportunity to spend more time with my son, who hadn't said "Fuck you" to me in months.

I was behind my clutter-free desk and Fred was across from me in the client's chair, an amiable balding bulldog whose resemblance to Edward G. Robinson came up more often than he would have liked. He was a sharp dresser, a habitué of Luigi's Custom Tailor shop in Van Nuys, though right now he was in shirtsleeves and suspenders. He had a few years on me and retirement was his favorite subject.

But not today.

"You really think there's anything good to be had," he said, the cigar in his fingers furthering a thirties gangster vibe, "out of poking around in this thing?"

This thing, of course, was Bob's murder.

"I have a client," I reminded him. "A longtime one in Pearson, and all he wants is enough for a few columns that can get him back his liberal bona fides."

"*If* he pays you," Fred said, sticking the cigar in the hole in his skeptical expression. "Look. We haven't had problems with the LAPD in years. We even have some ex-cops of theirs on the payroll. Why borrow trouble?"

I ignored that and flipped a hand. "You're the one who followed the Sirhan Sirhan case in the press. I was in Chicago minding my own business. What's your take?"

He grunted a laugh. "You were in that goddamn kitchen when the shit hit the fan. And you're asking me?"

I didn't say anything.

Fred put his cigar in the ashtray on my desk that was there for him and clients; I hadn't been a regular smoker since the war. The real one.

He said, "Sorry. I know you and Bobby were tight. I got a big fat tactless mouth sometimes. I just don't see what's to be gained. Professionally or personally."

"You didn't answer my question."

"What question?"

"What's your take, Fred? This thing has every earmark of a police cover-up. Looks like they're doing whatever it takes to quash any conspiracy talk."

His shrug was slow, elaborate. "That's easy. They're lazy. Not the rank and file—it comes from above, the brass and the D.A. It's a hell of a lot easier to prosecute a single individual for a crime than multiple defendants. All you gotta do is ignore evidence that doesn't fit the story you're tellin', then make your conviction."

"Tell me something I don't know. They have one man in custody—do they want to explain another shooter or two, slipping through their fingers? *Of course* the D.A. wants a quick win that the public can buy."

He threw a hand in the air. "Precisely."

"But what about the defense team, Fred? What about that slick prick shyster winking at me? What the hell does Cooper think *I'm* in on, anyway?"

Fred shrugged again, not so elaborate. "You should ask *him.*" He held up two fingers with the cigar twirling smoke in between, Winston Churchill style. "But I'll give you one thing —you can't take the gun evidence too serious. Their forensics guy, this Wolf character, is famous for giving the prosecution whatever it needs. You remember the Kirsch case?"

"Didn't make the *Tribune.*"

He filled me in. "Kirsch was a former Deputy D.A. who was tied up with a wife-swapping crowd in Long Beach. Some guy didn't wanna give Kirsch's wife back and Mister Deputy District Attorney shoots both of them in bed. His *own* bed, at that. It was a slam-dunk case till this Wolf character got caught sweetening the bullet evidence, and almost botched the whole thing."

From the intercom came the voice of our thirty-year-old starlet/receptionist, who lent the A-1 a pretty face when she wasn't doing a round of auditions.

"Your nine-thirty is here, Mr. Heller. In the conference room."

"Thanks, Evie."

I clicked off, and Fred said, "Your FBI buddy? Keeping things discreet?"

I nodded, getting up. "Yeah. He wouldn't want to be caught consorting with the lowlife likes of us."

Wes Grapp was the Special Agent in Charge of the FBI's Los Angeles Office, but before that he'd held the same post in Kansas City. That's where we'd met, when I was working for the family in the Greenlease kidnapping case back in '53. We'd gotten along well, sharing information with each other that helped the overall cause. For what good it had done.

Grapp had helped himself to the seat at the head of the table in the squarish room bisected by a conference table designed for a different space. The walls were bare flat plaster, pale green, no framed anything, as if to underscore the confidentiality of anything said here. The old-fashioned wooden blinds were drawn to keep sunlight and prying eyes out—after all, this nasty world of ours included binoculars and lip readers.

In his early fifties, Grapp dressed well—that gray suit was off-the-rack, but the rack was at Bullock's Wilshire—and the pleasantness of the features on the long narrow oval of his face was compromised by a prominent nose and high forehead that rose to a dark, receding Nixon-ish hairline.

He got to his feet, extended a hand, but retained his head-of-the-table position. After the ritual handshake, firm but not showy on either of our parts, we both sat, me at his right, Daddy's favorite son.

We exchanged small talk about family briefly, and the status of our mutual friend, Kansas City Cadillac dealer Robert Greenlease, who'd been ailing. Greenlease and his wife Virginia had endured the deaths of all three of their children, but Mrs. Greenlease was apparently finding solace in her church and charities.

"Not the best thing about our jobs," Wes commented. "The tragedies, particularly the ones we have to sift through."

I'd told him on the phone just what tragedy I was starting to sift through. Which had made it clear we'd need to link up away from his office.

"I have an appointment this afternoon," I said, "with Sgt. Manny Hermano. We've never met. He has an interesting reputation, considering he got entrusted with a high-profile investigation like Special Unit Senator."

Grapp's grin came quick and left the same way. "Yes, 'Shoot 'em Up' doesn't sound like a nickname you'd generally find attached to somebody heading up the inquiry into the assassination of a major presidential candidate."

"Particularly one named Kennedy."

A nod. "Particularly one...yes. I would imagine you're already aware that Sgt. Hermano has a relationship with the Central Intelligence Agency going way back. Actually, so does his superior, Chief of Detectives Houghton. And that's really all I can say on that subject."

Not a surprise.

I asked, "What *can* you tell me, Wes?"

He might have just tasted something foul. "Just that our role at the Bureau has been frustratingly limited. Homicide is a violation of state law and, from the start, the LAPD asserted its jurisdiction. We did have, *do* have, underlying jurisdiction through civil rights statutes...and certain federal legislation passed after November 22, '63."

I nodded. "Covering violence against a candidate for federal office."

His eyebrows went up and down, but his gray eyes remained placid. "Right. That pertains to the President, as well. Doesn't go far enough. I've been pushing for Secret Service protection for presidential candidates ever since Dallas."

"Maybe that will happen now."

"Maybe." That came out a sigh. "From the start of this one, absurd as it might seem, the LAPD called the assassination a strictly local matter. Still, I let Houghton know we'd be running a parallel investigation, and suggested two FBI agents accompany any of his teams in the field. He rejected that. Sgt. Hermano was to be point man. We were told everything had to go through him."

" 'Everything' covering what?"

His gesture might have been an M.C.'s introducing a guest artist. "All of our work. Scores of interviews around the country with anyone who'd known Sirhan since he came here as a child. In school, in Pasadena, or at the ranch in Corona, where he worked."

"And this got you what?"

His smirk had no humor in it. "Nothing of much importance, for all our digging. Oh, I could give you Sirhan's passport number, visa number, every damn number from Social Security to when he was booked at county jail. Even the serial number of his Iver Johnson revolver. Numbers that don't add up to jack squat."

I leaned forward. "And nothing of substance at all from those interviews?"

"Well. A gas station manager said Sirhan was a good worker, friendly and polite. The gent who employed him as a gardener said he was quiet and well-mannered. When he worked at a health food store, his fellow employee said they studied the Bible together and that Sirhan was 'a really nice boy.'"

My turn to smirk. "Sounds like what the next-door neighbors say when some guy kills his whole family after his wife didn't pass him the salt."

"It does. There's always people who never saw it coming… but this goes a little deeper. Sirhan was a member of the Rosicrucians, which Mayor Yorty inaccurately described as communist to paint Kennedy's killer a Commie. But a friend at college who headed up the local SDS chapter said Sirhan rebuffed efforts to recruit him into that radical group. Other friends found him not particularly interested in communism or even politics in general. He was keen on his schoolwork, and later, in making money."

"Doesn't sound like much of a political fanatic."

The eyebrows went up again and stayed up a while. "Well, he comes across that way in the notebook found in his bedroom at his mother's."

That had caught my eye in the newspapers; hell, it caught everybody's eye. "Where he wrote 'RFK Must Die' over and over again."

Grapp nodded. "But here's something the boys at SUS won't mention—their top handwriting experts and ours couldn't confirm it was Sirhan's writing."

"Do I detect some doubts, Special Agent Grapp?"

He shifted in his hard chair. "I just wish we hadn't been elbowed out of this one. The fudged forensics from that perjurer Wolf make me suspect there may be something to this second shooter talk...or at least we could've put our people, who are the best after all, into finding out the truth of it or not."

I smiled a little. "Somebody really doesn't want a conspiracy on this one."

"No, somebody doesn't. Keep in mind everything we came up with went to, and through, Hermano. He was the total arbiter. He was the one who decided which witnesses were worth believing, and was the personal polygraph expert who browbeat that Serrano girl into submission, her and others. They sent portable tape recorders out on every single interview they conducted, you know—*everything* got on tape...sounds impressive, right? Only Hermano and the D.A. culled it from 3,000 hours to 300 hours, for use in the court case, and deep-sixed the rest. Burned them like they did those photos."

"You heard about that, huh?"

"We don't miss much at the Bureau." He leaned forward. Almost whispering, he said, "But we do what we're told, and it came from the top to play whatever game the LAPD had in mind."

The top being J. Edgar Hoover.

Grapp sat back, his volume normal now. "I don't have to tell you, Nate, that you don't start with the perp and work backward, discarding everything that doesn't apply to putting him away. It's bad policing, and it's bad science."

The tableau in the Pantry flashed through my mind. "I saw that little bastard, Wes, banging away at the crowd...and I saw my friend fall, and lie sprawled on that filthy floor, his eyes staring into the inevitability of that moment. I'm not trying to clear Sirhan fucking Sirhan."

He patted my forearm sleeve. "Good for you. But if you find he didn't work alone, more power to you. Just don't set out with your mind made up, one way or the other. And, Nate? Do I have to tell you to make sure Hermano thinks you're on his side?"

"No, I get that. He didn't leave a trail of dead suspects behind him because he's open to discussion."

Cops and crooks alike called Parker Center—the police administration building at 150 N. Los Angeles Street—the Glass House. TV and movie fans knew it well, from the revived Dragnet if nothing else, so it seemed somehow fitting that 803, the big room on the top floor, should be decked out as a sound stage. Training films and the like had been the goal here, the walls asbestos woven with chicken wire, bare stanchions climbing to the network of pipes and ducts of a high, open ceiling.

Right now, however, it had transformed into an enormous office, a bullpen of a dozen or more desks without cubicles, surrounded by file cabinets, interwoven with assorted tables, charts, evidence boards, and Xerox machines. But this space, obviously designed to be a center of activity, had a ghost-town look, with only a handful of plainclothes officers at their posts, desktops empty but for an occasional cardboard box, phones wrapped in their own disconnected cords. The air conditioning was almost chilly, minus human bodies to soak it up.

"*Mr. Heller!*" a voice called, echoing from the back of the room. "*This way!*"

A stocky, fireplug figure in a suit and tie stood behind a metal desk, gesturing for me to come. I went down the central aisle of this all-but-abandoned outpost to that desk, which was bigger than the others, and given rather more breathing room. To one side, various chairs were assembled in a meeting area facing an evidence board that had been cleared but for a few photos of the Pantry, Sirhan and other related subjects.

Manny Hermano came out from around his big metal desk with a hooked-up phone and a few files fanned out like a poker hand. That suit wasn't cheap—Hart Schaffner & Marx maybe, a plaid olive number with a vest and darker green tie with red stripes.

He offered up a big white trying-too-hard smile under a nicely trimmed handlebar mustache, his dark thinning hair swept back over a rounded square face, his nearly black eyes bright behind glasses with heavy black frames, over which black thick eyebrows hovered.

We shook hands; he tried too hard there, too. But at least he was friendly.

"Have a seat, Mr. Heller," he said. He gestured to one of the chairs by the now nearly blank corkboard evidence display.

I sat and he came over and pulled a chair around to face me, not too close, leaning forward a bit, his hands folded and dangling between his knees.

"So," he said, his voice mid-range and husky, "Drew Pearson wants to tell the story of SUS."

That was what I'd indicated in the phone conversation we'd had this morning when I set up our meeting.

I said, "To a degree. If I may be frank?"

"Please."

"Basically, Drew wants to jump on the bandwagon, venerating Bobby Kennedy. He wrote some, well, unflattering things about Bob in the weeks before the shooting."

Hermano nodded, smiled a little. "What seemed like fair game politically became embarrassing in an instant."

"Shoot 'em Up" Manny was no chump. Grapp had filled me in: Hermano had a degree from UCLA, spoke French and Spanish fluently, and had authored a textbook on criminal investigation, teaching law enforcement classes one night a week at Los Angeles State College. And of course the CIA had used him as a teacher, too, in Latin America. Never mind what subjects.

"Mr. Heller," he began, and I stopped him.

"Nate," I said with a nod.

"Manny," he said with a gesture to the green-and-red tie. "In a way, it seems strange you'd come to me to learn anything about this crime. You were in that Pantry, when it all went down—a trained observer."

Was there something slightly arch in the way he said that?

"Being a trained observer only takes you so far," I said. "I think you know, Manny, just what a madhouse that Pantry became."

He shook his head sympathetically. "Never experienced anything like it myself, and I've been in more than a few tense situations in my twenty-two years on the job. All those shots fired, the chaos, so many people crammed in that small space. Unimaginable."

I opened a hand to him. "So you understand why the point of view of an investigator of your stature is of interest."

Yes, I was kissing ass.

He smiled again, a bandito in a sharp suit; leaned back and folded his arms. "And my conclusion, formed from a distance, and yours at the scene, are surely the same. You saw that little bastard blasting away, didn't you?"

"I did."

"Testified to that effect."

"I did. I believe I talked on the phone, from my Chicago office, to one of your people, by way of pre-trial preparation."

He nodded. "That's right. We were selective about who we advised the District Attorney to call among the eyewitnesses. There were so many of them, and a witness of *your* stature was high on our list."

My ass's turn to be kissed.

I said, "That was the primary role of SUS—case preparation."

"Correct. That and researching the suspect and his background. Which we did thoroughly—to the tune of over three thousand interviews, and the longest, largest and most expensive criminal investigation in LAPD history."

I tried to look impressed. "And what did you learn?"

He flipped a hand. "Sirhan was clearly a self-appointed assassin. He decided that Bobby Kennedy was no good, because he was pro-Israel and powerful. And Sirhan was going to kill him, at whatever the cost."

"Premeditation, then."

"No question. And he wasn't under the influence of alcohol or drugs at the time, nor was he legally insane. And we found absolutely no evidence of a conspiracy in this crime. Believe me, we tried."

I cocked my head. "Yet some say a conspiracy was indicated. Eyewitnesses—"

"The unreliable ones," he cut in, some edge now, "we worked

on till we proved them false, or they modified their statements when we accused them of publicity seeking. That Serrano girl was a flake. There was a waiter, this kid DiPiero, who claimed seeing Sirhan with a good-looking girl in the Pantry. But we wound up identifying the woman who we determined was where this polka-dot-dress nonsense started."

This was news to me. "Oh, then you found her, the girl in the polka-dot dress?"

He bolted to his feet and went to the evidence board where he snatched off an 8x10 from the surviving scraps. Proudly, he walked over and handed it to me.

"That's her. Schulte. Valerie Schulte. She was in the Pantry that night, all right, just not with Sirhan. Maybe you saw her."

I hadn't, but that didn't mean anything. But what did strike me as meaningful was the absurdity of this attractive young woman—a blonde who resembled Sandra Dee—being identified by anybody as a dark-haired girl in a white dress with black polka dots. In addition to her hair color, the Schulte girl was wearing a green dress with yellow polka dots.

Oh, and she was on crutches, her right leg in a cast.

He folded his arms and smirked, pleased with himself. "Took forever to get that kid DiPiero to come around and make the right I.D."

I decided then and there not to take Manny's night course in criminology.

I said, "Anything you care to share on the ballistics side?"

He batted at the air. "Oh, Wayne Wolf is a real pro. He can make forensics evidence get on its hind legs and bark. He worked all night, making a match from a bullet at the scene to Sirhan's gun! He's not the top man over at the lab, you know, but I knew to request him."

I bet he did.

I said, "You confirmed that Sirhan was seen using a gun of the correct make at various shooting ranges?"

A decisive nod. "That's right. We gathered 40,000 cartridge casings and Wolf examined every one of them, looking for a match."

"How many did he come up with?"

"Well, uh...none. But that was a long shot, wasn't it?"

Forty-thousand long shots, apparently.

I glanced around—only three desks were inhabited. All the cardboard boxes suggested moving day or a mass firing.

"Looks pretty slow around here now," I said. "But I'm surprised with the trial over, and the death sentence delivered, you haven't shut down already."

He shrugged. "Oh, by last September we cut back from forty men to twenty, and we're phasing out now. Should be out of here by end of July, with everybody back to their regular assignments. We're waiting to see if Mr. Cooper files an appeal, but confidentially we're told that's unlikely."

What struck *me* as unlikely was having an assurance like that from the defense attorney after a murder conviction.

"Well," I said, getting to my feet, "I think that's all I need. Thanks, Manny. It's been enlightening."

He walked me down that central aisle in the movie sound stage that had housed this farce.

A firm hand settled on my shoulder as we walked. "Listen, Nate. There's a favor you could do me."

"If I can."

"Could you ask Pearson to straighten out this nonsense about me returning to the LAPD as some sort of CIA sneak? These conspiracy kooks are trying to make it sound like I was brought back and planted into the RFK case so I could steer things around to a point where no one would discover a conspiracy. That's just not so!"

He opened the door onto the hall for me.

"These clever types are already getting together and cookin' up nonsense," he said, "looking to profit by demanding, 'What *really* happened? What *really* happened?' *Couldn't* have been one little man with a gun! Ready and willing to float their theories to a public that craves answers as big as their fallen hero."

Sounded to me like Manny believed in conspiracy after all.

NINE

I arranged to meet a certain controversial medical examiner at four P.M. at the Otomisan, a hole-in-the wall diner on East First Street in Boyle Heights. Just east of downtown Los Angeles near Little Tokyo, across the L.A. River, the Heights had provided a post-war home for a large Japanese-American community. A handful of red booths faced a counter with a dozen red-cushioned stools, vinyl seating split like sideways smiles. Vintage Japanese prints with grim faces shared the walls with wartime family photographs of smiling ones, despite stark backgrounds of barracks and barbed wire.

Thomas Noguchi said, "This area is one of the few places where my people could live in L.A., after World War Two, when they were released from the internment camps."

His English was precise with the lilt of a Japanese accent.

"Were you shoved into one of those camps, Dr. Noguchi?"

We were sitting across from each other in a booth; the middle-aged Japanese woman in an indigo-blue cotton top and matching slacks kept a discreet eye on us as she fussed behind the counter, these two suspiciously well-dressed men ordering beer and nothing else. It was the kind of place that had regulars and we weren't those.

About forty, Dr. Noguchi—his round, pleasant face not really fitting that slender, almost skinny frame—looked damn near dapper in a dark, sharp, wide-lapelled suit, his wide, thick-knotted tie navy striped with narrow white. His hairline, no gray in the black, curved above a high forehead naturally, not receding, at least not yet. Thick black eyebrows arched in permanent curiosity.

He shook his head. "No, Mr. Heller. I came over from Tokyo in 1952. But my wife Hisako and her family were in detention camps. I fear this history is fading for the current generation."

"Boyle Heights is a little off the beaten path for me," I said. "I don't mind meeting here, but I have a hunch you don't live in Little Tokyo."

"I do not. My wife and I have a nice two-story residence on Oxford in the Wilshire District."

"Can't be the Sapporo beer," I said. We'd already been served the bottles and glasses. "They sell that all around town."

He chuckled. "No. And it is too early to dine. Why I selected this setting we will get back to. First, let us discuss your topic of interest—my autopsy of Robert F. Kennedy."

I poured beer into my glass. "Might I begin by asking, Doctor, if the findings of your autopsy had anything to do with your recent firing?"

That invoked a modest Buddha smile. "It did. But there were sixty-one charges against me, including that I reveled in the publicity following the assassination. A jealous rival had me singing and dancing in my office while the Senator lay dying. Elated at the thought I would soon become famous."

"That seems unlikely. But admittedly we've just met."

The tiny smiled widened a bit. "I have read of you, Mr. Heller. They call you the Private Eye to the Stars...well, they are calling me the Coroner to the Stars now, so perhaps we have something in common. And yet I would imagine yours is not an appellation you have encouraged."

"No," I admitted. "But handling Marilyn Monroe's autopsy made yours inevitable, I'm afraid."

He filled his glass. "An inherent irony is not lost on me," he said. "I had performed the autopsy on Miss Monroe six years before, and now found myself making the death examination of an alleged lover of hers."

I knew more about that than I would share with the deposed medical examiner.

"Bob was a friend," I said. "I think you know I was there that night, in the Pantry."

He nodded, took a sip of beer.

Finally he said, "We speak of these people as if they descended from Mt. Olympus. But their frail humanity is something with which I am all too familiar in my profession."

"And in mine," I said. "I was Bob's bodyguard that night. But he insisted I not carry a gun. If I had, you might have conducted a different autopsy."

His eyes, a washed-out gray, conveyed great sadness. "To me, your friend and his brother represented the greatness of America. I respected their style, their leadership, the way they reached out to all ethnic groups as if to say, 'You too are Americans.' "

I smiled just a little—probably as close to a Buddha smile as I had in me. "His brother Jack fought in the Pacific, you know."

"I know. As did you, Mr. Heller. Bronze Star, I believe?"

"You do your homework."

"Even a doctor to the dead must do so. But in all honesty, I encountered you in my more casual reading. You do not appear to have made the medical journals."

I swallowed some good Japanese beer. "No. More like *True Detective* and *Confidential*."

"You are too modest. More than once in *Life*, at least once in *Look*. And the Sunday supplements. You harbor no resentment toward the Japanese?"

"Do you harbor resentment over the internment of your wife and her folks? I'm guessing yes but you don't obsess about it. What good would it do? There's an emperor and some generals I wouldn't mind knocking around some."

"We have that in common as well." He sipped beer again. "Speaking of journalists, you said on the phone you were looking into the case for Drew Pearson. What, might I ask, is Mr. Pearson's agenda?"

I shrugged. "Frankly, he got on the wrong side of this thing by blasting Bobby Kennedy politically in the weeks before the assassination."

The dark eyebrows flicked up and down. "Unfortunate timing."

"Drew does know there's some talk of a possible second shooter, which he may touch upon, but that's not the focus. He just wants to be able to discuss the tragedy accurately while elevating the memory of Robert Kennedy."

Noguchi touched his chest, lowered his head an inch or two. "It needs scant elevation in these quarters, despite the dancing I'm said to have done."

"Do you know why the results of your autopsy were withheld for many months and given to Sirhan's defense at the last minute?"

"I know only that it wasn't my doing."

He told me his story.

At Good Samaritan Hospital, at 3 A.M. on June 6 last year, the medical examiner had made his way through a heartbroken crowd whose vigil had turned into mourning. A security guard guided Noguchi and two deputies to the hospital's autopsy room. A team from the M.E.'s office was already there—investigator, chief autopsy assistant, photographer, with instructions to secure the appropriate hospital charts and X-rays and assemble the surgeons who had tried to save Kennedy's life. Also present were staff members of Noguchi's and the D.A.'s.

Noguchi had been advised by trusted peers from around the country that if Kennedy died, the medical examiner must take charge before the federal government rushed in, as they had after the JFK assassination, which had resulted in the President's body being flown to D.C. for an autopsy (by unqualified military doctors) so flawed it generated immediate cover-up rumors and conspiracy theories.

Conducting this important autopsy at the Good Samaritan was fine with the medical examiner—conditions in the basement at City Hall were cramped and dire. Noguchi had been begging for better conditions, making enemies of his bosses by telling the press that in his facility rats outnumbered microscopes.

"Senator Kennedy's body lay on the table," Noguchi said, "under a sheet. After removing the bandages from the deceased's head, I turned to the surgeons and asked what had become of the hair shavings—the scalp hair around the wounded area, shaved off before surgery? I knew that might contain critical evidence."

Noguchi had sent an investigator scurrying to the operating room to check; his emissary discovered the hospital staff had retained those little clumps of hair, which Noguchi's man placed in an evidence envelope.

"In the autopsy room I made an unusual request," Noguchi said. "Not normal procedure by any means, and the only time in the thousands of autopsies I have performed that I asked for the deceased's face to be covered. This was done with a towel. I needed to proceed with my work undistracted by my feelings for the Senator. I observed a moment of silence, head bowed in the traditional Japanese manner of respect. Then I began my work at the feet and worked my way to the head."

I frowned. "That isn't normal procedure either, is it, Doctor? Isn't the reverse more typical?"

He nodded, twice. "Yes, Mr. Heller, but this approach, slow, careful, can uncover important evidence overlooked if the wound gets all the attention."

First studied was a through-and-through gunshot, underneath and somewhat to the back of the right armpit. Traveling at an angle, the bullet (not recovered) exited through the front right shoulder.

Second to be examined was another wound an inch or so from the first; it surprisingly had not traveled in the same direction, rather crossing to lodge in soft tissue near the spinal column at the back of the lower neck. With a finger and thumb, Noguchi had removed the deformed .22 caliber bullet.

Third was the fatal bullet, its exact path impossible to probe. It had entered the skull an inch to the left of the victim's right ear, shattering into metallic shards. These fragments could not be matched to Sirhan's gun—to any gun—beyond establishing the caliber (.22). Unburned powder grains formed a circular pattern on the victim's right ear.

"This was unquestionably the most meticulous autopsy I ever performed," Noguchi said. "But, ironically, that very thoroughness led to a credible conspiracy theory, which did not endear me to my already vociferous critics."

The clumps of scalp hair retrieved at the medical examiner's instance had revealed gunpowder residue. And not just metallic elements, but soot.

Soot in the forensics sense is a collection of unburned grains of powder, burned grains of powder, and metallic fragments.

"Doctor," I said, leaning forward, "I saw it myself—the muzzle of Sirhan's gun was at minimum a yard away from Kennedy. Soot in the hair means the kill shot was within inches of Bob's head. Or closer."

With an almost pixieish smile, Noguchi asked, "Mr. Heller, are you familiar with the expression, 'in a pig's eye?' "

"I am. Also in a pig's ass."

"Well, the test I ran involved neither one—in this instance, it was a pig's ear. Actually, seven of them."

Seven pig's ears had been attached to as many padded muslin heads simulating skulls. With earmuffs at the ready, Noguchi directed a plainclothes detective to shoot at each faux skull, first a firm contact shot, second moving back a quarter inch…then half an inch…one, two, three, four inches.

"At three inches from the right mastoid area," Noguchi said, "we had a perfect match for the tattooed pattern of unburned-powder grains on the victim's right ear. And the shape of the entrance wound was nearly identical."

Noguchi's autopsy findings were not the only indication Sirhan may not have been the sole shooter: four bullets were fired at RFK, three hitting him, another tearing through his clothing; five other victims behind Bob were also shot (none killed), all the bullets recovered; and three more slugs wound up in the ceiling tiles. That indicated the trajectory of twelve bullets at the scene, with Sirhan's revolver holding only eight.

"Too many bullets," I said.

"So it would seem. But the LAPD insists the excess can be written off as ricochets. And you know better than most, Mr. Heller, the extent of the crowded excitement in that Pantry. What did the eyes of witnesses actually see? Did no one see what actually happened?"

I thought about that. Then: "Sirhan would've had to lunge toward Bob close enough to make the kill shot, not be noticed by anybody, and then lurch back into his prior position, to have fired at the distance witnesses reported."

"So it would appear." He opened a palm, tentatively. "The only other possibility would seem to be a second gunman, shooting from behind at close range, then slipping immediately away, attention diverted by Sirhan shooting from farther away, in front."

Soon it would be the supper hour and Japanese-American patrons in modest Western street clothes were trailing in; the little mom-and-pop diner would soon be filled, the bubbling oil for tempura welcoming an obviously regular clientele.

"Do you mind my asking," I ventured, "what sort of charges were brought against you? Your professionalism seems apparent to me. You must have a dark side I'm not sensing."

That Buddha smile returned. "You see my smile? I was accused of wearing this expression in the midst of mass disasters. I reportedly threatened a fellow employee with a knife. I dreamed aloud of how I might become even more famous if only a jetliner would crash into a hotel. And I longed to perform a live autopsy on my boss."

"Who doesn't?"

He leaned gently forward. "I suggested we meet here, Mr. Heller, because no other restaurant in town displays photographs of the detention camps. I was a child in Yokosuka when you were fighting in the Pacific. Would the residue of a not distant past erect a barrier between us? Would you assume a Japanese coroner had somehow botched so important an autopsy?"

"Of course not."

"I see that in your case, or at least sense it. But the ridiculous charges against me are what a friend has called 'plain, old-fashioned prejudice.' Or do you think I'm simply paranoid, thinking there are people out to get me because I'm Japanese?"

"I do not. I can't imagine you're going to let them get away with it, either."

His nod was on a tilt. "I've taken my case to the Civil Service Commission of our fair city...or at least we will see how 'fair' it is at the hearing I've demanded."

On the street, I asked the deposed medical examiner one last question.

"What does your gut tell you about the Robert Kennedy killing, Doctor?"

He didn't hesitate in answering: "My gut tells me Sirhan acted alone. But my 'gut' is not enough—forensic science must concern itself only with the known facts. Based on that, I cannot support the conclusion that Sirhan Sirhan killed Robert Kennedy."

Nita wrapped up a guest shot on a new show that would be on in the fall, *Marcus Welby, M.D.*, and just before eight P.M. dragged into my Pink Palace bungalow looking like a patient. But she was ready to be discharged after a shower and freshening up, decking herself out in a gold-red-and-black tunic top and black flared pants. I got into a two-toned striped yellow shirt with matching tie and a golden brown blazer, if you're interested. My pants did not flare. Much.

We dined at the hotel, in the timeless Polo Lounge with its dark green-and-white walls and tartan-plaid carpet, its horseshoe-shaped private booths overlooking the garden patio where lights on trees seemed to twinkle in time to the tinkling piano making background music out of Cole Porter, George Gershwin, Johnny Mercer and other standard bearers.

We shared the twenty-bucks-plus Beverly Hills Salad De Luxe, a decadent concoction of crab legs, shrimp, avocado, tomato, romaine lettuce, and Thousand Island dressing. I mean to make no judgment about my female companion, but she ate most of it. I was busy recounting the encounters I'd had since seeing her a thousand years ago this morning—Fred Rubinski and Wes Grapp at the A-1, Manny Hermano at Parker Center, and Thomas Noguchi at the Boyle Heights diner.

This would be our third night together, assuming she stayed over once again. I'd learned quite a bit about her. She'd been married to a director—I inwardly cringed because my ex-wife was now married to one of that breed, although hers did film, and Nita's TV—but she made a point of it having been over for years. She had no kids and informed me, too lightly, she was "cheerfully barren," the result of an illegally performed abortion in her teen years.

"And now," she said, "after a fairly successful run, even if I never did land a series...I'm at a crossroads."

"Really? Paused for a train, or just waiting for your turn at an all-way stop?"

"Take today," she said, dismissing my question for the smart-ass rhetorical thing that it was. "A pretty decent role. A woman with some scary symptoms that Robert Young explained away. Nice man, by the way...a little moody. Anyway, I'm just a throwaway, filler stuff, really."

"What about 'there are no small parts, just small actors'?"

"Stanislavski knew what he was talking about. But I'm afraid even the small parts will dry up for this small actress. Nate, I'm...going to be forty-three in a month. Tell anyone and I'll have to kill you."

I waved that off. "Don't worry, honey. Knowing that, I'm not about to be seen in public again with an old bat like you."

That made her laugh. I liked that I could make her laugh. And I liked her. She was upbeat and sad, a tougher combo to pull off than the ingredients of the Salad De Luxe. Which was excellent, by the way. She'd started talking, leaving room for me to eat, finally.

"Truth is," she said, "I'm heading into that no-gal's-land of ingenue roles I'm too old for and character parts I'm too young for."

"Didn't you say something once, about needing a sugar daddy?"

Her smile was almost a kiss. "That's what I was hinting at."

We laughed about that, and variations on the theme, as we kissed and petted like kids—not in the Polo Lounge, but on top of my made bed at my bungalow in the low lighting that was kind to a miserable old bastard like me and a supple not-young doll like her. I fondled and kissed her in intimate places that are none of your fucking business and she did the same with me. We undressed each other, which was sexy if awkward, and then were under the sheets.

After some quick clean-up in the bathroom, she returned in just bra and panties, neither terribly substantial, just pink fluff really, and crawled under the covers and went almost instantly asleep. I took another shower, warm not hot, got into my pajamas, black silk, and padded out in my slippers to get myself a ginger ale in the darkened living room. I preferred Coca-Cola but the caffeine was not a risk worth taking. As an afterthought, I added some vodka.

I took my glass out on the patio. The night was cool enough that the robe was a good idea. I sat at a glass-topped, white wrought-iron table. Put my right ankle on my left knee and exposed some ankle. That the patio was smallish made it feel protected. Beyond a low stone wall lay a gently rustling tropical garden whose greenery was enlivened by exotic flowers, palm trees lording over all against an unimpressed deep blue sky, its starry tiara askew.

She made me jump a little, she'd been so quiet, slipping out onto the patio in a pink Beverly Hills Hotel bathrobe. It fit her nicely, belt knotted at bellybutton, feet bare, dark brunette hair tousled, no makeup at all.

As she sat on the wrought-iron chair next to me, she was laughing lightly.

I tried out a tiny grin. "Am I that funny?"

"I was just thinking."

"Oh?"

"I don't remember ever being with a man who wears pajamas. Much less silk ones."

"You, on the other hand, seem simply made for terrycloth. Luckily I had a lady's robe handy."

"Luckily," she agreed. "Some past guest must have left it."

I nodded. "Another sweet young thing who'd probably never seen an adult male in silk jammies before."

"Except maybe in the movies."

"Except maybe in the movies. Just how many men not in jammies have you been with, young lady?"

"Did you want a full report on my past amorous liaisons, Mr. Heller?"

"We have time, Ms. Romaine."

"I doubt that. You think I rolled up all those TV credits without staring at a ceiling or two?"

It was all very light but there were contradictory undercurrents. Melancholy. Fondness. Regret. Loss. Possibility.

"This poking around," she said.

"Hope you enjoyed it."

"Not what I mean. Looking into…what you're looking into. It sounds like I got you into something…dangerous."

"Danger is my business. Trouble is my middle name. Granted, they laugh at my passport…."

"I mean it, Nate. This is big. Full of risk. I shouldn't have… what I mean is….You can stop here. You can stop *now*. Before we can't sit out here like this without wondering what every rustle of leaves is about."

"Nita. That's lovely of you to say. And you *are* the one who got me pulling at a string or two on the sweater. But it's turned into a job, for a longtime client. Perhaps I shouldn't have brought you up to speed. Perhaps you're the one unnecessarily at risk."

"I'd like to stay...up to speed. Help you, if I can. If it makes sense."

We sat quietly. She reached for my drink and sipped.

"That's more than ginger ale," she observed.

"A hint of vodka."

"More like a kick."

Fronds rustled, but nobody tried to kill us.

"Before you were born," I said, "my first job as a private investigator took me to Miami. I'd been a plainclothes detective before that, youngest on the Chicago PD, and I'd attracted some attention. Got me clients right off the bat. One of them was Anton Cermak."

"Who?"

Maybe she was past forty, but she was still so very young.

I said, "The mayor of Chicago. He got himself in trouble with the Outfit."

"The what?"

"You're a child. The Chicago crime syndicate. He got in bed with the wrong faction and he tried to have a man called Frank Nitti killed."

"Him I've heard of. He was on *The Untouchables*. I did one of those."

I decided not to tell her that Eliot Ness had been a close friend. That could wait. This wasn't about name-dropping. Not that she'd know many.

"Anyway, young lady, if you check the history books, a little foreign guy with bushy hair and a dark complexion took a pot shot at Franklin Delano Roosevelt, who I assume you've heard of. This was not long after FDR won the presidency. The assassin's name was Zangara and he had some half-assed political motive, anarchy or some such bullshit."

"But he didn't kill Roosevelt. That much I know."

"He didn't kill Roosevelt. The history books say Giuseppe Zangara missed and accidentally hit Mayor Cermak, who was shaking hands with the President Elect at the time. Zangara was a Sicilian who thought he was dying of cancer, by the way, and they say his family lived well after Giuseppe went quickly to the chair. There was a second shooter at Miami, ready to back him up. Pretty standard procedure for certain types of assassinations. Bottom line, Mayor Cermak was killed just a few weeks after two of his crooked cops were sent to shoot Al Capone's successor, Frank Nitti. They'd pulled in another cop for back-up without telling him the score. That was me. That was what initiated me going private. I had to go to the hospital where Frank Nitti lay fighting for his life and convince him I wasn't in on it. Did I mention Cermak had hired me as a bodyguard?"

Halfway through that she had clutched my hand.

I looked at the stars. "What do they call that feeling—déjà vu, right? Well, all day long I've been feeling it, and I think I felt it that night in the Pantry, too, wrestling with that little bushy-haired prick, but I didn't let it in. But Nita...*I've been here before.* And the Cermak kill went down in front of a crowd of people, a packed amphitheater, and everybody saw it and nobody saw it, not really. So I have come full circle, baby, and I don't like it. It's like I've spent all these years learning everything and nothing."

She got up and came over and sat in my lap and put her arms around me and buried her face in my neck. I could feel the tears.

Muffled, she said, "Is that all true?"

"Yes. It's true. You *are* a child."

She stayed on my lap with her arms around me, but she pulled away to look at me with the big brown eyes in the lovely makeup-free face. "How far are you going to take this?"

"Us? Or this?"

"Both."

"Far as I can get away with."

"It's cute when you call me 'Baby.' "

"Is it?"

"Very Bogart."

"Him you've heard of."

"Tell me something."

"I'll try."

"Can a sixty-something man get it up twice in one night?"

I lifted her off my lap.

"Let's go in and see," I said.

TEN

The Riviera Country Club, a verdant ribbon between Pacific Palisades and the Pacific Ocean, had been around since the late '20s, a haven from L.A. traffic and a sanctuary of solitude interrupted only by the crack of metal or hardwood golf heads connecting with balatá-coated balls. That and, of course, the cries, moans and obscene outbursts of frustrated members and guests. Arnold Palmer called the Riviera "one of the great tests of golf." I called golf itself a colossal pain in the ass.

I disliked the so-called sport with the intensity of those who loved the game, but playing it, and playing it well enough not to be an embarrassment, was a requirement of doing business in certain circles. So was losing more holes than you won.

The main clubhouse, a rambling array of light-tan, red-roofed Mission-style structures, offered the expected balcony view of the driving range, chipping area, putting green, and practice bunker. The bar afforded a tucked-away, high-ceilinged, predominantly male refuge of mahogany paneling, piped-in Rat Pack music, and two-tone green-striped upholstered easy chairs in little private groupings, matching chairs at tables and on higher legs at the bar. You could get shit-faced here in style.

I'd ascertained their 8:30 A.M. tee time by way of a call to Grant Cooper's law office, pretending to be a colleague. But I had no desire to chase Sirhan Sirhan's attorney and his prosperous peers around the golf course, dodging balls and navigating white-bark trees. Eighteen holes, plus dropping off their clubs and freshening up in the locker room, should put them at this posh version of the traditional nineteenth hole before lunch.

From the balcony beyond the bar, I'd seen their pair of golf carts storm the citadel, and twenty minutes or so later they trooped in, four men in their early sixties wearing pricey casual clothes intended for men half their age (though few could have afforded them)—lightweight sports jackets with large-collar button-down shirts, stripes or solids or in Cooper's case brown-and-orange plaid. Their flared slacks, tastefully gray or tan, offset the offenses. I was in a light-blue-and-white-striped sport coat, navy tie, and white slacks, so I was only marginally less guilty.

I had commandeered an easy chair by a fireplace—neither I nor it were lit, even if I was deep into my second vodka gimlet. As the foursome collected cocktails at the bar, I caught Grant Cooper's eye. Took him a second or two to make me, but then I smiled—applying medium wattage—and waved him over. He reflexively returned the smile and excused himself with his peers, an uplifted hand conveying he'd only be a short while.

The prominent attorney was tall and slender with a deeply grooved oblong face, eyes glittering dark behind heavy black-framed glasses, his steel-gray hair swept back above a high fore-head. He set a martini down on the coffee table between us.

"Mr. Heller," he said in a baritone with an edge, as I stood and we shook hands across that low-riding table. "I believe we've never met outside the courtroom."

"That's correct." I gestured to an easy chair positioned oppo-site. "Would you sit for a moment? I have a few things I'd like to go over with you."

Cooper shrugged, affable if wary. "Nothing unpleasant, I trust. I already took a beating on the back nine."

He sat. Folded his arms and got comfy, resting an ankle on a knee. White leather loafers—Pierre Cardin, I'd wager—and orange silk socks. "Don't recall seeing you here before. Are you a member?"

"No, my L.A. partner, Fred Rubinski, is. I'm in Chicago more often than not."

"The A-1 Detective Agency, isn't it?"

I nodded. "I wanted to ask you a few questions about the Sirhan case." I briefly explained I was doing background research for Drew Pearson.

"Pearson has a reputation," he said through a slice of a smile, "as something of a muckraker, Mr. Heller. Bit of a scandal-monger."

"Make it 'Nate.'"

"And 'Grant.'" He produced a pipe from one sport coat pocket and a tobacco pouch and matches from the other. "Is that why he's digging into the RFK assassination? To pay tribute now that Bobby Kennedy has acquired sainthood status?"

I pretended to be mildly amused by that. "Exactly. And you're in a position to share an insider's look at the case."

A thick black eyebrow arched. "More so than the late Senator's personal bodyguard?"

"That's not something I'd care to advertise."

"But you *were* there that night, which is more than I could say."

"I was in the Pantry," I admitted, "but like most people present, I don't really know what I saw. It was like the stateroom scene in *A Night at the Opera* but with guns."

A smile flickered. "Well, one gun, anyway."

I put on a thoughtful face, not at all adversarial. Sat forward, hands loose in my lap. "Actually, that's something I've been wondering. *Could* there have been a second gun, do you think?"

He waved that off as he waved out his match, his pipe lighted. "Nonsense. Conspiratorial bunk."

"But couldn't you at least have raised the possibility in court?"

A curt head shake. "Going down that path would've killed us out of the gate."

Of course, they'd been "killed" anyway.

Staying reasonable, I said, "I've spoken to Medical Examiner Noguchi. He says there were powder burns on, and behind, Bob's right ear. That and the other gunshot wounds indicate the shooter stood right behind him. And we both know Sirhan was in front of him, several yards away."

The attorney gestured with pipe in hand, the exhaust fumes aromatic in a way that said money. "You said it yourself, Nate— that was a madhouse. No two people reported the same thing, and my client was under attack even as he kept blasting away. Weren't you one of the men who tackled him, and didn't it take Rosey Grier and the rest of an impromptu football team to take that little assassin down?"

Sirhan's lead defense attorney's description of his client: "that little assassin."

"Took a group effort, all right," I said. "That runt was almost supernaturally strong. But I'm wondering—meaning no criticism, just trying to put things in perspective—why you didn't bring the autopsy evidence into court?"

He studied me.

Finally, coldly, he said, "We got hold of it very late."

"Still," I said, "you didn't really use Dr. Noguchi's findings at all, beyond establishing homicide."

Cooper seemed openly irritated now; both feet were on the floor and he was edging forward on his comfy chair. "I wouldn't trust that little Jap farther than I could throw him, though I wouldn't mind trying. He's a self-aggrandizing, publicity-seeking *former* Medical Examiner these days, you know."

I squinted at him, as if I didn't already have him well in focus. "But you kept the autopsy photos *out*..."

The heavy eyebrows hiked. "Because that grotesque material would have been obscenely prejudicial to the jury!"

"Those autopsy photos would have demonstrated the kill

shot came from behind—you could have absolved your client
of the murder itself, if not the general assault."

Cooper goggled at me. "Absolved him of the murder of a
man he killed in front of dozens of witnesses? My goal wasn't to
try in vain to plead the innocence of somebody who stood a few
feet from the Senator and emptied a gun at him, wounding five
others in the process!"

"What *was* your goal, Grant?"

His brow knit. "To prove diminished capacity and keep him
out of the goddamn gas chamber."

"How did that work out?"

Cooper reared back, his eyes flaring behind the heavy black
frames. "How did your *bodyguard* assignment work out, Heller?"

I raised a surrender palm. "Fair enough. Then can I assume,
with a client on Death Row, you're going to appeal?"

He grunted. "Why bother? The judge ran a tight ship. We
did our best. Do you think I enjoy losing a client to the gas
chamber? It's never happened to me before."

A sentence of death never happened to Sirhan Sirhan before
either, but that "little assassin" wouldn't get a second crack at
improving his batting average. Not courtesy of a crusading
defense attorney who didn't bother mounting an appeal after
suffering a Death Penalty verdict.

"Neither one of us," I admitted, "served our clients all that
well."

"On that much we can agree." He seemed about to get up,
clearly annoyed that a conversation that began well had so
quickly degenerated.

I raised a hand as if I were being sworn in, in court. "I have
just a few other things."

He frowned. "I notice you've not been taking notes on this
journalistic fishing expedition."

"Would you prefer I did? I wanted to keep things informal. Off the record. Strictly background."

For a moment he thought, then: "No. That's all right. Go on."

"Why did you stipulate to the ballistics evidence?"

He flinched, taking a rabbit punch the ref missed. "Mr. Heller…"

"Nate."

"Nate. It was irrelevant to our defense. We stipulated to almost everything evidentiary that the prosecution introduced."

So I'd noticed.

"You almost certainly could have kept the 'RFK Must Die' notebooks out," I said. "They were seized in an illegal search, after all. And even if you couldn't, you could have questioned whether Sirhan wrote them—no handwriting expert could say that he did. And this Wolf character is a notorious ballistics hack for the prosecution, narrowly escaping a perjury charge in the Kirsch case. Yet you made no effort to impeach his 'expert testimony.' "

"I thought I'd made clear," Cooper said tightly, "that our goal was strictly one of proving diminished capacity. Our client wasn't always happy with us on that score…there were, as you may know, some outbursts from him in court. He claims, not entirely convincingly, that he has amnesia about the shooting itself. The path we took seemed the only way to save his life. And, yes, we failed to do that."

I tossed down the rest of my gimlet and got to my feet. "Yeah, yeah, and I stink as a bodyguard and maybe we can buy each other drinks or play eighteen holes sometime and meanwhile we'll just write it off as the cost of doing business, that little prick taking the fall for Christ knows how many other shooters in that pantry."

He bristled, looking up at me. "The cost of doing business… in what way, for God's sake?"

"Oh I don't know. The cost of you not doing jail time for possession of stolen Grand Jury transcripts in that Friars Club card-cheating scandal. Of avoiding disbarment over what the LAPD has on you. Of keeping your big-league mobster clients like Johnny Roselli happy, though what's in it for them I couldn't tell you. Not yet anyway."

Now he was on his feet, tall enough to glare right at me, dark eyes sparking under black eyebrows that blended into the upper black rims of his glasses in twin thick strokes as if applied by a master caricature artist.

"Those are the kind of careless remarks, Nate, that can get you in trouble in court…and out of court."

"Is that a threat, Grant? Have you forgotten that I'm from Chicago? That I know Johnny Roselli, too?"

He got very close; I could smell the English Leather. He spoke softly, almost whispering.

"Maybe you need to think, Mr. Heller, about whether you want everything I know about Operation Mongoose and certain anti-Castro efforts on your late friend Bob's behalf coming out before you get too goddamn fucking mouthy."

"Well, I guess I know at least one thing, Mr. Cooper."

"Oh?"

"Why you winked at me in court."

I gave him a cocky little salute and got the hell out of there. But I just might have been shaking a little.

After lunching with Nita at Canter's on North Fairfax—she had auditions all afternoon—I headed back to my A-1 office to take meetings unrelated to the Kennedy inquiry. But midday Will Harris, our forensics consultant, returned a call I'd left the day before. Will had retired from the FBI last year and opened up shop in Pasadena as a freelance criminalist. He'd been recommended to us by Wes Grapp.

I told him I was researching the RFK assassination for Drew Pearson and would like to go over some photos and documents with him—the material Sgt. Shore had slipped me out at Griffith Park the other day.

Will was past fifty but sounded younger thanks to enthusiasm and a boyish tenor. "I guess I know why you're calling *me* about it."

"Do I?"

"You mean you don't know?"

"Know what?"

"You really don't know? My last job for the Bureau was helping work the crime scene at the Ambassador just hours after the killing. I took my twenty-year retirement the next week."

I leaned back in my desk chair. "That may be a helpful coincidence. Can you make it to the Bradbury Building yet today?"

Instead of answering that, he said, "How would you like a tour of the crime scene?"

"I've seen the crime scene."

"You only *think* you have. Look, there's somebody at that hotel you should talk to. Let me make a call. Think a doddering old boy like you might be able to get yourself out of bed in the middle of the night?"

"Sure. To pee."

"Or not to pee is the question. I'll call you at the Beverly Hills—usual bungalow?"

"Yup," I said, and gave him the direct phone number.

"It'll be around two A.M.," he said. "That's a working kitchen, obviously, and any other time but the middle of the night would be hard to arrange, not to mention noisy as hell."

"I'll wait for your call. In the meantime, how about I messenger over this packet of photos and documents?"

"It's a plan."

❀

I had an early dinner with Nita at Musso & Frank's—with plenty of film/TV industry people around for her to smile at—then followed her Fiat in the Jag out to Studio City and her little house where we loaded up enough things to move her in for a week or two at the bungalow. She'd pick up her mail every couple of days and check her service for messages. This was only Day Three of my investigation and our relationship, but things were moving fast.

We went to bed early and mostly lay there talking, getting to know each other better, and she began questioning me about the famous crimes and infamous people I'd encountered over the decades. I didn't tell her everything because there were more dead men and lively women than could reasonably be believed, even with the bullet scars and my enduring good looks as evidence.

Her family history bore echoes of my own: born in Brooklyn, daughter of Jewish immigrants from Europe, previous generations suffering murders, pogroms and brutal discrimination that finally chased her father's family out of Russia.

We were still talking when my travel alarm went off at one-thirty A.M. I got up, threw off my pajamas and got into fresh underwear, button-down Polo, slacks and Italian loafers, tossed some water on my face, toweled off, and was about to go out when she sat up, her breasts challenging her nightie.

"Aren't you taking a gun?" she asked.

"I'm going to a hotel, not the Alamo."

"We've both been to that particular hotel before. And you have a way of getting yourself in Dutch. Or were those stories you told me bullshit?"

"There were elements of truth."

But she did have a point. I was wading into some choppy

waters, inhabited not by sharks but the likes of the Company and the mob and maybe even a Palestinian assassin or two.

So I put my holstered nine millimeter on my right hip— shoulder slings were just too damn uncomfortable at my age— and tossed on a Pierre Cardin sport coat over it.

She said, "You know what Miss Kitty tells Matt Dillon don't you?"

"No. What?"

"Matt…be careful."

"What if my name isn't Matt?"

"Be fucking careful."

Walking through a hotel in the middle of the night, particularly a sprawling one, makes a haunted house out of it and a ghost of you. Of course, a tragedy haunted the Ambassador, turning it into a collective terrible memory. *Would Hollywood's Hotel ever recover?* I wondered. *Was the Cocoanut Grove on its way to yesterday?* Already a certain seediness was showing, as if the grand old palace was slowly rotting from within.

My footsteps were a ghost's, too, silent on the red-and-black carpet, the after-hours low lighting dulling the yellow of walls and pillars, fountains shut off and gurgling faintly as if in final death throes, leather furnishings and scattered ferns and an occasional classical statue or grand piano adding to the ghostly aura, objects from the past refusing to give way to the present.

The Embassy ballroom, when I moved through with my foot-steps like echoing gunshots, was barely lighted at all, despite the chandeliers hanging like crystalline jellyfish, and when I stepped through the curtains just beyond where Bob had urged us on to Chicago, the slanted corridor's ebony was spookily dis-rupted by the outline in light of the double doors we'd gone through to where Sirhan Sirhan had been waiting.

I pushed through to my past where the faint blue glow of

buzzing fluorescent lighting awaited. So did a little man in a white bucket cap, red-and-white aloha shirt, chino shorts and sandals. Studying a clipboard of fanned-back pages, Will Harris wore round-lensed wireframe glasses and looked a little like a white Sammy Davis Jr.

"We have about an hour," he said by way of greeting, "before the cleaning crew comes in."

Right now, the big adjacent kitchen was as abandoned as the one on the *Titanic* right before it went down. The Pantry, with only Will and me populating it, still seemed small.

I went over to him—he was standing near where Bob had fallen—and we shook hands, a quick but firm handshake.

"Try to imagine," Will said, eyes large and buggy behind the lenses, "eighty human beings jammed into this space."

We were in the most open area of the Pantry, with only an ice-cube-making machine to the right compromising the space and with the kitchen itself off to the left. The major difference, besides the absence of bleeding bodies, was the floor wasn't filthy. Perhaps what had happened here had shamed the hotel into treating this space with respect.

"I don't have to imagine it," I said. "I was one of them."

"My point being," he said, peering over the top of the wire-rim glasses, "the notion that once the shooting started anyone would see much of anything but bedlam is specious at best."

"If you got through those pilfered papers," I said, nodding to the clipboard in his hands, "you know the LAPD came up with ten sightings of the girl in the polka-dot dress, several with Sirhan."

He pointed to the stainless-steel serving table. "Yes, including that they were both standing up there, waiting...well above eye level. Who would be looking in their direction, not Robert Kennedy's?"

I shrugged. "The girl was a curvy number, they say. But getting a look at the next president of the United States might upstage her."

Will clunked the clipboard down on the ice-making unit. "Let's start with the 'official' bullets, according to this prosecution shill Wolf…who I personally warned Deputy D.A. Fitts about, although he probably already knew, after that Kirsch case."

The little criminalist held up two fingers—whether a hippie peace sign or Nixon's victory gesture was in the eye of the beholder. "We have two bullets entering RFK's right back. These remained lodged in the body. That's bullets One and Two."

Now he held up three fingers. "Another bullet entered the victim's right back with an exit wound out the right front. This passed through a ceiling tile and was lost in the ceiling interstice. Bullet Three."

Four fingers. "Another bullet passed through your friend's suitcoat, right shoulder, on an upward path, not entering his body but going on through to strike victim Paul Schrade in the forehead. Thankfully not fatally. Bullet Four."

Five fingers. "Another shot hit the right hip of bystander Ira Goldstein. Bullet Five."

Two hands employed now, chest-level against the aloha colors, a forefinger of the left added to the displayed five digits of the right. "Another bullet entered Goldstein's left pant leg but not his body, struck the cement floor and hit another bystander, Erwin Stroll, in the left leg. Bullet Six."

Seven fingers. "Another bystander, William Weisel, was struck in the stomach. Again, not fatally. Bullet Seven."

Eight. "Another bullet first hit a ceiling tile, then wounded bystander Elizabeth Evans in the forehead. Bullet Eight."

I said, "Your fourth, sixth and eighth trajectories make damn little sense."

He batted the air as if at an irritating fly. "They're not *mine*—

it's that clown Wolf again. Here's just one example—that fourth bullet had to pass through the Senator's suitcoat, at an 80-degree upward angle. Schrade would need to be nine feet tall to take that hit where he was standing."

I thought about all of that. "Sirhan's .22 held eight bullets. Sounds like the prosecution had to make eight bullets sing and dance to keep the count down."

Will gave up half a grin. "And they did it with audacious imagination—have to give 'em that. But let's keep the count going, shall we?"

"Who's stopping you?"

He tapped the first page of the clipboard where it rested on the stainless steel counter. "The autopsy indicates *two* bullet tracks in the victim's brain from *one* entry point—in court, the prosecution took care to call the two bullets 'fragments,' as if they added up to one. Not to confuse a layman, but a twelve-millimeter 'fragment' from the victim's brain could not have fit through the barrel of a .22 revolver. I don't believe it was a frag, rather a flattened .22 bullet...which of course adds a ninth bullet."

"Forensics experts might disagree on that," I pointed out.

"Possibly—one like Wolf, in the bag for the prosecution, sure as hell would...and did." The little man in the bucket hat glanced around. "Let's have a look at those swinging double doors where you and the Senator and his party came in."

We took the few steps over there and I frowned. "This door frame looks new—did they paint it?"

"It is new. The original had a pair of bullet holes here, about two inches apart..." He pointed to the center door frame, about his shoulder level. "...one above the other."

"Yeah. Yeah, I remember noticing that in the photos."

Will indicated the left vertical side of the door frame, where a photo had shown two LAPD officers identifying two more bullet holes, a bit lower than the center post ones, staggered.

"There was also a small caliber bullet lodged in the door jamb," Will said. "If you're keeping track, we're up to fourteen bullets now. And that doesn't address the ceiling tiles, which you may note all look fresh and clean…replaced after a number of tiles were removed as evidence."

I reared back. "Why would they be considered evidence unless they had bullet holes?"

"You're not as dumb as you look, Nate. Of course, you might expect those tiles, and that original doorframe, to be in the evidence locker at Parker Center."

"And they aren't?"

"No, they've all been destroyed. Recently, right after the trial. Space issues is the reason given. That wasn't information I dug out of the material you gave me—I still have sources at the LAPD. But let's be generous. Let's say I'm wrong and only one bullet entered Robert Kennedy's brain and fragmented. Let's say any bullet holes in the ceiling tiles were ricochets made by the official bullets. That still brings us up to…" He counted on his fingers.

"Call it too many bullets."

He nodded. "Fair enough. Listen, if I can get my hands on Wolf's test bullets, who knows what I might find? But I can tell you this much right now—at least two .22 caliber guns were used here. The kill shot came from behind, close-up, but you knew that. The surviving gunshot victims were mostly in front of RFK. And it's highly unlikely any of Sirhan's bullets hit the Senator…*if* Sirhan was firing bullets."

I frowned. "What else could he have been firing?"

"Blanks. Creating a diversion, one hell of a distraction. And with another shooter or two in the room, would you have wanted

Sirhan firing willy nilly at a crowd *you* were part of? Eyewitnesses report his weapon producing long, visible flames, some recall getting hit by the residue of what might have been flash-burn paper."

I'd been one of them.

At the east end of the Pantry, a sturdy-looking blond man in his early forties in a gray suit and thin blue tie came suddenly in; he had the confidence of someone who worked here and I wondered for a moment if he'd come to toss us out. Then I recognized him, though we hadn't exactly met: this was the hotel man who had led Bob off the stage and later joined in with Grier, Johnson, Plimpton and me, among others, in subduing Sirhan.

"Nathan Heller," Will said, gesturing to me with one hand and indicating the newcomer with the other, "this is Karl Uecker, maître d' at the Cocoanut Grove."

Uecker came forward with a tight smile and we shook hands, traded nods. I said I remembered him and he said he remembered me.

With a hand on the maître d's shoulder, Will smiled and said, "Karl arranged this for us tonight. And I wanted you to chat with him about what you both witnessed."

I said, "I'd like that."

Karl nodded and started right in, his German accent thick but easily penetrable: "I was guiding the Senator by the hand, you know. I believe I was closest of anyone to him, with the exception of the security guard, who was just behind us."

I asked, "Did Sirhan at any time position himself behind the Senator? If so, did you see him fire his weapon?"

"No! No! He was never an inch from Kennedy's head—that's ridiculous. I would have seen it. And for that little man to get close enough for that, he would've had to pass by me, and he didn't! After his second shot, I get hold of Sirhan very tight and push him against the serving table while the Senator staggers back, hit."

Will said, "Tell him the important part, Karl. The part you weren't asked about on the witness stand."

His light blue eyes were wide. "That guard has his gun out! I don't think many people saw that. And I yell at him, 'You must be crazy to wave a gun around in this chaos!' "

I'd seen that, too!

With a satisfied smile, Will said to me, "That security guard, Thane Cesar, was in a perfect position to take those shots from behind your friend Bob. Maybe you'd like to talk to Mr. Cesar? I made a few calls and can give you his address."

"Please," I said.

ELEVEN

Chicken ranches, dairy farms and apricot orchards dominated the Conjeo Valley back when Thousand Oaks—a tourist court got out of hand—surrounded a farm that rented trained animals to the movies. By a decade ago, it had developed into a quiet community of several thousand, known for extending a warm welcome to film productions in the market for typical Americana. The L.A. suburb's population now numbered near thirty thousand, thanks in part to the technology-driven Newbury industrial park.

Yucca Lane, a short narrow excuse for a working-class street, had never attracted Hollywood (or any) attention, its shabby little houses hiding behind coyote brush and other scrubby native greenery. I tooled my Jag around a massive gnarled oak that stood mid-lane like an ancient witch playing traffic cop. Then I pulled into the driveway behind the yellow mid-'60s Chevy Chevelle, a muscle car starting to look a little flabby.

The same might be said of its apparent owner, who sat in a metal lawn chair under the overhang of the entry area of the low-slung modest gray clapboard-and-brick ranch-style adorned with a small, struggling lawn.

When I'd called Thane Eugene Cesar's number, he started out wary but warmed up when I introduced myself over the line. He said he'd read some articles about me and was fine with me stopping by. His attitude did not change when I explained, almost as an afterthought, that my reason for coming was to gather background information on the RFK assassination for a national columnist.

"About time," he'd said, adding, "I have a story to tell," followed by an odd little inappropriate laugh, *huh-hah-hah*.

He had a matching metal chair waiting for me with a small Styrofoam cooler between. Lurching to his feet as I emerged from the Jag, he wore a rather childish striped t-shirt, khaki shorts and sock-free sneakers, a slightly pudgy six-footer with a pleasant, boyish face, dark brown hair and a skinny mustache riding an overbite smile. I made him for his mid-to-late twenties.

I was in a seersucker sport coat over a sports shirt, splitting the difference between casual and business. He had a can of Brew 102 in his left hand as he offered his right for me to shake, which I did. He squeezed hard then went limp dishrag at the close.

"I saw you interviewed on Jack Paar," he said, then added that late-night host's famous catchphrase, "I kid you not!" Followed by the *huh-hah-hah*.

"Yeah," I said. "That was a while back. Got to meet Charley Weaver and Dody Goodman."

He sat in the creaky metal chair and gestured for me to help myself to its mate. "Did you get their autographs?"

"Uh, no. Charley Weaver is not a real guy."

"Well, sure he is."

"I mean, he's an actor. It's a role he plays. Thank you for talking to me, Mr. Cesar."

"My friends call me Gene."

"And I'm Nate."

"Hey, feel free to help yourself to a beer."

"I just might, a little later." No way in hell. Brew 102 was a local beer that had somehow managed to capture the taste of smog.

"Listen," my pal Gene said, "I should apologize for not inviting you in. But the place is a mess. Joyce, the wife, left me for a clarinetist last week."

"Well, that's a shame."

He rolled his eyes. "Yeah, and I'm pitiful when it comes to housework. I wouldn't want you to think I'm a slob or something. Anyway, it's nice out here. Nice day."

This was Southern California. Of course it was a nice day, as long as you weren't drinking Brew 102. Which incidentally was called that, the brewery claimed, because they had to try 101 times before they hit perfection.

"A jazz player," Gene said.

"Pardon?"

"The clarinetist. Tough to compete with."

"I can see where it would be."

He swigged 102. "She took the kids. Do you think that's fair? She runs off with a clarinetist and snags the kids, too?"

"Seems a little much."

A dog barked down the street.

"You know I seen you that night," Gene said, eyes narrowing. "But I was too wrapped up in my work to introduce myself or anything. But you was in that crowd behind us, Bobby Kennedy and me."

"I noticed you as well," I said. But the truth was, he'd mostly been a blur in a gray uniform and cap, one of those invisible people we don't really see as we move through our daily lives. And my attention had been elsewhere than on a nonentity good guy like Gene Cesar.

"You know I always wanted to be a police officer," he said, sending a distant look past me. "Studied police science at community college. But security guard's as close as I ever got. See, I had an ulcer going back to high school. I was 4-F because of it. You was a Marine, right? And a police officer? Before being a private eye?"

He *had* read some of the articles. I said all of that was correct, then began the daunting task of keeping Gene here on track.

"So," I asked, "how long have you been doing security work?"

A shrug. A sip. "That's only part-time. I saw an ad and jumped at it—I was in deep shit for money at the time, I mean, two little kids? A mortgage? *Huh-hah-hah.* Really I'm mainly a maintenance plumber out to Lockheed in Burbank. You got to have a security clearance from the Defense Department for that, you know. You're on call for that whole goddamn facility, when you're on duty. It's like...like being in the military."

Lockheed in Burbank, aka the Skunkworks, was the home of the U-2 spy plane. Could this plump plumber somehow be tied to the CIA? No, that was ridiculous....

I asked, "When did you start with Ace Guard Service?"

"About six months before that night at the Ambassador."

His first deception: from the LAPD documents, I knew Thane Eugene Cesar had started at Ace in late May '68, a few days before the assassination.

"Could you tell me about that night, Gene?"

"Sure. It's not the kind of thing you forget, is it?"

"No it isn't."

I work days at Lockheed, mostly. I'm on nights this week because of vacations, you know, filling in. But on June the fourth I get home, like usual, about 4:30 p.m. Supervisor from Ace calls and wants me to work a shift from six to two in the morning at the Ambassador. I'm tired, havin' already worked a full day at the plant, but the Supe twists my arm.

I get to the hotel about six-oh-five p.m. and report to the head of security there, William Gardner, who posts me at the main doors of the Embassy Ballroom. I'm standing at the main

door of the ballroom and at about eight-thirty, quarter till nine,
Jack Merritt…another Ace guard?…says to me, 'You know, I
got a funny feeling there's gonna be big trouble here tonight,'
and I look at him and say, 'Why?' And he says, 'I just got that
feeling.' I just laugh that off, but maybe he knew something I
didn't, huh-hah-hah.

Around nine, Gardner moves me downstairs to the Ambas-
sador Room to mingle with the crowds and keep an eye on
things. And, you know, keep them from going upstairs to the
Embassy Room, which is already filling up. Anyway, I'm only
there maybe twenty minutes. Then Gardner comes back down
and takes me up to the kitchen area.

At nine-thirty, I get reassigned to the east doors of the
Pantry, which lead to the Colonial Room, where the press is. At
maybe eleven-fifteen, I get moved to the swinging double doors
to the west, near the backstage of where the Senator is speaking.
Nobody replaced me at the east doors, by the way. Anybody
could have walked in during the hour before the shooting — I
couldn't exactly monitor both ends of that damn Pantry. Where I
was stationed was kind of cool, though….How so? Well, I could
hear Milton Berle cracking jokes and makin' Rafer Johnson and
Rosey Grier split a gut, laughing.

Yeah, I guess you could say I was distracted. Sure, that Sirhan
character could have wandered in. Yes, I was supposed to be
checking badges and passes, but like I said, I couldn't be at both
ends of that Pantry at once, could I?

When the Senator comes down from the hotel through the
Pantry, east end, on his way to make his speech, I hold back the
crowd as best I can. Then I position myself by those double
doors waiting for the Senator's return.

When the speech is over — they pumped it in on loudspeakers
in the kitchen — I go through the swinging doors and pick up the

Senator in that slanted backstage hallway, a couple feet from the double doors. That maître d' is leading Bobby by the right hand into the Pantry and I fall in behind 'em and take hold of his right arm, just below the elbow, with my right hand. We all just start pushing through the crowd. No, no, Kennedy never even looked at me. He was looking ahead at the people and cameras.

I'm right behind him all the way down to the stainless-steel serving table, on his right side, and when we get there, he reaches out and turns to the left to shake hands with some bus-boys. My hand sort of broke loose, away from his arm, and of course I grab it right back again because people was all over the place.

Now, I just happen to look up right then and I seen an arm and a gun stick out in front of us, out of the crowd, y'know? Five shots get fired off, I seen the red flash from the muzzle, and I duck because I was as close as Kennedy was. So close I got powder in my eyes from the flash! I grab for Bobby, throw myself accidentally off-balance and fall back against the ice-making machines. Then the Senator falls right down in front of me and I turn around and I seen blood coming down the right side of his face and I scramble up to my feet, draw my gun and go to the Senator. I look up and Rosey Grier and Rafer Johnson and a bunch of people—you was one of them, wasn't you, Nate? —are beating the shit out of this Sirhan guy. I was scared. I admit it. I was shaking, you know, physically shaking, the way you feel after a car accident. Another security guard stops me and says, 'Let's get out in front of this and stop the pandemo-nium.' We get out of there.

No, I did not see Sirhan's face. He was so short, he was standing behind other people and all I could see was his hand and the gun poking out.

Didn't get a good look at the gun, no. I knew it wasn't a .38

when it went off, because I've shot a .38 and a .22 and you can
hear the difference.

Oh, I'd say I was four feet from the gun when it went off and
Senator Kennedy was two or three feet.

"Did anyone," I asked, "come up and squeeze between you and
the Senator during all the bedlam?"

"No. People was getting shot and falling, though. It was
crazy. Just fucking crazy."

(Among the pilfered LAPD materials was the transcript of a
radio interview with Thane Eugene Cesar fourteen minutes
after the shooting, which concluded thusly: "What kind of
wounds did the Senator suffer?"

"Well, from where I could see, it looked like he was shot in
the head and the chest and the shoulder."

This made Cesar the only witness to describe accurately the
location of RFK's three wounds.)

I asked, "Were you carrying your own weapon that night,
Gene?"

He shook his head. "I had a .38 that Ace issued me. They
like the larger caliber. Better stopping power."

"Did the LAPD confiscate that weapon?"

Another head shake. "No. Or the sidearms of the other two
security guards in the room, neither. Those guards was plainclothes, by the way. I was the sole man in uniform."

"According to police reports, you owned a .22 like Sirhan's,
but sold it months before? Is that right?"

"It is. A Harrington & Richardson .22 revolver. Sold it for fifteen bucks to Jim Yoder, a Lockheed pal who was getting ready
to retire and move to Arkansas, which he did....You sure you
don't want a beer?"

A baby was crying somewhere.

"No thanks." I shifted in my metal chair and it squeaked. "Gene, I don't know if you're aware of this, but I was Robert Kennedy's security chief that night."

His eyes popped like a squeeze doll's. "Jeez. Shit. I *didn't* know."

I smirked in self-reproach. "Kind of makes us both bodyguards who dropped the ball."

His soft face turned hard. "I don't accept that! And you shouldn't either, Nate. I know all about Bobby refusing to have any armed security seen with him. Gardner, the Ambassador security chief, made that clear. The Senator did *not* want to be photographed that way!"

"Oh, I know."

His turn to smirk. "Bobby probably woulda had a shit fit if he seen an armed guard like me sidling up behind him, *huh-hah-hah*. I was told in no uncertain terms I was strictly there for crowd control. But that Pantry was so packed and risky, he was probably glad for any help. No, you shouldn't feel guilty about that. I don't."

"No sleepless nights?"

He slapped at the air. "Hell no. Well…I had my share of nightmares, dreamin' I was back in that sardine can with bullets flying every fucking which way. But Senator Kennedy got himself killed with his dumb-ass ideas about keeping the cops out and security to a minimum. Hope I don't offend you saying so."

"Not a RFK fan?"

That overbite smile looked at once childish and sinister. "I definitely wouldn't have voted for Bobby Kennedy because he had the same ideas his brother John did, and JFK sold this country down the river. I think all of them Kennedys are the biggest crooks who ever walked the earth. They literally gave the country away to the Commies, the minorities, the Blacks."

1

I twitched a smile. "A Nixon man, then."

He slapped the air again. "Oh, fuck *him,* too. I voted for Wallace!"

George Wallace, the notorious segregationist ex-governor of Alabama, had won five states in 1968 with his third-party campaign.

My host gulped some beer, sat forward. "Shit, man, I worked my ass off for ol' George—passed out handbills, made donations, you name it. Bobby Kennedy getting shot isn't the tragedy—*George Wallace* losing the election is the tragedy!"

I squinted at him. "Yet you were right there, protecting Bobby Kennedy that night. Risking your life to do so."

He leaned back, slapped his pudgy chest. "Because it was my job! Just because I don't like Democrats don't mean I go around shooting them every day, *huh-hah-hah*."

How often *did* he shoot them, I wondered?

"Sorry," he said, and that soft face that had turned hard softened back down. "If you was his security chief, you must've been a Kennedy man. I don't mean no offense."

"None taken. Like you, I was just doing my job. Filling in for a guy." I smiled and lied through my teeth: "Can you imagine how much better off we'd be in this country with George Wallace as president?"

He toasted me with his 102. "Fuckin' A. That Wallace didn't take shit off *nobody!* I'm fed fucking up, and a lot of people I work with feel the same. Shove us too far and, one of these days, we're gonna fight back. If we can't do it at the ballot box by getting the right man in to straighten this shit out, then we've got to take it in our own hands. I can't see any other way to go!"

"I hear you."

He squinted at me, the upper lip with the skinny mustache

curling. "The black man, these past four to eight years, has been shoving this integration shit down our damn *throats*…so we've learned to *hate* him, the black man. And one of these days, at the rate they're goin', there's going to be a civil war in this country. It's going to be white against Black….and let me tell ya, *huh-hah-hah*—the blacks ain't *never* gonna win!"

SUS chief Robert Houghton, in a news release announcing the shutting down of the official investigation, had said, "No one with far right-wing connections was inside that kitchen pantry."

Good to know.

"Why the hell," Nita asked, "would Cesar be so candid?"

We were tucked away in a corner of the multi-tiered Miceli's, perhaps Hollywood's most popular Italian restaurant. The walls were brick, the woodwork carved, the windows stained glass, the ceiling a nest of hanging Chianti bottles, the tablecloths red-and-white checkered, and the red leather of the booths of a vintage going back to the defunct Pig 'n' Whistle from which they had been salvaged when my old Chicago crony Carmen Miceli opened the place in 1949.

"Maybe I'm a brilliant interviewer," I said.

We were sharing an antipasto salad and a bottle of Campione Merlot.

"Perhaps he's trying reverse psychology," Nita said, frowning. She looked young and cute in her gold-red-black print tunic top. The Cher-style eye makeup was over and now the big brown eyes were helped only by some minor mascara and a little light green eye shadow. Her dark hair was back in a ponytail.

"You mean," I said, "if my new best friend Gene Cesar killed Bob Kennedy, he figures to sound innocent by being open about his contempt for the victim. Interesting."

She gave me half a smirk. "You make it sound silly but there might be something to it."

"Another possibility," I said, forking a black olive, "is the guy's a dope."

"If he's a dope, who would trust him with an important assignment like this?"

I chewed the olive and swallowed. "Excellent point."

I had already filled her in on a phone conversation I'd had at the office with forensics guy Will Harris, reacting to Gene Cesar saying he'd got powder in his eyes due to Sirhan's gunfire. Will said this was impossible at the three-foot range Cesar claimed; however, the powder could have been blowback… from Gene's own gun barrel.

I'd also asked Will to check on the sale of Cesar's .22 to his Lockheed pal who moved to Arkansas. Maybe we could buy it back and do some testing. He was on it.

"My buddy Gene," I said to Nita, "was just behind and to the right of Bob when the shots were fired. If he's telling the truth about where he was, relative to Bob, then either the shooter had to be between him and Bob, or Gene did it himself."

She frowned in thought. "Could he just be remembering it wrong? You said his various statements—particularly about the shooting itself and the immediate aftermath—are inconsistent."

"They are. The LAPD materials include four distinct versions—not wildly different, but…different. Sometimes Gene gets knocked down, other times he doesn't. Sometimes the maître d' bumps into him, other times he doesn't know who it is, just 'somebody.' But we can be sure about his positioning—there's strong evidence he was standing very damn close behind Bob."

"What evidence?"

I gestured with a breadstick. "Cesar was wearing a clip-on tie. Photos of him earlier that night confirm as much. And remember that terribly sad photo of Bob on his back and the busboy comforting him? Cesar's clip-on tie is on the cement near Bob's outstretched right hand."

Her hand came up to her mouth. "As if...as if...in a moment of struggle...."

"Bob yanked the tie off his assailant's neck."

She pushed her share of the salad aside; put her chin in a hand and an elbow on the tabletop. "You think Cesar was some kind of...hit man?"

I flipped a hand. "Could be part of a radical right-wing group. A second shooter assigned to make sure Bob bought it if Sirhan failed. Or Gene could have taken advantage of the moment to put one into a public figure he despised."

She made a face. "None of that sounds right."

"No. It doesn't."

Her perfect eyebrows went up. "Could it have been an accident? Cesar draws his gun in response to Sirhan's shooting and it goes off and kills the very person he's trying to defend?"

"What, three times? Actually, four, 'cause one went through Bob's clothing without hitting him."

She pursed her lips. "Okay. Not a good theory."

"Not a good theory. But what is?"

We shared a pizza (Miceli's Special, "Everything But the Oven"). Somehow we managed to come up with both an appetite and some conversation unrelated to the tragedy that brought us together. She'd had another round of auditions today and was up for a role on *The Brady Bunch*. And she had a callback on *Mannix*.

Over the last of the wine, I said, "We're obviously getting somewhere."

"You mean in our relationship?"

I smiled a little. "Sure. But what I mean is, whatever was really going on in that Pantry is starting to show itself. So far I've just been sniffing around the edges of this thing. But I have enough now to put the entire weight of the A-1 behind a full-on investigation, and talk to my pal Wes Grapp at the FBI, assuming the Bureau isn't a part of a government cover-up. And then of course there's Pearson, who'll be up for funding it, considering just how big this is."

"That sounds like good news," she said.

"Doesn't it?"

We toasted.

Back at the bungalow a call was waiting for me—Jack Anderson. Didn't matter what time I got in, I was to get back to him. Pleased with what I had to tell him, I dialed direct from the bedroom phone. Nita, already in her nightie, was pillow-propped up next to me as she read *Airport*.

"Jack," I said after he answered. "Good to hear from you. I wanted to report in, anyway."

"Afraid that's no longer necessary."

"Oh?"

A long silence. A sigh.

He said, "I take it you haven't heard the news."

"What news?"

"Drew…Drew had a heart attack this morning."

"Oh hell."

"Died on his way to the hospital."

The world without Drew Pearson in it was suddenly a smaller place.

"Damn….I'm sorry."

Weary sadness oozed across the wire like a gas leak. "We'll talk later, Nate, but that'll have to be the end of this current assignment. I'm going to be picking up the reins on the column and working to just keep the boat afloat...if you'll forgive the mixed metaphor."

My hand was tight on the receiver. "Jack, I'm getting somewhere on this thing. Are you sure...?"

"For now, at least, yes. Timing isn't right, and even if it was, I don't know if I have access to the funding. You need to face it, Nate. The RFK inquiry is kaput."

PART THREE
The Go-Go Dancer
with the Zebra Rug

April 1969

TWELVE

The following morning at the A-1 office in the Bradbury Building, I rounded up Fred Rubinski and got my other two partners on a conference call—Lou Sapperstein in Chicago and Bob Hasty in Manhattan.

"So," I said, rocking back in my desk chair, "we don't have a client."

From the speaker phone, Lou said, "How much do we have invested in this?"

Lou had been my boss back in Chicago on the Pickpocket Detail in the early '30s. He was past retirement age and understandably skeptical about throwing good money (or time) after bad.

"I've only been on it for a few days," I said. "We can walk away clean."

Bob Hasty, half a decade younger than me, said from our office at the Empire State, "Who you trying to kid, Nate? You have a lot more invested than a few days. We all know Bobby Kennedy was your friend."

Hasty had worked Homicide in D.C., which is where I knew him from, when he was with Bradford Investigations, with whom the A-1 was affiliated. I'd hired him away to run the New York office.

In the client chair, a third of a cigar stuffed in his face, Fred asked, "What's the upside here? If we decide to pursue this thing just to be good goddamn citizens or something?"

"Better publicity," I said, "than helping Errol Flynn beat that statutory rape rap."

Fred grunted. "Old news."

Lou said, "I wouldn't care to see you dead, Nate."

"Nor would I," I admitted.

"But," the speaker phone went on, "if there's more to this than just some lone-nut Arab taking out a pro-Israel politician, you'll be wading into dangerous, murky waters."

I said, "You left out 'bloody.' "

Fred said, "From what you've told me, Nate, the LAPD either botched this out of sheer incompetence or they're covering something up for their pals at the CIA. How is making enemies of either of those fine upstanding institutions good for business?"

"With a client," I said, "we have a certain amount of cover, not to mention funding. As it is, all I have are suspicions. That's why we're talking, fellas. Staying on this is hard to justify."

"No it isn't," Hasty said. "You're the boss. You *are* the A-1, both in the public perception and in the legal sense."

With a tinge of reluctance, Lou's voice announced, "Hasty's right. We three partners put together don't add up to your percentage of the business. It's not a democracy. This is your decision, Nate."

A knock at the inner office door prompted a "Yes?" from me.

Our receptionist, Evie, apparently between auditions, stuck her pretty blonde head in. "There's a gentleman out here to see you, Mr. Heller. He doesn't have an appointment but seems to think you'll see him. What should I...?"

"What's his name?"

"Ronald Kiser."

Fred and I exchanged glances. A reporter for *Life* magazine both here and abroad, Kiser had been the Sirhan Sirhan defense team's investigator. He was an interesting guy, having trained as a Jesuit before winding up a married journalist. I knew him a little, the A-1 having provided security for him when his insider reports on Vatican II got him death threats.

I signed off with Sapperstein and Hasty and told Evie to send Kiser in. And I asked Fred to stick around, which he did, repositioning himself on the sofa under the wall of framed press accounts and signed celebrity photos, leaving the client chair empty and waiting.

Kiser came confidently in, a youthful forty or so, a short but formidable figure in a conservative gray suit and darker gray tie; under a blond burr haircut and behind dark-rimmed glasses, the pleasant blue-eyed features on his round face often wore a smile. But not today.

"Mr. Heller," he said as he approached the desk and held out his hand. "Apologies for just dropping by."

I got up, shook the offered hand, and reminded him that he was Ron and I was Nate and to have a seat.

I gestured to my partner on the couch. "I believe you know Fred Rubinski."

They nodded to each other, as Kiser settled into the client's chair.

"I was sorry to read about Drew Pearson's passing," he said in a steady baritone. "He was a force of nature. And you knew him well, I know. Did a lot of work for him over the years."

"That's so. He was a damn tightwad and a hypocritical old Quaker, but I'll miss him."

"You'd been doing a job for him lately, I understand."

I nodded. "How is it that you…?"

"Grant Cooper mentioned it. Well, warned me, I suppose." He took his glasses off and cleaned them with a handkerchief; though possibly myopic, his gaze was direct. "Are you, uh, going back east for the funeral?"

"No. We're sending flowers."

Kiser leaned in, folded his hands and set them on the edge of my desk. "If I might ask…are you intending to go forward with your investigation?"

"Jack Anderson tells me the *Washington Merry-Go-Round* column won't be pursuing that line of inquiry, so…no."

"Would you be open to taking on a new client in the matter? *Life* wants a series of articles and so does *Paris Match*. Plus, I'm going to be writing a book about the case. I can't think of anyone more qualified and appropriate than you to be out there gathering info while I start the writing. With something this topical, it's important to strike while the iron is hot. I can meet your standard fee and cover all expenses as well."

Fred was sitting on the edge of the couch. With the stub of cigar stuffed in his cheek, he looked like Edward G. Robinson playing a managing editor in a '30s movie.

"I need to know where you're coming from," I said, coolly, "before I can decide anything."

A smile made a brief appearance before retreating. "Well, *Time/Life* has authorized a ten-thousand-dollar retainer to get us started. Would that be sufficient?"

My partner was salivating, but I needed to make sure this wasn't some kind of payoff. Kiser had been part of a defense team that just might have sold their client down the river. Maybe this offer was about finding out what I'd learned and hushing it up.

"Excuse me, Ron," I said, and went over to Fred and took him by the arm, eased him up from the couch, and walked him out.

On the other side of the door, I said, "Talk about *deus ex machina*."

He blinked at me. "What the fuck language is that?"

"Latin, and I'll let you know whether it means stroke of luck or screwed sideways."

Back in my office, I resumed my position behind the desk and asked, "Tell me, Ron—how did you come to be the investigator for the Sirhan Sirhan defense?"

Well, my first reaction was strictly emotional. After the news bulletin about the shooting knocked me on my ass, I cried and cursed and threw a glass across the room, wanting to do something, anything, besides just sit in front of the TV choking on rage and sorrow. So I pulled myself together and called Life's *L.A. bureau and got enlisted on the spot.*

First assignment was to head out to interview Sirhan's brother at his apartment in Pasadena. This was maybe twenty-four hours after the assassination. I had a photographer along but the brother wouldn't cooperate, and he later told the police we'd tried to strongarm him. Which was bullshit. The cops ignored that as well they should. I believe that was the last good decision on the case the LAPD made.

Next I got a call from Al Wirrin, the ACLU's chief counsel in Los Angeles. An assassination isn't a free speech issue, obviously, but Wirrin wanted to make sure Sirhan got a fair trial.

'Is it true Grant Cooper's a pal of yours?' Wirrin wanted to know.

A top-flight criminal lawyer like Cooper was just what Sirhan Sirhan would need. I said I knew Cooper, which I did from several stories I'd worked on involving him, and then sort of horse-traded—told Wirrin I'd put Cooper in touch if Wirrin could get me in to see Sirhan.

Did I know Cooper had represented mob guys? Sure I did. I didn't think much of it at the time—he was dealing with Phil Silvers in that Friars Club card-cheating case and that didn't make Cooper a comedian, did it? Later, I had some second thoughts...when was that? When we wound up with two mob-

connected lawyers on the team. This other one had been Mickey Cohen's mouthpiece. That was a bit unsettling, but what really bothered me was Cooper's approach. How so? Well, he was one of those hale fellows well met, all smiles and friendly personality, adding up to nothing much.

Look, in Cooper's defense, we couldn't have had any more eyewitness evidence against Sirhan if God had taken snapshots, so it wasn't like we were trying to deny this was the guy who shot Bobby Kennedy. It's just...the defense team took the LAPD's word on everything. Cooper didn't challenge them once!

And if I'd bring something up, like the possibility of a second shooter, or a conspiracy, Cooper'd just brush it off—took everything the prosecution handed us at face value. He was fine with stipulating to the killing. He said his only concern was saving 'this wretched boy's life.'

So the defense emphasized the psychological side of things, exploring Sirhan's mental and emotional state, leading up to and including the killing. As far as actual evidence was concerned, Cooper had a very poor grasp of it.

I was told to gather all the background material on Sirhan I could to establish the defendant's mental state for the psychiatrists and psychologists working the case. I wound up interviewing Sirhan almost every day for six months before, during and after the trial...far more often than any of the attorneys did.

Like any good interviewer, I kept things open and friendly, and after a while Sirhan loosened up. I heard it all—his life story, all his aspirations, his dreams, his high hopes, his dashed hopes.

He's no idiot. Quite intelligent, really. Well-read, books all over his little cell. If I used a big word on Monday, on Tuesday he'd use it back to me, correctly. Our conversations went all sorts of places, religion, philosophy, politics...but he never veered from his story that he did not remember killing Robert

Kennedy. He didn't deny it—he even said, 'I must *have done it!' But he didn't remember a damn thing.*

Hell no, I don't think he did it alone! He was such an unlikely assassin….kind of a chickenshit, really. Like when he worked as a grocery boy in Pasadena and got pissed off at the owner, and claimed he called the guy a goddamn son of a bitch. 'You said this to his face?' I asked him. Sirhan said, 'No, I said it under my breath, so he wouldn't hear me.' What the hell kind of macho assassin is that?

When I would get into the idea of possible involvement of others in the assassination, he would get evasive. I think he was lying about that. But I don't think he was lying about not re-membering the shooting itself.

Even Dr. Diamond couldn't break through that. Who? Dr. Bernard Diamond—the shrink the defense team brought in to ascertain Sirhan's mental state…to try to learn what happened through hypnosis. Diamond almost immediately found out Sirhan was an incredibly easy subject. Went under so fast, so deep, that keeping him conscious enough to answer questions could be tricky.

You're right, Nate—achieving that kind of rapid hypnotic state does generally indicate prior hypnosis. But as far as Diamond was concerned, he seemed to be more interested in implanting 'memories' than recovering them.

After countless sessions, Diamond came to what I consider to be an unlikely conclusion—that Sirhan programmed himself to kill Robert Kennedy. Diamond based this in part on Sirhan having fallen off a horse back in '67. No serious injuries but occasional blurred vision and some chronic pain…and the loss of a lifelong dream to become a jockey.

The fall seemed to engender changes in behavior—the talkative, polite Sirhan turned withdrawn and irritable. During this period,

Sirhan saw numerous doctors, without relief. He also became interested in self-hypnosis and mysticism. He joined the Rosicrucians, an organization that is itself fascinated by the occult and mysticism. There's a three-month gap leading up to March '68, by the way, where Sirhan just drops out of sight.

I believe Sirhan really doesn't remember shooting Robert Kennedy, that he probably killed Kennedy in a trance and was programmed to forget that he'd done it, and also programmed to forget the names and identities of others who might have helped him do it.

During the trial, I wanted Grant Cooper to at least expose the jury to this possibility, and share various clues that Sirhan was, in fact, not himself that night, that he might have been acting under other influences, possibly programmed under hypnosis. We had tape-recorded all of Sirhan's hypnotic sessions, so those could have been played for the jury, who could make up their own minds.

But Cooper said, 'They're never going to believe that! Anyway, I'd be a laughingstock. Drop it.' That was a huge disappointment to me during the trial. Even Dr. Diamond backed off from that theory, that Sirhan was a 'Manchurian Candidate.' I'm not sure why—I think because he didn't want to look silly.

"Instead," Kiser said, "Dr. Diamond fell in with the other defense psychologists in saying Sirhan was a paranoid schizophrenic. But Cooper's whole approach, of pleading diminished capacity, sailed over the jury's heads."

I'd been leaned back in my desk chair, taking all this in. Kiser seemed to be finished, so I asked, "What are you after from me, Ron?"

He bounced a fist off my desk—not enough to make anything jump, but making his point. "Keep digging. Keep looking. The whole idea of a conspiracy was ignored in that trial. Actively kept out by the defense! In the meantime, I'll get to work on my book, my insider's look at the case and how it played out in court, and my own investigation, as far as it got. So. What do you say?"

"I say make the check out to the A-1."

"Good. Good. Where will you start?"

"By asking if you can get me in to talk to Sirhan Sirhan."

"I can try."

"Try hard. In the meantime, I'll look into that 'Manchurian Candidate' angle you mentioned."

The morning fog had long since burned off and the sky over the beach in Malibu was a perfect, nearly cloudless light blue over a gray-blue ocean so calm it seemed to shimmer more than roll, the surf brushing in against the sand in a foamy teasing tickle. It was in the low sixties and my suitcoat was unbuttoned and I'd left my shoes and socks in the Jag. The geometric modern house nearby might have been a set left over from a science-fiction movie. This was a perfect day in a part of the world where perfect days were one thing that didn't require special effects. Who wouldn't be happy here?

"When Bobby Kennedy was killed," the tall, movie-star-handsome film director said, "the lights in a part of me went out, too."

John Frankenheimer might have still been standing here where I'd left him almost a year ago, only now the loose shirt and chinos were pastel, not earth tones. His left hand was in a pocket and his right hand held a shot glass with an inch or so of golden brown liquid in it. You didn't have to be a detective to figure out that was Scotch.

"With Bob," he went on, "I felt I was part of something. That I could change the world. He made an idealist out of me. Then suddenly he was gone and nothing mattered."

He was just a little drunk.

"We're thinking of moving to France," he said. "Evans and I have always loved Paris."

He was referring to his actress wife, the redundantly named beauty Evans Evans, that gorgeous brunette who would have made any husband's life tolerable anywhere. Wichita, Kansas, for example, where he'd told me they'd be heading next week, to start production on his new film—*The Gypsy Moths*.

"I'm looking into the possibility," I said, "that Sirhan Sirhan was Laurence Harvey."

In *The Manchurian Candidate*, Harvey had portrayed a brainwashed innocent programmed through hypnotism by Communists to assassinate a presidential candidate.

Frankenheimer gave me a sharp look that had a smile in it for just a moment. "George always said our movie was possible. I'm not saying he was wrong."

George Axelrod, the screenwriter of *The Manchurian Candidate*.

The director shrugged in elaborate cynicism. "But suppose that *is* what happened to Bob? Who's going to do something about it? Nixon?"

"Maybe I'll do something about it."

He chuckled and finished his drink. "You really take this private eye shit seriously, don't you, Heller?"

"I have my moments."

"I need another drink."

In my opinion he didn't, but I followed him back to the coldly futuristic house anyway. Soon we were sitting by the pool where I'd seen Bob napping on a beach chair less than a year ago. And a lifetime.

The lovely wife, in a bright orange-and-black print top and pale yellow shorts, brought me a rum and Coke I appreciated but hadn't asked for—in a glass, on ice, with a lime slice. She'd remembered how I'd liked it from my previous visit last June. To her husband she delivered a fresh couple of inches of Scotch and threw in a secret look to me that said she was worried about him. He'd married well.

I was pretty prosperous now, but still couldn't picture needing a swimming pool with an ocean in my back yard. Of course I was more Chicago than Hollywood, so I cut my host some slack. Their ways were different out here.

"Something odd," Frankenheimer said, "that sticks with me."

"Oh?"

"The press reported that Sirhan Sirhan was inspired to kill Bob after seeing him in a documentary with a pro-Israel stance. I made that documentary."

Jesus.

"But something doesn't add up," he said.

What did in this thing?

"That documentary aired two days after Sirhan's journal entry where he writes 'RFK Must Die' over and over. How does a documentary that hasn't been broadcast yet inspire an assassination?"

I had no answer for that. No one did.

"How well did you know Bob, Nate?"

"Pretty well. Better than some."

He was looking past the pool at the ocean. "You know what I liked about him? That he was funny. That he was shy. That he was dedicated. How he would listen for a long time and then respond quick, right to the point. He loved that movie, you know."

"*Manchurian Candidate*?"

Frankenheimer nodded. "So did Jack. His brother."

Glad he cleared that up.

The director clicked in his cheek. "We wouldn't have got it made without Jack."

"Oh?"

"Nobody in town wanted to touch it. Too controversial. Too far out. I had Sinatra all lined up to star in it and he and Jack were still close at that time. Frank approached him and Jack said he loved the book. He had only one question—who's gonna play the mother? Frank said we're going after Angela Lansbury and Jack thought that was perfect. We had a deal with United Artists the next day."

"I'm surprised you got Jack Kennedy's okay."

"Why's that?"

"MK-ULTRA isn't exactly the United States government's shining hour."

Frankenheimer frowned in surprise. "How much do you know about that, Nate?"

"I know it's an expansion of Project Bluebird and Project Artichoke, which both studied using hypnosis in interrogation. Some say they were looking for a way to manipulate foreign nationals into carrying out political assassinations. How come you know about it, John?"

He saluted me with his glass. "You first."

I had to gather my thoughts a little, but finally I said, guardedly, "Back in '53, I had a client, a CIA scientist, who was a part of MK-ULTRA, and who wound up going out a high window and taking everything he knew about the program with him. That's all I can say on the subject, but I know about MK-ULTRA, all right."

"Another botched bodyguard assignment, Nate?"

I pretended that didn't cut. "Why, didn't you ever have a box-office flop, John?"

"Not one that went out a high window." He raised the hand that didn't have a drink in it, palm out. "Sorry. That was uncalled for."

"No. That was an honest enough response. So it's your turn—how is it *you* know about MK-ULTRA? I don't figure it's made *Variety* or the *Hollywood Reporter* yet."

His gaze was hard. "I think you know."

"Yeah. I think I do. I don't figure that novel you based your movie on was the be-all and end-all. You'd have researched the hell out of it. That would be your way."

Slowly he nodded. "We hired a consultant. On paper he was impressive—Dr. Joseph W. Bryant, head of the American Institute of Hypnosis, one of the acknowledged founders of modern hypnotherapy. He worked for the military during the Korean War, counteracting enemy brainwashing, and after that for the CIA in the area of psychological warfare—mind control, behavior modification. A number of prominent attorneys have used him as a consultant on major cases, including F. Lee Bailey on the Boston Strangler. And he's consulted on several other motion pictures, though not as major as ours."

"Impressive—on paper. How about off the page?"

His sigh turned into a rueful laugh. "A flake. His 'institute' is an office on the sleaziest stretch of the Sunset Strip. Already this year the California Board of Medical Examiners found him guilty of using hypnosis to examine more than just the minds of female patients, which got him a five-year probation."

My eyebrows were up. "And this was your consultant?"

He shivered, sipped his Scotch. "I shouldn't have used him for research—I should have researched *him*. Oh, he was knowl-edgeable, all right, and helpful as hell. I think there are few secrets in that world of hypnosis and mind fucking that he doesn't know. But he's an oddball to say the least. Amish beard. Weighs about four hundred pounds. Quotes the Bible here and Dr. Kinsey there."

" 'In my Father's house are many mansions.' "

Frankenheimer sent the rest of his Scotch down his throat. "I wouldn't encourage you to look into him, Nate, if it wasn't for a radio program I happened to hear in the early morning hours after the shooting."

"I couldn't sleep, either."

He stared at the sun-glimmering surface of the pool. "I was up all night, twisting the radio dial in search of any news about Bob and his condition, the arrest of the assailant, any damn thing. I stumbled onto a phone-in show on KABC and who should be the guest, but my old associate...Dr. Joseph W. Bryant."

I frowned. "This was about the assassination?"

"Not directly. But when the subject came up, briefly, Bryant made an offhand comment that gave me a chill."

"Yeah?"

Dark mournful eyes fixed on me. "Bryant said it sounded to him like the assassin may have been acting under a post-hypnotic suggestion."

THIRTEEN

On its bluff jutting into San Francisco Bay, San Quentin Prison would have offered inmates a spectacular vista if its high walls hadn't denied them of it. What it provided instead over four-hundred-thirty-two acres were barbed wire, gun towers, and four massive cell blocks, its welcoming white-and-black castle-like facade a cruel joke. A fifth cell block, the maximum security one, was euphemistically called the Adjustment Center, as if perhaps chiropractors were on staff and not grizzled guards.

Accompanied by one of the latter under a clear blue mid-afternoon sky—I'd had a pleasant three-hour drive here—I passed by a guardhouse through an area of administrative buildings and staff housing. We strolled through the prison's original gate, a portico erected to accommodate a horse and buggy—San Quentin was, after all, built in 1852 (by prisoners who would then inhabit it)—and entered a plaza with a chapel on the right and cell blocks to the left; up ahead was the hospital.

In the old tower that housed Death Row, I met with Inmate B-21014 in a small off-white visitation room while two guards waited just outside. The slightly built figure sat at a modern wooden table, his left wrist cuffed through a metal loop. The walls were a pale yellow and, behind the seated figure, two windows let daylight filter in through trees and barred windows. His gaze was serene but I had to squint a little through the sun to get a fix on him.

Self-composed but with a nervous, embarrassed smile, he'd

have seemed childlike if he'd been any smaller. His hair had been trimmed back to subdue the wild, bushy look, and he wore a blue denim prison fatigue top and blue jeans with black canvas shoes. His skin tone was the kind of bronze the white kids on Malibu Beach would kill for.

I had seen Giuseppe Zangara—he preferred being called Joe ("I'm American citizen!")—in his cell in Miami in 1933. He had been the same size—115 pounds, five feet five—with the same faint smile. Another little foreigner who had shot his way into history. The déjà vu of it curdled in my stomach like a bad meal.

Abruptly—almost making me jump—the prisoner got to his feet as best he could and bowed, awkwardly clasping his uncuffed hand to the other as if in prayer.

"Sirhan Sirhan," he said, head lowered.

"Nathan Heller," I said, and thrust my hand across the small table and he accepted it. He gave it a politician's pump, three firm shakes that belied his otherwise shy manner.

His small smile seemed poised to break into laughter, though it only did so once—through much of our meeting, it remained the same. It was the bewildered smile of someone who couldn't quite believe what was happening to him.

He said, "You are working with Mr. Kiser, I understand."

"I am," I said, as we both sat. "With Grant Cooper not seeking an appeal, Mr. Kiser has picked up the ball. He's not an attorney but, as what's left of your defense team, he's interviewing possible representation for you."

"And writing his book," Sirhan said.

A tinge of amused contempt there.

"And articles," I said, somewhat defensively. "He's funding these efforts, after all. May we begin?"

"Might I ask a question first, sir?"

"Of course."

His head cocked to one side. "You were one of those who tried to stop me, sir, were you not?"

"Yes."

The smile again. "Then why would you try to help me now?"

I served up half a grin. "I'm being paid to."

He laughed. "The American way."

"Yes. But you'd be wise to keep in mind that Robert Kennedy was a friend of mine."

His face lengthened the smile away. His head gave a quick snap of a bow. "Sir, I share your sorrow."

"Then let's start there. What did you think of Robert Kennedy?"

He was a prince, sir, Robert Kennedy—heir apparent to his late brother's throne. I admired him very much. I loved him, sir. For all the poor people in this country, he was the hope.

And I stand with the poor people of this country, sir. The minorities. I am a poor person myself. I am not rich. Otherwise, sir, would I be in this position?

After the Arab-Israeli war, I had no identity, no hope, no goal, nothing to strive for. I simply…gave up. No more American Dream for me. I was an Arab! A foreigner in this country, sir. An alien. A stranger. A refugee.

That was the setback I suffered, sir. After the Arab-Israeli war, I could see that everybody in America loved a winner… and when the Israelis won, it made a loser out of me. And I did not like that one bit.

When my sister came down with leukemia, I would come home after college classes to take care of her. When she died, I became terribly depressed. I quit school. Worked as a waiter, a cook, gardener, gas station attendant. I hung around the race-tracks, gambled a little. One day I saw a note on the bulletin board at Santa Anita offering a position as an exercise boy. I had always dreamed of becoming a jockey. It meant a new start! I was into life, sir, not death—watched horses being born. Such a life-affirming experience.

One foggy Sunday, my horse was flying and I couldn't make the turn—saddle was loose or something. I never felt the fall. No pain, sir—I was unconscious. Next I knew I was in a hospital bed with a concussion. Stitches under my chin and next to my eye.

My family says I changed. It's true I felt different. I wasn't the same.

When did I buy the gun? That would be early last year, sir. This was my first purchase of a gun, but I was familiar with them because of Cadet Corps training in high school. I fired M-16s, .45s, .22s. I could tear a gun apart and put it back together. We used to have competitions. And I could shoot.

When I heard reports of Kennedy's pledge to send jet bombers to Israel...that was in May, sir, I believe...it made me terribly mad. This man I admired seemed suddenly a villain to me. A killer who wanted to throw bombs on people and destroy them and their country. The very weapons he condemned in Vietnam, he would donate to Israel! It seemed paradoxical to me, sir. I could not believe it.

I could have shot him right then, I was so terribly mad. But only in my mind, not in deed. The notebook? I believe the notebook is mine. I just don't remember writing those things.

I frankly don't remember much of that time at all, sir, leading up to the shooting. If the horses had been running that night, I would have been down at the track. But they weren't and I went downtown to watch a Jewish group's parade celebrating the one-year anniversary of their victory in the Six-Day War. I'm not sure whether I was just going to watch or heckle or what—I wasn't going down there to shoot anybody. I know that much, sir. But I had misread the advertisement and found the parade was going to be held the next night.

Yes, sir, I will try to remember as much as I can. But it is like a dream. No, not a nightmare, not till the very end.

I park my car and start wandering around. I notice lights are on in a storefront window and crash a celebration for a Republican candidate running for U.S. Senate. It's not much of a party, though. Someone suggests a better one going on for another Republican candidate at the Ambassador Hotel across the street. I go over there. That's where things start to get dreamlike.

I recall a Mexican band, a lot of brightness, a lot of people. I'm getting tired, it's getting hot, very hot. I want a drink. I see a makeshift bar and a bartender in a white smock. Looks like Abbott in Abbott and Costello, but Latin. We don't speak, we just nod. I seem to know him. He gives me a Tom Collins in a tall glass. I drink it while I am walking around. It goes down like lemonade. I guzzle it and order another. He makes it and I walk around and after I drink I come back and it's like a routine between us. Like I'm a regular customer of his. When he sees me coming back, he knows what I want.

I begin to feel even more sleepy. I'm no drinker, I'm small, and it gets to me. Woozy, I go out to my car. I'm surprised I make it there. I feel too drowsy to drive and decide to go back and get some coffee. I'm told I took my .22 Iver Johnson from the glove compartment and moved it into my pocket. But I don't remember doing that.

Don't remember walking back to the hotel either, sir, but I must have. I do remember some of what followed. I start searching for coffee. I need coffee bad. I ask about coffee at the bar and an attractive woman sitting there says she knows where the coffee is. She takes me by the hand and leads me behind the stage where Senator Kennedy is speaking.

She is so pretty. I decide to try to pick her up. I'm fascinated by her looks. I'm getting very sexual ideas about this girl and make up my mind I'm going to make it with her tonight. She doesn't lead me on—it's my job to woo her. She never says much, but she's very erotic. I feel consumed by her. She is a seductress with an unspoken availability. Yes, sir, a white dress with black polka dots.

A big shining coffee urn and cups are back there and I pour coffee for us. I remember wondering how I'd pay for it. Then a man with a clipboard and a big, full face, who seems to be in charge, points in the direction of the Pantry and the girl acknowledges his instructions.

I follow her like a puppy into the Pantry, still sleepy, very sleepy. Bright lights, shiny surfaces. I'm flirting with her and she sits on the steel table with her back to the wall. Her thighs, her legs, are right there in front of me. I am just looking at her, trying to take her beauty in. Trying to figure out how to hit on her. That's all I can think about, how I'm fascinated by her looks. She's sitting, I'm standing. Busty, looks like Natalie Wood. Never says much. It's so very erotic. I'm consumed by her.

Then she pinches me. It's startling—like a wake-up call. Like when you're stuck with a pin. It snaps me out of my doldrums and yet I'm still sleepy. She points back over my head and says, 'Look, look, look!' I turn around or did she spin me around? There are people coming through the doors. I am puzzled about what she is directing me to. Doesn't seem relevant, just people streaming in. She keeps motioning toward the back, more and more animated.

No, I wasn't thinking about Senator Kennedy! Didn't even know he was in the hotel. Then I am dreaming I am at a target range. I didn't know I had a gun but I saw targets, circles, circles. I think I fired off one or two shots. They say I called Bobby Kennedy a son of a bitch, but I don't remember doing that.

The next thing I remember is people on top of me, choking me, and getting my ass kicked….You were there, sir.

You must remember that part.

"Even after only a handful of sessions," Dr. Eduard Simson-Kallas told me, "it became clear to me that Sirhan Sirhan is no paranoid schizophrenic. No psychotic. Not at all."

I was seated across an uncluttered desk—a single notebook, a pen, a phone—from San Quentin's senior psychologist in his small wood-and-plaster office with the only other furniture a chaise longue with a chair at its head, patient/shrink style. With luck I wouldn't be asked to lie down. The wall behind him bore framed diplomas from Stanford, NYU, University of Louisville, UCAL Berkeley and Heidelberg University. Mixed in were a portrait of his wife and kids and a fancy ribboned certificate that said he'd been a Lieutenant Commander in the Estonian Army.

About fifty, Simson-Kallas was slender, a man of average height but with nothing else average about him—not the blond hair that left most of his head bald with a curly shock in back, not the penetrating close-set dark eyes under fuzzy caterpillar eyebrows nor the prominent nose, full lips and rounded chin. His houndstooth jacket and white turtleneck announced him as his own man.

So did his opinions about Sirhan Sirhan.

In what I assumed was an Estonian accent—vowels over-pronounced—he spoke above tented fingers.

"Paranoid schizophrenics," he said, "are almost impossible to hypnotize. They're too suspicious, they don't trust anybody, not even friends or relatives. They can't concentrate, they can't follow instructions. They make poorest subjects for hypnosis."

The accent had him dropping articles here and there, too. Not always but enough to add to the foreign feel.

I said, "Sirhan is supposedly in the most easily hypnotized group."

The caterpillars rose. "Oh yes. Sirhan is one of the most hypnotizable individuals I've ever met. He is grade five on hypnotism scale—less than ten percent of Americans rate grade five. When defense psychiatrist, Dr. Diamond, gave him a post-hypnotic suggestion, Sirhan jumped around like a monkey and climbed cell bars."

I grinned. "I don't know, doctor. I've seen that kind of thing in nightclub acts, where the subject is just going along with the gag."

"That is possible," he granted. "Sirhan could have been clowning or trying to fool them. He had little respect for Dr. Diamond, who like several others on the defense team was a Jew. As an Estonian émigré, it didn't take me long to gain Sirhan's trust—my people are neutral on the Middle East. He was extremely eager to talk to me. I tested him and found his IQ was 127, not the 89 presented at the trial. That low score came from his not trusting the Jewish doctors testing him."

I said, "Yours can't be a popular opinion in law enforcement circles."

He shrugged. Folded his hands. Rested them on the blotter. "I have not advertised it, but I'm working on a lengthy affidavit outlining my findings. The chief psychiatrist here agrees with me—he too does not see Sirhan as psychotic or paranoid schizophrenic. Nothing in Sirhan's test responses indicate that."

I frowned. "That diagnosis was at the heart of the trial."

His dark eyes flared. "Conduct of mental health professionals in this case is appalling! Errors, distortions, even probable manipulations of facts. That trial was, and will go down as, the psychiatric blunder of century."

"It could be argued," I said, "that Sirhan's attorney, Cooper, was just pursuing the best legal strategy. To present Sirhan to the jury as mentally ill and protect him from the death penalty under California law."

He waved that off. "The assumption that the jury could not accept a defense of hypnotic programming is absurd in this case. The grounds were substantial. Not taking that approach is unjustifiable on a tactical basis."

I wasn't sure he was right about that, but didn't press it, asking, "What about the general belief that you can't commit an act under hypnosis that you wouldn't do otherwise?"

"There are numerous famous cases that put the lie to that belief. If a hypnotized subject is convinced, for example, that he is acting in self-defense, of course he will kill."

I opened a hand. "Sirhan seems to think he was dreaming of being at a target range."

Simson-Kallas nodded. "And he frequented such ranges— had done so that very day. This is consistent with programming. So is his show of superhuman strength that night, his serene expression as he emptied his gun on the crowd, his composed, relaxed behavior at the police station after his arrest—all of this is consistent with a hypno-programmed state."

"What about this girl in the polka-dot dress? A kind of handler, you think?"

He nodded three times. "Yes, and a trigger. You can be programmed that if you meet a certain person, or see something specific, you go into a trance. Those drinks were almost surely drugged. An individual under the influence of barbiturates, particularly with increased dosage, would go through three stages: a slight sedative effect...a more pronounced cloudiness, even amnesia...then slurred speech, disrupted thought patterns, poor coordination, with a lack of awareness of painful stimuli. All of these conform to Sirhan's behavior that night."

"There's talk of self-hypnosis."

"Yes, and he has practiced that." He lifted a forefinger. "But this young man is not devious enough to have killed Robert Kennedy on his own, under any circumstances. He was prepared by someone. He was hypnotized by someone. He was there to draw the attention of the others in that Pantry. His role was to provide an obvious simple explanation to the crime that would prevent others from asking questions."

I cocked my head. "And he did have a motive."

Just one nod this time, some sadness in it. "Sirhan does display great emotional distress reliving his childhood in Israel, when he lived in an area that took heavy bombing during the '48 Arab-Israeli conflict. He witnessed atrocities that scarred him, no question."

"So he does have definite deep feelings about Palestine and Israel."

This nod was in slow motion. "He does. To me, however, his comments about Arab-Israeli politics have a strangely rote feel—like an actor reciting his lines. He doesn't speak with the hesitancy and rephrasing common in genuine expressions of thought and emotion."

I was nodding now. "Which could have been played upon by his programmers. How long would that kind of programming take?"

He frowned. "I would say a few months. There seems to be a period of about three months leading into the assassination where Sirhan's movements are largely unknown. That programming wouldn't require him disappearing off the face of the earth, being shipped off somewhere into the hands of some mad doctor. No, it might be akin to a job he took, meaning he would not drop entirely out of sight from his friends and family. But many hours each day would be devoted to this programming."

I locked eyes with him. "The question is, doctor, would he have been a willing participant?"

The caterpillars rose again. "More to the point is, *how* willing? I have attempted to get through the barrier concerning those three missing months and get nowhere. Just that during that time he isn't working and at night occasionally sees friends from his college days, spends time with his family…but what of the days?"

"Let's get back to 'How willing?' "

A one-shoulder shrug. "He may have thought he was involved in study of mysticism, magic, philosophy, metaphysics, all areas of interests of his, dating back at least to his interest in the Rosicrucians. Perhaps he was told he could play a role in pro-Arab activism. And he might have known he was being prepared to participate in an assassination. None of that matters."

That rocked me back. "Well, of course it matters!"

He calmed me: "I mean, in the sense of understanding that Sirhan Sirhan was deprived of a fair trial. That he was at best manipulated by unknown programmers under false pretenses, or at worst was just another cog in a wheel."

"But an important cog."

Another nod, again of the slow-motion variety. "An important cog. How do they say it in the old private eye movies, Mr. Heller? He was set up to be a patsy…to take the fall?"

That got a smile out of me—not much of one, but a smile. "What do *you* think, doctor?"

A long sigh. "I think Sirhan Sirhan has always been a loser. He failed at Pasadena City College. He played horses and lost.

He wanted to be a jockey and fell off a horse. He finally found a role he was suited for."

"Political assassin?"

"Arab hero. He likes to say he doesn't remember killing Robert Kennedy, yet he takes pride in helping Arab refugees by doing so. And yet...."

"And yet?"

"He is willing, eager, for me to hypnotize him and find out what really happened. He says over and over, 'I don't know what happened. I *know* I was there. They tell me I killed Kennedy. But I don't remember!' It is the only time an emotion really comes through."

I let some air out. "He does recount everything in a frustratingly passive way."

"Like he's reciting from a book. And where are the details? Yes, there's a girl he wants to sleep with, and the Tom Collins drinks and the coffee in the urn, but what else? A psychologist looks for details. If a person is involved in a real situation, there are always details. I've been doing this for twenty years, Mr. Heller. Other murderers I've interviewed speak with great expression and in horrific detail about their crimes."

"And all you get out of Sirhan," I said, "is that he was hoping to get laid."

"Well, he did get screwed," the doctor said.

FOURTEEN

Nita was still sleeping the next morning when I made the call from the bungalow's living room to attorney F. Lee Bailey in his Boston office. We were old friends—I'd been his investigator on the Sam Sheppard re-trial a few years ago and the A-1 had handled a few minor things for him in the meantime. I told Lee only that I was trying to get a bead on Dr. Joseph W. Bryant and he didn't pry about the reason.

"Well, I can tell you this about him," he said in his mellow courtroom baritone. "Bryant may be the most brilliant man alive in the field of hypnotism—certainly the most knowledge-able and imaginative."

"How did a New England lawyer happen to connect with a Hollywood hypnotist?"

"Back in '61, in San Francisco," Bailey said, "Melvin Belli put on a hypnosis seminar for trial lawyers with Bryant the star attraction. Bryant hypnotized three of us, myself included, and instructed us to hold out our right arms while he droned on about how our arms were feeling numb. I was just waiting for something interesting to happen, and only sensed my arm being lightly rubbed. When Bryant brought us around, we each of us had hypodermic needles stuck through the fleshy part of our arms."

"You're kidding."

"Not a bit. He informed us this was an example of hypnosis as anesthesia. The punctures had not caused bleeding. He removed the needles painlessly, sent us to our seats and re-sumed the lecture. *That*, Nathan, is what brought Dr. Bryant to my attention."

"And then you pulled him in on the Boston Strangler case."

"Yes, but before that to assess another strangler—the so-called Hollywood Strangler, Harvey Bush, who'd killed three elderly women. Bryant's theory was that Bush hated his mother and was killing her over and over. In Bush's cell, with the prisoner in a hypnotic trance, I played the role of the mother. The son of a bitch attacked me and if Bryant hadn't been there to grab him, Bush would have made victim number four out of me."

"Were you in a dress like Tony Perkins at the end of *Psycho*?"

"Very funny, Nathan. Now as to the Boston Strangler, Albert DeSalvo, it was Bryant himself who nearly became a victim. After repeatedly telling the hypnotized DeSalvo that the victims represented him strangling his daughter over and over—for diverting his wife's love from him to her—DeSalvo clutched Bryant by the throat. Bryant grabbed his attacker's shoulders and shouted, 'Sleep!' And that did the trick."

"Well. He would seem to be the genuine article."

"Oh, he's that, all right. But I'd never use him in court. Wouldn't dare put him on the stand."

"Why not?"

"He's too damn full of himself. A pompous ass. A showboat."

Of course Lee had been called all those things, too.

"And then," the attorney went on, "there's his sexual proclivities, which any competent prosecutor would use to impeach him. He's on probation now for hypno-hanky-panky with female clients. And his receptionists are a parade of bosomy bimbos right out of a Russ Meyer movie—they last in their well-paid jobs only as long as they can take it. Apparently not all women are attracted to tubs of lard."

"*That* heavy, is he? I heard 400 pounds."

"An exaggeration. Really, I wouldn't put him past 380."

"Can you buy this character working with the CIA?"

"Hell, Nathan, he *bragged* about it! That doesn't make it necessarily *true*, of course—he's an insufferable egotist and shameless grandstander."

Again, charges that were frequently leveled against Lee, but I was too gentlemanly to point that out.

"Let's just say," Lee said, "his eccentricities do not outweigh his genius."

I thanked the attorney for his help, rang off, and went into the bedroom. The shower was going in the adjacent john. I stepped in there just as Nita was stepping from the shower looking like Botticelli's Venus but black-haired and better. I helped her dry off and maybe we fooled around before getting into casual clothes and taking breakfast in a booth at the Polo Lounge.

Nita was eager to catch up on my visit to San Quentin—she'd been asleep when I got back last night—and took it all in with wide eyes and smart questions. But when our food arrived, our conversation stopped and she seemed blue, only eating half of her veggie Eggs Benedict.

I'd had no trouble putting away the Dutch apple pancake and figured whatever was troubling her could be dealt with by me expressing a little interest. "Any auditions today?"

That only made her look more glum. Her youthful green-and-black striped top was upbeat but she was bringing it down.

"Yes," she said, her smile pained. "A salesgirl on *Here's Lucy*. At her age, Lucille Ball tends to hire older younger actresses, so I have a shot. Nate, I've auditioned every day this month and haven't landed a damn thing."

"What about that *Marcus Welby*?"

"That audition was last month. The shoot was this week. Nate, I'm just too…too *in between*—not an ingenue, not a matron. I feel like I'm chasing my tail."

I reached across and patted her hand. "Let me do that for you."

She smiled, laughed a little, but withdrew her hand. "I'm just frustrated, that's all. And I'm not doing you any good, either."

"Could've fooled me."

She sighed. "I mean…begging you to take on Bobby's assassination. If there's nothing there, it's a waste of time. If there *is* something there, it's dangerous. No, *fucking* dangerous."

"Look. I have a client, paying real money. I'm not working for you, I'm working for him. And when I'm finished with this thing, why don't you come back to Chicago with me."

She smirked. "Chicago? What's in Chicago?"

That hurt. "Well, me."

Her expression melted. Now she reached for my hand. "Oh, I'm sorry. Sweetie, I'm sorry…."

"There's a lot of theater back home and I have connections. They shoot movies there all the time. Think about it."

She was nodding. "I will. I definitely will."

Soon she was off in her little Fiat after a bit part in a sitcom, an episode of which I would only watch if she were in it.

In the yellow pages I found the office of the American Institute of Hypnosis at 8833 Sunset Boulevard and spoke with a pleasantly ditsy receptionist, making an appointment for two P.M. That allowed me time to call Ron Kiser and bring him up to speed on my conversations with Frankenheimer, Sirhan Sirhan and Dr. Simson-Kallas. But he had nothing new for me.

The afternoon was cool and I met it in a lightweight navy blazer, Polo shirt, gray slacks and Italian loafers. I parked the Jag on Larrabee and walked toward Sunset and around Mad Man Muntz's off-kilter rectangular glass box on the corner with its beautiful girls in fishnet stockings and short skirts ready to sell you a four-track car audio system. The Strip's sidewalks had no shortage of hippie kids, but this was nothing compared to what it would be after dark, when the Whisky a Go Go up the street drew them like bees to honey. Or maybe sheep to grass.

I strolled past a long white building across the top of which in red were the words

The Classic Cat

next to a marquee promising BIGGEST TOPLESS SHOW IN THE WEST. Next door, as if on another planet, a wide, almost digni-fied two-story building presented itself, its lower facade brown brick, above which, under a row of windows, it said

AMERICAN INSTITUTE OF HYPNOSIS

against the smooth pale concrete face of its upper floor. At right—comprising a vertical third of the structure—a checker-board of windows made room below for the white front door a few steps up from the street.

This was the Sunset Strip, all right.

I went into a waiting room big enough for a dozen and inhabited by a lone receptionist at a desk that had a phone and date book on it and nothing else. The mahogany paneling didn't quite go with the Scandinavian modern chairs lining the walls, their oak frames bearing green cushions. On one wall in a mas-sive frame, each phrase stacked, were the words:

CLINICAL HYPNOTHERAPY

HYPNOANALYSIS

PAST LIFE REGRESSION

CRIMINOLOGY

and

SEX THERAPY.

On the opposite wall in a matching massive frame was a photographic portrait hand-colored of (if the bronze plaque below could be believed) Dr. Joseph W. Bryant, Jr. This was a photo circa late '50s or early '60s and depicted its heavyset subject in a black business suit and tie, black-rimmed glasses, short brown hair high on a round, puffy-cheeked head. Like the building, almost dignified.

I crossed wall-to-wall carpeting to the reception desk, where a redhead in a green low-cut red-paisley dress was beaming at me with full, red-lipsticked lips and bright copper-eye-shadowed green eyes behind a pair of black-rimmed glasses like Bryant's in his portrait, apparently strictly to suggest professionalism. Her bosom, a third of which was showing with the braless rest no mystery, would make a lesser man gasp. I merely goggled.

"Nathan Heller," I said. "I have a two o'clock with Dr. Bryant."

"You're with life!" she burbled. Her smile was so wide the number of toothpaste-ad white teeth showing seemed improbable.

I didn't understand her at first, then got it: I'd said on the phone I wanted an interview for *Life* magazine.

"Sit where you like, honey," she said, gesturing, jiggling. Her flesh was white with faint red freckles. "The doc'll only be a minute."

"I like the view from here."

Even more teeth! "I bet you do."

"I don't believe the size..."

"Oh, they're real!"

"...of this place. How many people work here, miss?"

"Call me Alice." She took off the glasses and tossed them on the desk, to lessen the distance between us. "How many work here, regular? Two. The doc and I. Other doctors come and go. Mostly it's patients. A lot of patients, but he cleared the afternoon for you."

"Only two people on staff? A facility this size?"

"Well, there's a lot goes on upstairs. A recording studio with a control room, TVs, multiple tape decks. A closed-circuit set-up to treat three patients at once, at locations anywhere in the country. Examination rooms, patient rooms. We have more couches than a furniture store."

Oh, the stories those couches could tell.

The phone rang and she said excuse me and smiled (she was the kind of girl whose smiles were almost always accompanied by a shrug), putting on the unneeded glasses to make an appointment for a private session. I strolled over and had a closer look at Dr. Bryant's portrait. He reminded me of someone. Oliver Hardy minus the Hitler mustache? I'd try not to become his Stan Laurel.

"Mr. Heller!"

The commanding voice came from a tall fat man in a yellow polyester sports coat with a knotted red neck-scarf and red-and-black-and-yellow plaid pants and pointed brown shoes who stood filling a doorway behind the receptionist at her desk, his fists at his waist like Superman. His glasses were rimmed in heavy red and thick lenses magnified his dark eyes, his shaggy rust-brown hair swept back, the blister-pale Ollie face framed by an Amish beard. He looked like the host of an oasis in a mirage when you'd been crawling across the desert a really long time.

He didn't look much like his framed portrait of maybe ten years ago, but this was Dr. Joseph W. Bryant, Jr., all right, pushing at 400 pounds hard, putting the hippo in hypnotist.

"Dr. Joseph W. Bryant, Jr.," he confirmed pleasantly as he proffered his hand. I took and shook it, a clammy thing reminiscent of a pet's rubber squeeze toy.

He gestured for me to enter and I did, with him closing the door behind us. The office was good-size, its walls at right arrayed with framed diplomas and clipped magazine and newspaper articles about its inhabitant; at left were framed posters of three films—*Tales of Terror* with Vincent Price, *Dementia 13*, and *The Manchurian Candidate*, on all of which he'd been a consultant. A shrink's couch was against the back wall. To the right of his desk, where he could swivel, was a console with microphones and push buttons and knobs and dials arranged in a wide V. The area in back of the console was curtained but glass could be glimpsed where the curtains joined.

"You would be the famous Private Eye to the Stars," he said jovially as he settled into his chair. He was like a department store Santa with questionable intentions.

"That does follow me around," I said, taking the client's chair he'd indicated with a pudgy palm. Or was that "patient's" chair? At least I wasn't shown to the couch.

"I suppose it's inevitable we should meet," he said, a twinkle in the lens-magnified eyes.

"Is it?"

"Private Eye to the Stars," he said with a modest flourish of a hand, "meets Hypnotherapist to the Stars."

I didn't know of any celebrities he'd treated and the framed pictures on the wall didn't include any. Maybe he'd been on some of the film sets.

Still, he must have read something in my expression because he added, "I refer of course to the celebrity likes of Albert DeSalvo and Carl Coppolino."

The Boston Strangler and a convicted wife murderer.

I smiled, nodded, said, "Our mutual friend Lee Bailey sends along his regards."

"Very kind of him." Bryant was reaching for a pipe in a holder of several. "We shared some very interesting, and if I might say, hair-raising experiences. I can share some of those with you, if you like, for your article."

"Not necessary. Lee has already filled me in."

He lighted a match. "If you wish a direct quote or another point of view, don't hesitate to ask."

"I'd like to talk to you about hypnosis," I said, taking out a pad and pen, to pretend to take notes, "as it pertains to therapeutic work."

"Certainly."

"I notice you list criminology," I said, with a gesture toward his outer office, "as one of your specialties."

A confident nod. "I'm very much an expert in the use of hypnosis in criminal law." He had the pipe going now. The smoke smelled pleasant, floral and sweet. And expensive.

"Of course," he continued, "I'm probably the leading expert in the world on hypnosis itself. It's hardly surprising the LAPD would call upon me from time to time. Or the lawyerly likes of Melvin Belli and our friend Lee."

I asked, "How would you define hypnotism for the layman?"

Bryant rocked back, challenging his chair. "Hypnotism is an increased concentration of the mind, a supreme relaxation of the body, and an enhanced susceptibility to suggestion. Sometimes drugs are employed, but often not."

"You offer sex therapy as an option, I see."

He nodded several times, firmly. "Sex and religion are my chief interests, hypnotism merely a means to an end. Seeing that term 'sex therapy,' you most likely took notice of how physically attractive my receptionist is…and, this is off-the-record you understand, but I admit to making a habit out of hiring my current bed partners as receptionists." He chuckled. Puffed his pipe. Leaned across chummily. "When a relationship breaks up, I need to cast for both roles, so to speak."

Yuck.

I asked, "You did a *Playboy* interview, didn't you?"

His grin didn't have as many teeth in it as his receptionist, but it was Cheshire-like just the same. "I did. But then *you're* a friend of Hugh Hefner yourself, aren't you, Mr. Heller? Perhaps I should call you 'Nate' and I should be 'Bill.' "

"Sure, Bill. Yes, Hef is a client. Going way back. And, well… I've dated a few Playmates and Bunnies in my day."

"Or rather in your nights." His smile was as cute as a kitten. A dead kitten. "I am convinced the best way to get to know a woman, really *know* her, is at a deep emotional level. This requires sexual intercourse, of course. Oh, don't mistake me for some sort of sybarite. I'm an ordained priest in the Old Roman Catholic Church, which some dismiss as a fire-and-brimstone sect, and a frequent guest preacher at fundamentalist churches all around Southern California. *That* you can quote me on."

"Perhaps we should get back to the kind of subjects *Life* magazine is interested in as opposed to *Playboy*."

He let out a single *Ha!* "Yes. Perhaps we should!"

I said, "You mention religion as your other obsession. What does religion have to do with hypnotism?"

The big buggy eyes got bigger and buggier. "Only everything! The prophets produced their visions by a form of autohypnosis and, in the Middle Ages, most of the prophets who heard the voice of God actually disassociated their own voices and heard themselves. Many elements of hypnosis remain in religion today—the chanting testimonials, the flickering candles, the cross as a fixation point."

This mumbo-jumbo I couldn't care less about, but I said, "Interesting. Let's back up, though. I could really use some background about your work for the government."

He waved his pipe like he was in the backseat of a convertible in a parade. "Certainly. During the Korean conflict I was chief of all medical survival training for the United States Air

Force, which translates to 'Brainwashing Section.' Accomplished great things there. Stateside, I established this institute in 1955, started our teaching program in 1958, and in 1960 began publishing a medical journal devoted to our work here."

"By 'great things,' do you mean your groundbreaking work in brainwashing? Both in rehabilitating our military personnel who'd been prisoners of the enemy and developing techniques that could be used against those enemies?"

He stiffened just a little, scratched the Amish beard at the chinny chin chin. "That's substantially correct. But you understand I can't provide detailed information about any of it— we're talking about research and events that remain classified years later. Definitely top secret."

I tossed a casual hand. "Perhaps you could talk in more general terms. For example, how does one go about brainwashing a subject?"

He thought about that briefly, then pontificated: "Well, you have to have control over the person, either lock them up physically or dupe them into cooperation. You may have to use a certain amount of physical torture or else deploy what we might call mental gymnastics. And there is the use of long-term hypnotic suggestion, probably drugs, and so on. Under these situations, where you have all this going for you—like in a prison camp or in a controlled seemingly positive environment —you can brainwash a person to do just about *anything*."

"Literally anything?"

He gestured with pipe in hand. "Come now, Nate—you're not naive. The government programs people to kill all the time— enlists them into the army, tells them killing is for their country's own good, and the recruits, the draftees, don't doubt any of that a bit. And Uncle Sam doesn't have to use hypnosis to put it over."

I nodded. "It becomes rote. The way Sirhan Sirhan shot Bobby Kennedy, for example?"

He looked hurt for a moment, a big put-upon baby, then scowled, looking nothing like a baby at all. "I am not going to comment on that case because I didn't interview that particular subject."

"Not for the LAPD? Not for the CIA?"

"Not for anybody!"

I leaned in. "The chief psychologist at San Quentin suspects you did."

His mouth tightened into a sphincter. "I just *told* you I *didn't* hypnotize Sirhan. I don't have an opinion because I *didn't treat him.* You've got a lot of misconceptions about hypnosis and here you are, trying to find some ammunition to put that same old crap out, that people can be hypnotized into doing all these weird things and so on...the old Svengali stuff...and I am not going to be party to it, not for *Life*, not for *Playboy*, not for the *Journal of the American Institute of Hypnosis*! I don't want to be quoted by you at all. I don't want to be in your goddamn article. Because I have no desire to be laughed at."

I turned over a hand. "You've had to bump up against ridicule from the beginning of your career, Bill, and you've fought back with facts. What is your opinion? Did Sirhan indulge in self-hypnosis, as one of his defense psychiatrists believes? Or was he programmed to kill? Brainwashed by an expert?"

He got to his feet; it was like watching a film of a building implosion play backward. "This has been gone over fifty million times. If that's all that you have got to interview me about, you are wasting my time and yours. This interview is *over*."

He came around the desk, and I wondered if this soft-looking but nonetheless heavyweight creature was going to take a swing at me.

No. He stormed out—of his own office!

For a big fella he moved fucking fast. He was halfway down the reception area by the time I slipped past Alice, who looked up with big green eyes and asked, "Did you want to schedule another appointment?"

I did not answer.

He was out the door already and by the time I got outside, I couldn't see him, looking side to side and across the street and…

…Jesus, he was right next door, heading into the Classic Cat, home of the biggest topless show in the West.

FIFTEEN

I followed him. I wasn't exactly sure why—I'd probably gotten everything out of him I might expect to, but the hypnotist shrink had bolted from his office in what seemed like panic. His next move might prove of interest, so out on the Strip I walked past the Classic Cat's valet parking and went in under the marquee to enter between two bouncers in tux vests, skinny black ties and bulging muscles. No cover charge, a freestanding sign immediately told me, but the unlisted price of the two-drink minimum would no doubt make a strong man blanch.

It took me a moment before I realized I'd been in here before—not when it was a strip joint, but the Jerry Lewis Restaurant, which the comedian had opened to thumb his nose at his old partner who had Dino's elsewhere on the Strip. The decor had been luxurious but the fare average, and now Dean Martin was still dishing up drinks and food while his old partner's joint was offering topless dancers and a little combo playing Louis Prima castoffs, and Jerry didn't even get a slice.

Remodeled into a fairly plush nightclub, the Classic Cat was a long, rather narrow space. The foyer had a coat room to the right, some offices, and a display area of life-size posters of dancers interspersed with framed 8x10 blow-ups of celebrities on visits to the premises—Jim Arness, Adam West, Bob Crane, Doug McClure, and (oddly) Lana Turner. Pool balls were clacking at left, a bar separating this area from a small stage with seating. Past Roman columns the space opened up to accommodate a black-curtained sea of pink-cloth-covered tables facing a large stage angled across the upper left corner. Occasional cursive pink neon high on walls reminded patrons where they were and guided them to the restrooms and exits.

I did not spot Dr. Bryant in the smaller stage area, where a blonde with enormous piles of hair danced pert-breasted top-less in a glittery G-string and matching heels while a bored Latin in a tux played a rhumba number on a grand piano, the band in the main room far enough away to do little more than provide a discordant contrast. The audience was sparse but attentive, some college boys in letter jackets between classes and a few actors in sport coats between gigs…way between, in some cases.

The main showroom was perhaps a third full, mostly busi-nessmen and tourists, women among the latter group, giggling embarrassedly, their men keeping the drinks coming. The dancer here had a ton of brunette hair framing a lovely face and spilling down her bare back. Tanned all over, she was coyly covering her breasts with her arms while she wore only the lower half of a Dorothy Lamour pastel sarong as she managed to summon considerable grace swaying in heels before a zebra backdrop while the little combo (Raul and the Revelations) butchered "The Lion Sleeps Tonight."

Somehow she was bridging the South Sea Islands and Darkest Africa just fine and when she entwined her hands behind her head it was as if to make sure we could all see her natural gifts included no scars where breast met bone or around the edges of prominent puffy areolas. The nipples themselves were scolding fingertips. God had made all that, not a plastic surgeon. Nice going, God.

I was standing off to one side and she noticed me. I admit I was staring—she was a striking woman but also something about her was nagging at my mind—and she smiled just a little across the vastness of the room. Or was I just another dipshit patron imagining a stripper had just connected with me?

The good doctor in his yellow sport coat and knotted red scarf was seated at a table near the stage, but didn't seem to be watching the production. He overwhelmed his chair, a bear on a unicycle. A waitress pretty enough to perform here delivered Bryant a drink that he hadn't had time to order; it was a silly looking thing in a tall glass with a bunch of fruit pieces on a cocktail stick. He ignored it, but my impression was this was a regular customer's automatic order.

On stage, the tall busty brunette—well, she was in heels, so maybe she wasn't tall exactly, perhaps five six—was wrapping up her set. Soon she was deftly scooping up dollar bills that had been tossed on stage during her performance, bowing to her applause, and slipping off.

An M.C. in a striped sport coat, white slacks and out-of-date early Beatle haircut emerged from somewhere to tell his microphone that they'd just seen the incredible Marguerite and that next on the Classic Cat main stage would be that sweet Southern belle, Dixie. The zebra backdrop went up and a Confederate flag unfurled down. Pixie-haired Dixie, blonde, strutted out wearing a Johnny Reb cap and a gray excuse for a vest and a red bikini bottom. Also, for those keeping score, red cowboy boots. The band began to play a bump-and-grind version of "Dixie" and for comic relief sang out, "I wish I was in Dixie!" at appropriate inappropriate moments, which prompted her to smile and waggle a finger at them and her bottom at the audience.

I settled in at a table toward the back. A stunning redhead waitress took my order for a rum and Coke.

"Why aren't *you* up on the stage?" I asked her, just being friendly.

"I'm saving myself for my wedding night," she said dryly.

I had that coming.

Dixie was still strutting, her vest not yet doffed, when Marguerite came out from a stage door wearing a long diaphanous black robe over her stripper garb. She walked straight to Bryant and sat, and he leaned in, talking to her intently. Now and then he would stop and sip his stupid drink through a straw. Marguerite just listened, then shrugged, got up and went back the way she came.

That might have been a failed negotiation for a table dance, but I didn't think so. Those two seemed to know each other.

Bryant sat through Dixie's three numbers, not watching the stage, just leaning on an elbow and occasionally sipping through his straw. There was something childish about him. Like Fatty Arbuckle in the silent movies—you know, the cheerful fat man who got accused of rape.

A chirpy voice asked, "Table dance, mister?"

The pert-breasted blonde from the smaller stage, weighted down with all that hair and wrapped up in a white gossamer robe open over a sparkly bra and matching G-string, beamed down at me. She looked so young I was ashamed of myself. Nonetheless, I asked her how much and she said five dollars. I told her I had ten for her if she would just sit down and kept me company for a while.

"Actually, I'm glad to sit down," she said.

"And I'm glad for the company."

She looked at me with big sky-blue eyes under over-the-top fake eyelashes and light blue eyeshadow. "My name's Susie. Are you from L.A. or just visiting?"

"I'm from Chicago."

"What do you do?"

"I'm a private detective."

That stopped her for a moment. "I don't have any married boyfriends, actually. At least, if I do, I don't know it. And if I did know it I wouldn't want to talk about it, even for ten dollars."

"I'm not on that kind of job."

"What kind of job are you actually on?"

"You see that fat slob, Susie?"

"I see that overweight gentleman, yes."

"Do you know him? He works next door. He's a hypnotist."

"I know who he is. Actually, I worked for him a while."

I blinked. "As a receptionist?"

"How did you know?"

"I told you I'm a detective."

"He was always trying to...you know. Fuck me. Actually."

"And you didn't want to actually fuck him."

"No! Would you?"

"Hell no. What was he like?"

"Horrible. Sweaty. A real bragger."

"What would he brag about?"

She made a disgusted face that still managed to be cute. "About helping the police and stuff. He actually said he caught the Boston Strangler."

"Did he."

"And some other strangler. And you know that terrible man who killed Bobby Kennedy?"

"Sirhan Sirhan?"

"Yes, Sirhad Sirhad. He said he actually hypnotized him."

"Did he."

"He did. For the police, probably. He works with the police a lot. He said he actually helped put him away, Sirhad Sirhad."

Sometimes you strike gold in the most unlikely places.

I got out my billfold and gave her a twenty.

"I don't have change," she said apologetically.

"Actually, Susie," I said, "I don't need any."

"You're nice." She got up, leaned in, gave me a kiss on the cheek.

Best twenty dollars I'd spent in a long time.

A dancer I'd seen in Chicago, Haji, was doing her exotic thing on stage, Raul and his Revelations struggling to cope with Martin Denny's "Misirlou." She proceeded to perform a belly dance that was too good for this clip joint.

In the middle of Haji's act, Bryant got up and went out fast, his beeline not taking him anywhere near me, though I ducked down just the same. When he made it to the door, I got up to follow him again, but somebody put a hand on my sleeve.

"Baby please don't go," Marguerite sang, doing Cher. She had the same kind of low, throaty voice, not at all like Susie's chirp but at least as appealing. And she was just enough older than Susie to make me not feel immediately guilty.

I asked, "Did you have something in mind?"

Marguerite was in a sleeveless white top and a black-and-white checked miniskirt and white vinyl go-go boots with a matching white purse on a chain strap slung over her shoulder. She was probably twenty-one, twenty-two—in this day and age that was the equivalent of forty.

"I thought we made a connection," she said archly. "You looked at me, I looked at you. Remember?"

"I remember," I said. "Very 'Some Enchanted Evening.' "

"I don't know what that is," she admitted and sat.

"An old guy reference," I said and sat. "You don't look like you're getting ready to go back on stage."

"No. I was just filling in for somebody. I'm done for the day."

"I'm Nate, by the way. Or Nathan. Want a drink before you head home?"

"Why not?"

I motioned my wait-for-her-wedding-night waitress over and ordered up a Harvey Wallbanger for Marguerite and a second rum and Coke for me.

She put her hands together piously; she had very long, very
red, very pointed fingernails. "I saw you talking to Susie."

"Nice kid."

"Little young for you."

"So are you."

Her shrug was ageless. "But not *jailbait* young. The management pretends not to know she's on fake I.D. I've never seen
Susie talk to a man for so long a time. You must be quite the
conversationalist."

"I'm fucking articulate, haven't you noticed?"

Her dusty-rose lipsticked lips puckered into a nice smile.
"You do have a way with words."

She had Cher eye makeup on to go with her voice, but it
gave me a pang—she looked uncomfortably like Nita on our
first meeting in the Senator's suite at the Ambassador.

"What on earth," Marguerite asked, leaning in, "was there to
talk about with that airhead? I mean, she's sweet, and probably
a fun little piece of tail. But she makes Goldie Hawn look like a
rocket scientist."

"That's just an act. Goldie Hawn is very smart."

"Susie isn't. You can't have taken *that* much time negotiating
your way into her panties. What's your game?"

"You seem to want to know a lot about me."

She lifted her chin and looked down at me; she had a cute
pug nose. "You do interest me. Most men in the afternoon sit
close to the stage. You were halfway out the door. You ashamed
to be looking at naked young women, Nathan?"

"Utterly."

"Do you spell that with two d's?"

We both laughed. I was liking her. She was smart, maybe not
Goldie Hawn smart, but not bad for a place like this.

"Actually…to borrow Susie's word," I said, "I was inquiring
about your next door neighbor—Dr. Bryant?"

Her eyebrows went up but her eyelids didn't. "Ah. Our friendly neighborhood shrink. What about him?"

"Ask me what I do for a living first."

"What do you do for a living first?"

Goldie Hawn had nothing on her.

"I'm a detective. Private. Just checking up on him for a client."

She poked a long red nail at me, like she was about to tickle the tip of my nose. "So *that's* why you're here. Not to look at naked girls. To find out about Dr. Bryant. And here I thought I was the one you were interested in!"

Our drinks arrived.

"If I *were* interested in you," I said, "how much might it run? If you have a college fund or something."

She just looked at me. Had I offended her?

"A hundred dollars," she said. "My place isn't far. But let's have our drinks first. At these prices, we can't afford not to. And, anyway, I'm just getting to know you."

After a five-minute stroll from the Classic Cat up tree-lined Alta Loma, ending in a cul-de-sac, an unlikely garden oasis materialized just steps away from the chaos of the Strip. Once I'd taken in its Spanish-inspired white exterior walls and orange-tile roof, and gone arm-in-arm with Marguerite through the canopied entrance—

1200
SUNSET MARQUIS

—the residential hotel gave off a distinctly druggy cast. Beyond its unadorned open reception area, the large patio and pool welcomed skinny long-haired pasty-faced rockers in black t-shirts and black jeans clinging to shadows and sprawling on lounge chairs beneath patio umbrellas like vampires shy of the sun.

English accents buzzed here and there like mosquito nests, and now and then a familiar show biz face would appear among the hippie rabble—Mike Nichols, Bill Cosby, Van Heflin. And me without my autograph book.

The rooms were off the pool and Marguerite was in one of them. The furnishings were (as advertised on a cheap sign outside) attractive, but in a modern way that had immediately dated. The place had a kitchenette and the walls bore posters of Marilyn by Warhol, Jane Fonda as Barbarella, and The Doors at the Whisky a Go Go.

My hostess led me to an orange floral sofa without armrests in front of a low-slung glass-topped coffee table that had marijuana makings spread out like do-it-yourself party favors.

Marguerite perched next to me, rolled a joint, lit it, offered it to me, I declined, and she said, "You aren't one of those stuffy older generation types, are you?"

"I'm not a narc. That's the best I can do."

She laughed. I wasn't crazy about the sweet smell of the smoke, but it wasn't an issue.

Helpfully, she asked, "Can I get you something to drink? I could make you a Seven and Seven."

"No thanks."

She made a mock "hurt" face. "Oh. All business. Boring!"

"Business first. Fun time after."

"All right. Let's see the color of your money."

I got out my billfold and gave her a crisp hundred.

"Fancy!" she said and tossed it folded onto the coffee table. She slipped an arm around my shoulder. "You want to fool around? Or did you want to know more about the doc?"

"Let's start there. Anything you care to share."

She frowned coquettishly at me. "What do you want to know for? Some husband whose wife got hypnotized and then came home with a hickey? He's really harmless, the doc. He puts them under and feels them up and, you know, Chubby gets a chubby."

"This isn't about that. It's more about his work for the LAPD and the CIA."

I'd laid that out there bluntly but she didn't flinch.

"I imagine Susie told you about how he caught the Boston Strangler," Marguerite said. "Or anyway says he did."

"Yeah. And the Hollywood Strangler, too."

"He's big on stranglers, the doc. And that rich guy who killed his wife, Bryant helped the defense with that one, too, he says. But the guy went down for it anyway. The doc says if he'd been brought in sooner he could've got that guy off."

"Not in a sexual way, I hope."

"Ha! I should hope not. Listen, I hope I didn't lure you out here under false pretenses. I don't really know anything more than Susie probably already told you, about him helping the LAPD. As far as the CIA goes, he brags about that a *lot*, but isn't, you know, specific."

"Susie mentioned Sirhan Sirhan."

That stopped her for a moment, but just a moment. "The creep who shot Bobby Kennedy? The doc did say something about that. I think he hypnotized that guy for the prosecution, getting ready for the trial or something."

"Funny. His name doesn't turn up anywhere in the court transcripts, and several other hypnotists and psychiatrists do."

She shrugged. She placed the joint in an ashtray and cuddled up. "Now you know everything I know."

"About the doc, maybe."

"I dig older guys, y'know."

"Do you."

She kissed me; it was a sticky, sexy thing, but when she put her tongue in my mouth, it tasted like weed. Still, it went on a while and those long nails clawed sensually at my hair and then one pricked teasingly the back of my neck just as the kiss ended.

"Ow," I said, softly, with a smile.

"You just sit there. Did you like my zebra dance? At the Cat?"

"It was swell."

"You just sit there!"

She got off the couch and padded over to a portable stereo on a stand. She knelt and thumbed through LPs in a rack below, and in that short white skirt was something to see. She made her selection and started it playing. Herb Alpert and the Tijuana Brass—"A Taste of Honey."

There was no striptease. She just stepped out of the black-and-white miniskirt, kicked it away, and then out of her sheer panties and kicked those away too, then pulled the sleeveless white top off and smiled a little, well aware of the impact her full breasts could have on a man. Now all she wore were the white go-go boots, and she began a little pony dance.

Goddamn, she was a lovely thing. Unlike the poolside rockers, she was tan everywhere except where her bikini had kept her legal, and her pubic bush was a defiant thing, curling black against white flesh, as wild and tangled as the garden grounds of the Marquis.

And I won't lie to you. I was hard. I considered fucking her to keep things honest—you know, credible. To demonstrate that this was about more than just me pumping her, so to speak, about Bryant.

Maybe if she hadn't been brunette. Maybe if she hadn't looked a little like Nita, maybe I could have been the old randy Nate Heller. But seeing this incredible, available young thing (definitely not *sweet* young thing) in the altogether only made me think of Nita. Had I really gotten this old? Or had I finally grown up?

Now *I* was the one being hypnotized, by her undulating hips, by the swaying ripe fruit of her breasts, by the promise of red slightly-smeared-from-that-kiss lips as she inserted a finger in her mouth and sucked on it and widened her eyes in an effect both comic and erotic. But I would be damned if I'd fuck her.

And I didn't.

But to be honest with you, it wasn't my sudden superior moral sense, not entirely. It had much more to do with the world going bleary and me passing out.

When I woke up it took me a full minute at least to get my bearings. I was groggy, a mental thickness cut only by the blinding blade of a headache. I sat up and tried to recognize the surroundings. The lights were low, only a desk lamp on and the shape of a man, a big man, seated behind the lamp's glow.

"Are you feeling better, Mr. Heller?"

Bryant!

And this was Bryant's office....

I was stretched out on the patient's couch. My blazer was off and slung over a chair nearby. My mouth was cottony and my alertness was coming back but the headache had gone from a blade to banging. My right arm hurt at the joint. I got into a sitting position and my hands found my head as I leaned over, wondering if I was going to puke. Somehow I managed not to.

The fat man in the yellow sport coat, the red scarf loose around his neck now, came over into the dim desk-lamp light. He put a hand on my shoulder.

"You just take it easy now," he said. "Marguerite called me, worried about you. You passed out, for some reason. With a man your age, why that could be a stroke!"

"Back off! Let me get up."

He edged away, holding out his palms. "Certainly. I helped her bring you here. I, uh, had to give you a sedative. You began to get violent in your sleep and yet I couldn't rouse you. You may feel some aftereffects. You may want to call for a ride. Can I do that for you?"

"Fuck you," I said to him, and grabbed the blazer and got into it as I stumbled out of his office and into the unpopulated waiting room, the redheaded receptionist gone. I crossed the distance to the door, which seemed like a very long way.

"*Mr. Heller!*" he called.

But I was gone.

Out on the Strip was darkness streaked by headlights and neon, hippie kids milling, laughing, smoking, long-haired creatures of the night. I somehow got to my Jag around the corner and sat in it for a while before attempting to drive.

I touched the back of my neck.

I had turned down the joint and I had turned down a drink, but when I'd given into that kiss, and she'd pricked me on the neck, I should have known.

Something in her nail polish hadn't been by Maybelline.

PART FOUR

Welcome to Survival Town

April 1969

SIXTEEN

Someone was stroking my hand.

My eyes came open, lids going up like reluctant curtains, and sunlight was filtering painfully in through the foliage hugging the bungalow. I resisted the urge to close my eyes again and instead took stock.

I was on top of the bed, on the comforter, with Nita's side looking slept in. Right now Nita was sitting beside me, studying me, her smile one of concern. My eyes burned and sludge was creeping through the inside of my skull like the Blob looking around for Steve McQueen to smother.

"What time is it?" somebody said. Me, apparently. The words had not come trippingly off my tongue. More like tripped.

"A little after ten," she said. "If we want breakfast at the Lounge, you should get up and throw yourself together. They stop serving at eleven."

I sat up. It was no harder than lifting the back end of a Buick by the bumper. "What...what time did I get in?"

"I'm not sure. I went to bed early, around ten, and you must've crawled on top of the covers sometime after that, and didn't wake me. You're fully dressed, by the way."

I was! Still in the navy blazer, Polo shirt, gray slacks, even my shoes.

Nita seemed a little amused if still concerned. "You must have really tied one on."

Her dark hair was ponytailed back and she was wearing no makeup at all; even in her early forties, she put every one of the

Classic Cat girls to shame. Her pale pink PJs took pity on my
burning eyeballs.

"What were you up to, anyway?" she asked lightly. "You didn't
leave a note or anything…sorry. I don't have a right to—"

"Sure you do," I said. "I was picking up strippers at the Classic
Cat on Sunset."

She made a face and slapped my chest gently. "Oh, you. Get
dressed. Let's have breakfast."

We did.

I took time to shower and shave and, by the time I threw on
a fresh Polo, light blue sport coat and navy slacks, I was func-
tioning again. A good thing, too, because Nita's daisy-print
denim jeans, not at all offset by her white blouse, might have
made my eyeballs fall out.

Then, when we were having a cup of coffee in the bungalow
breakfast nook, I told her everything that had happened yesterday, leaving a few choice bits out, like Marguerite's bare-ass
dance in her little Sunset Marquis living room. Even so, there
was plenty for Nita to get wide-eyed about and the part I liked
best was when she gave me shit for going out without a gun. I
couldn't remember another woman ever doing that.

"This Bryant character said he gave you a sedative," she said
through angry little white teeth. "What *kind* of sedative…?"

I touched the front of my right elbow where it still hurt some.
"Scopolamine, probably. Maybe sodium pentothal. Probably
threw in a few of his hypno tricks."

"What could he have found out?"

I shrugged. "Not much, really. For once it's a blessing I'm
not a better detective—I don't have anything that would elude
any decent investigator. Worst of it might be confirming I've
been working to expose what really happened in the Pantry."

She added a little more cream to her coffee. "Seems to me,"

she said, a sip later, "he's confirmed his own complicity. Isn't drugging you an admission of guilt?"

Shook my head. "Not really. That lardbucket has all kinds of things he wants kept concealed. Just because Bryant told Betty and Veronica he programmed Sirhan doesn't make it true. And, anyway, he doesn't seem to have told them that, exactly—they think he hypnotized that bushy-haired little Palestinian for the cops or maybe the prosecution."

"Where does that leave you?"

I raised my cup of coffee in salute. "Now that I'm human again, I'm going to drop by the Sunset Marquis and have a little chat with Marguerite. If I can turn her against the doc, I'll have something to hold over him. There's no way she could have had any idea she might be an accessory after the fact to a political assassination."

She cocked her head. "Couldn't she?"

"I don't follow."

She was smiling as she leaned in. "Nate, didn't you tell me there was something about her that was nagging at the back of your mind?"

"Yeah."

Nita opened a palm. "She's a curvy brunette in her early twenties, right?"

"Right."

"With a pug nose?"

My mouth dropped open and words came out. "Oh. She could be the girl…"

"…in the polka-dot dress."

Nita insisted on going with me. Maybe because of what she'd said, I slipped off the jacket and slipped on the hip-holstered nine millimeter. The jacket wasn't custom-tailored for that, but

I was returning to the scene of the crime and certain corners
needed cutting.

We crossed the nondescript Sunset Marquis lobby, decorated by a scattering of framed black-and-white rock band
photos—I knew some of the groups because of my son Sam
(Byrds, Doors, Turtles)—to the simple front desk. Seated
behind it reading *Rolling Stone* was a handsome brown-eyed
guy in his late thirties, very tan, in a blue blazer and white
YARDBIRDS t-shirt.

He looked up and gave us a polite smile. "Help you, folks?
We have suites available. It's only suites here, no single
rooms."

"Is Marguerite in?" I asked. I'd never got a last name.

He smiled, tossed the newspaper-style magazine on the
desk; he looked a little like Tom Jones, the singer, not the
Albert Finney character. "That's her stage name," he said. "Her
real name is no secret, though. It's Elaine Nye. But she's out."

"Are you the manager?"

"Manager. Owner. Chief-cook-and-bottle-washer. Well, not
really cook, though."

"When do you expect her?"

"Three weeks?" It was a question. "She's got a booking."

"Happen to know where?"

"Sure. Vegas."

"Would you know where in Vegas?"

A shrug. "Could be any one of half a dozen places. Check the
Vegas Yellow Pages."

"Let my fingers do the walking?"

"Yeah. I'm not being a smart-ass—I just really don't know."

"Okay."

"She left this morning. Her and a carload of luggage. Doesn't
travel light, Elaine."

I got a twenty out of my billfold and slid it across the counter like a card I was dealing in Twenty-one. "I'd like a look at her room, if I could."

"You're Nate Heller, aren't you?"

This fucking Private Eye to the Stars thing was getting to be a pain in the ass.

I said, "Yeah. Twenty not enough?"

He waved that off. "Don't want your money. You're a friend of Hef's, right?"

I blinked. "I am."

"Hefner's a friend of mine, too. I built this place as a hotel to go along with the Playboy Club on Sunset. His out-of-town talent stays here. Listen, I'll let you look around in Miss Nye's digs, but you can't take anything."

He fetched a young woman in the office behind him to take over and walked us out and across the Astroturf that edged the pool, past assorted pale druggies, to Marguerite's room. Elaine's room. He unlocked the door with a master key and gestured for us to go on in.

The only thing that had changed was the grass on the coffee table, absent now; even the Herb Alpert LP was still on the record player, silent now. Nita watched, arms folded, exchanging a nervous smile with the manager/owner, and I checked around. The clothing in the closets and chests of drawers was a little light; the owner was right—she'd taken a lot with her. How many tops did a topless dancer need? The refrigerator had been divested of anything that might spoil. Three weeks had probably been a decent guess.

My search came up with nothing.

The only thing I found was a matchbook in the ashtray on the coffee table. It said:

PUSSYCAT
A'
GO-GO
IN THE HEART OF THE STRIP

Different Strip.

That I took, with the manager/owner's permission.

Our next stop was close by: the American Institute of Hypnosis. Nita went in with me and I approached the desk, where Alice the redheaded receptionist in the black-rimmed, probably window-glass glasses beamed at me like the old friend I was. This time about half of her bosom was on display in a green and pink geometric dress. The upper half! Get your mind out of the gutter....

"Oh, I'm sorry, Mr. Heller." I never saw so many goddamn teeth. "Dr. Bryant is attending a seminar and then a retreat. He won't be back until next week."

"A seminar where, if I might ask."

"Sure. Ask away!"

"Where is the seminar?"

"Didn't I say? Vegas."

"Know where he's staying or anything?"

A shrug. "Just Vegas."

Back out on the street, Nita said, "Did you see the rack on that girl?"

"I missed it," I said. "I was too wrapped up in the teeth. You don't do auditions on the weekend, do you?"

"No."

"Good. Then I have a sudden urge for a Las Vegas getaway."

She took my arm and cuddled up right there on Sunset in front of God, the hippies, the winos and everybody. "Aren't you afraid of taking me with you into the lion's den?"

"I'm afraid *not* to take you. The lions might come looking."

✻

We packed quickly, didn't even change our clothes. By one P.M. we were on our way via Route 66, with a stop for gas and burgers at Roy's Café & Motel at Amboy, and on to Highway 91, mountains and occasional little towns breaking up the desert monotony. The Jag was air-conditioned but we barely needed it, the weather in the low eighties. We played cassette tapes of Frank Sinatra by way of preparation for my return to a town I'd known since it was a bump in the road before Ben Siegel transformed it into modern Las Vegas, getting killed for his trouble.

Nita slept the last hour or so, waking up in time to see the sign announcing

WELCOME
TO *Fabulous*
LAS VEGAS
NEVADA

just as desert desolation was getting muted by dusk and a flowering of neon began. Initially it was gas stations and mom-and-pop hotels, like the Galaxy and Desert Rose and Lone Palm; but then came the spread-out casinos with their elaborate signs and black-letters-on-white marquee attractions: **HACIENDA** (Comedy Riot 1969, Hank Henry and Topless Models); **TROP-ICANA** (Folies Bergère, Julie London); **ALADDIN** (Minsky's Burlesque '69, Ink Spots); **DUNES** (Casino de Paris, Mills Brothers); **FLAMINGO** (Paul Anka, Myron Cohen); and at left, where we turned in, **CAESARS PALACE** (Anthony Newley, David Frye).

Set back from the Strip, Caesars' crescent-shaped central tower was fronted by a curved casino with symmetrical wings that swung outward, vaguely suggesting a Roman forum. A vertical plaza of Italian cypress trees and towering fountains bathed in turquoise light sprayed columns of water. At the passenger drop-off larger-than-life statues—Greek, Roman, and Renaissance figures mixed with shameless abandon—guarded enormous front doors.

Inside, body builders in Roman soldier garb and curvy ersatz Liz Taylor-style Cleopatras greeted us. To the left an underlit, stingily ventilated reception area encouraged guests not to wait for their rooms to be readied but rather to enter the cool bright sunken casino where slot machines and gambling tables sang their tuneless percussive song. Sexy waitresses in toga dresses were delivering guests gratis cocktails beneath a domed ceiling and a massive crystal chandelier in the shape of a Roman medallion.

Our room, however, was ready and turned out to be a modest example of the fourteen-story tower's 680 rooms: decorated in a style that might best be characterized as Spartacus Meets the Jetsons, the blue shag-carpeted (with matching furnishings) split-level suite had a dining area, grand piano, crystal chandelier, assorted statuary, and spiral staircase that led to a balcony encircling the living room. The sleeping quarters included a round bed, a mirrored wall and a Jacuzzi. The walls were mostly patterned gold, though at one point were interrupted by a red wall any San Francisco whorehouse would be proud of.

We stood in the living room hand in hand, like two pimply teenagers trying to get up the nerve to go into the homecoming dance.

I asked, "Decadent enough for you?"

"Nearly," she said.

We got into swimwear, robes and sandals and went down to the Garden of the Gods, a vast swimming pool designed in the shape of a Roman shield. The pool was lined with towering white columns, lights at the base of which made nighttime swimming a dreamy, romantic affair. We were not the only couple down here but crowded it wasn't. The most impressive effect, however, came from a full moon, lording over it all like a massive glowing poker chip.

Nita's long dark hair was pinned up, her curvaceous figure nicely displayed in a hot pink Peter Max-type print one-piece. My trunks were green and black Tiki-style. Together we were stylishly headache inducing.

We leaned against the side of the immense pool and kicked gently at the nearly bath-warm water and tried not to feel like we were on vacation. Wasn't easy, with that full moon reflecting off the rippling water's surface.

"So what's the plan?" she asked.

"Try to get a line on this supposed seminar of Bryant's. And we should be able to catch up with Marguerite or Elaine or whatever she's calling herself at the Pussycat A Go-Go."

Her dark eyes widened. "You, uh, want me to stay behind for that? Might be hard to work your charms on a 'dame' with a date along."

I batted that away. "I've charmed that girl all she's going to get. I might get rough with her, and if that would give you a bad opinion of me, then maybe you should go up and laze around our debauched suite till I get back."

Her eyes narrowed and so did her smile. "No, I think I'd like to see you at work. Might give me a better sense of just what I'm getting into."

"Not a bad idea at that."

"...is that guy looking at us?"

"You're worth looking at, but what guy?"

"Right behind us, past the columns and under a big umbrella at a little table. Unless you don't think it's suspicious, avoiding the sun after dark. But you're the private eye."

I glanced behind me. The man seated at the metal table saluted me with his drink—a Gibson, no doubt. He was at the far edge of middle-age, with a gap-toothed resemblance to actor Robert Morse of *How to Succeed in Business*. But the business Edward "Shep" Shepherd was in was spying.

Of course, in those orange Bermuda shorts and that Hawaiian short-sleeve sport shirt—not to mention the sandals without socks—he might have been on vacation. On the other hand, I would imagine he might turn up at many a vacation spot with business in mind. He was a man of medium height, medium build, medium in every way, his blond hair mostly gray now.

"Shit," I said softly.

"Someone you know," she said. Not a question.

"Old friend. The kind you hope never to run into."

"Too late to duck him."

"I wouldn't bother trying. Swim a little. I'll be back." With any luck.

She nodded, flashed me a look of concern, then swam off.

I got out, went for my towel nearby, dried off a little and padded over to where Shep was sitting, waiting. I pulled up a deck chair.

"Nathan. Imagine running into you like this."

"Imagine."

"How's that boy of yours doing? Sam? Still in school?"

"Still in school."

"My two are grown and turning me into a grandfather."

"And you're in Vegas why?"

He sipped his drink. Yup, a Gibson, the onion long gone. "Helping out the Atomic Energy Commission on a few matters. Now I'm catching up with an old friend."

"And here I thought we weren't speaking."

"Well," he drawled, hauling out that Southern accent he leaned on when he was playing nice, "I was hopin' I might make our past differences up to you by puttin' you on the right track."

"What track is that?"

His smile showed no teeth; in fact it was barely a smile at all. "Thought it might interest you to know that the same cabal behind Jack's death? Is also responsible for Bobby's. Smoke?"

He offered me a Chesterfield from the pack. He was talking about the two Kennedy brothers, in case you fell asleep in the second reel.

"No thanks," I said. "I gave up smoking after Guadalcanal. But then you know that. You know everything, don't you, Shep?"

He raised a palm. The smile widened to that gap-toothed Bobby Morse look. "I'm not here to tell you to stop doing what you're doin'. In fact, I hope to point you in the right direction. What needs to be done is better comin' from you than me, because I have certain waters I have to swim in. And you're never sure in such waters who's a minnow and who's a piranha."

Laughter from down a ways echoed across the pool.

"Colorful," I said. "Mind spelling it out?"

He sipped the Gibson. "You care for somethin' to drink, Nate? There's a little gal in a toga around here somewhere."

"No thanks. Tell me about minnows and piranha, Shep."

"Certainly." He spoke so softly I could barely hear him. "Now where was I? Ah, yes. So the same rogue elements in the Company who took JFK down are involved in the RFK kill. That simple. And that complex."

The Company, of course, was Shep's employer—the Central Intelligence Agency.

"Okay," I said. Casual. Stomach clenched.

A toss of a hand. "Let's start with a piece of information I *don't* have. Are you still friendly with Bob Maheu?"

Robert Maheu had been, when I met him, a Washington DC private investigator, a former FBI man who counted the CIA among his clients. He had contacts within organized crime circles and I had reluctantly worked with him in lining up certain key mob figures in the misbegotten plan to take Fidel Castro out. Obviously that effort failed, and I now viewed Operation Mongoose as less than my finest hour.

"Maheu and I were never friends," I said. "I was pleasant, I was professional, but he's a reckless, dangerous son of a bitch."

Shep's eyebrows rose slowly, as if heading to his scalp to hide. "Do you know what your non-friend Maheu is up to now?"

I shrugged. "He's right here in Vegas, isn't he? Running casinos for Howard Hughes?"

For those who have been living beneath a rock: business magnate Howard Hughes was a record-setting pilot, engineer, film producer, kazillionaire, and did I mention a crazy-ass eccentric recluse? In recent years he'd extended his financial empire to include Las Vegas real estate, hotels, casinos, and media outlets, moving in at the Desert Inn in '66. In seclusion.

"Yes," Shep said, "but Maheu looks after more than just casinos. You met with Thane Cesar, I understand?"

That Shep knew this didn't surprise me. He'd known I was in Vegas, hadn't he?

"Yes," I said, "but what does a nonentity like Cesar have to do with Howard Hughes?"

A young woman's laugh bounced across the water.

He leaned forward. Pointed a gentle forefinger. "Nate, I'm not going to connect the dots for you. But I am gonna provide you with a few extra dots. Let's start with Thane Cesar making occasional trips to Vegas where he's tight with a Hughes employee name of Hal Harper."

I frowned. "Hal Harper? Former LAPD guy? Lost his job in that police brutality scandal?"

A nod, a smile. "That's the one. These days he heads up Hughes' personal security detail. Say, uh…didn't you do some work for Howard Hughes yourself, years ago?"

I nodded. "Must have been '47, '48. Hughes hired me to deal with a starlet who was blackmailing him after their relationship went south."

The eyebrows went up again. "Were you successful in that endeavor?"

I shrugged. "I paid her off. Warned her that I thought Hughes was capable of just about anything, and to cut her losses accordingly. Which is why I never did another job for him. We never had words or anything—just told him it wasn't my kind of gig and he accepted that."

Another gap-toothed smile, a shake of the head. "That explains something."

"What?"

He gestured open-handedly. "Why Hughes has expressed respect for you. I think you should have a little talk with him, Nate."

"Easier said than done."

Shep cocked his head. "Maybe not for you."

"And why would I want to talk to that screwball?"

"Maybe to see just what Thane Cesar is to the Hughes organization. Oh, and to ask him how it was that he came to hire damn near all of Bobby Kennedy's staff after the assassination. You did *know* that, didn't you?"

"…I did not."

He raised the forefinger again, but in a teacherly fashion this time. "First talk to Maheu. He may be able to get you to Hughes. Insist that he try."

I was confused, but I managed, "All right."

He looked out at the pool. "That's a nice looking gal you got there."

Nita was swimming, her stroking arms graceful, her kicking feet rhythmic.

"*I* like her," I said.

"You should show the little lady a good time. Take her out tonight." Shep slipped his hand into the breast pocket of his Hawaiian shirt and came back with two tickets. "My treat. Anthony Newley and David Frye at 9 P.M. Dinner show. Like the kids say, be there or be square."

He handed them to me.

Who doesn't like free tickets to a top Vegas show? But how much, I wondered, were these free tickets going to cost me?

SEVENTEEN

A Circus Maximus waiter took us to a booth in a row of VIP seating elevated just behind the packed perpendicular-to-the-stage long tables where you got to know your neighbor a little too well. On the other hand, Nita and I found ourselves practically swimming in our plush gold-leather approximation of a Roman chariot, where a RESERVED card with "Heller Party" on it meant I probably could have skipped the generous tip.

The walls of the thousand-seat supper club, lined with pillars and statuary, were decorated with golden legionnaire shields. Actual (well, ersatz) Roman soldiers were positioned along the red-velvet-curtained stage, keeping an eye on the crowd, hands on the hilts of their swords. Possibly they were there to keep out the Ritz Brothers, who were working the nearby Nero's Nook lounge. Those boys could get rowdy.

The crowd was a well-dressed one and we fit right in. Her hair up, Nita was a curvy knockout in a slim sequined black evening dress with bare arms. I was in a gray Botany 500 suit, cut to accommodate the shoulder-holstered nine millimeter. I hoped the Roman guards wouldn't notice.

The grub was good. Nita partook of the Boneless Breast of Poulet de Bresse, which was Capon Breast in Sour Cream Sauce on Savory Rice (much better than unsavory rice) and I had the Broiled Filet Mignon Caesar Augustus with Champignons in a Triumphal Laurel Wreath. Rare.

We'd started with marinated herring and closed with Baked Alaska, after which Nita said, "What the hell are we doing here, Nate?"

"I saw Newley in *Roar of the Greasepaint* on Broadway," I said. "He's terrific."

"That's not what I mean and you know it."

I said with a shrug, "I'm surprised myself. I figured either Shep would show up personally or we'd be sharing this booth with somebody else. Somebody significant."

"Such as?"

"No idea." Really, I did have a hunch.

She leaned close enough for me to make out the Chanel No. 5 even in a room that was already smoky. "This isn't your style, is it? You're more the small jazz club type."

"Or blues den, in Chicago. Yes, that's right. Playboy Club's as close as I come to this, and their showroom back home's fairly intimate. This Ben Hur hokum is designed for the tourist trade."

That amused her. "Then why are we here?"

An affable mid-range male voice said, "Because this is the house that Jimmy Hoffa built, and Nate gets comped on his room....Sorry. Didn't mean to eavesdrop."

The owner of that voice slid into the booth on my side. His hairline a memory, the brown of the surviving sides turning gray, Robert Maheu looked like just another vacationing businessman in his conservative blue suit, white shirt and red-and-blue striped tie. A tad heavyset, he was a pleasant, dark-blue-eyed, usually smiling individual whose knob nose and reflective bald head gave him a vague resemblance to actor Karl Malden.

But this was no vacationer—as Howard Hughes' surrogate, he was one of the real movers and shakers in Vegas. Hell, in Nevada. And the reason for this VIP booth was mostly his presence, not that of the almost famous private eye and his sort of well-known actress companion, to whom I introduced him.

Maheu said, big smile, charming as hell, "You look very familiar to me, Miss Romaine. Have we met?"

"You might have seen me on TV," she said, smiling, pleased to be nearly recognized. "I'm an actress."

"She's been on every one of your favorite shows, Bob," I told him. "You watch all the ones with pretty girls, right?"

He said to her, "Don't listen to him. I've been happily married since 1941 to the lovely Yvette. Have you ever done a *Mission: Impossible*?"

"I have," she said, nodding, brightening further.

I said, "He's bragging now. That show's based on him and his DC agency. He used to assemble teams for the Company."

He leaned across me and smiled, whispering to Nita: "That's CIA....Of course your private detective friend here was the inspiration for *Peter Gunn*, so I can't really hope to one-up him."

She asked, "What did you mean about Jimmy Hoffa?"

Maheu grinned; he had a great smile. "Tell the girl, Nate."

"Hoffa put twelve million into Caesars," I said. "They couldn't get financing anywhere else. Borrowed it from the Teamsters Pension Fund."

"Hoffa's a great man," Maheu said, meaning it. "But Nate's probably told you all about that."

She shook her head, looked from him to me. "No, he hasn't."

I said, "I did some work for him, oh, back in the fifties."

Was Maheu being cute? Could he know that I'd been working undercover for Bob when I got in good with Hoffa? That was still the kind of thing a guy could get killed over.

Maheu's smile softened into something vaguely menacing and his attention was off Nita and onto me. "I would think you'd be looking hard at Jimmy Hoffa about now, Nate...in regard to Bobby Kennedy's passing, I mean."

What a very creepy way to put it: as if RFK had died in his damn sleep or something.

"Hoffa has an alibi," I said, a little arch.

Maheu's bald head reflected light. "You mean, he's been inside Lewisburg for over two years, with another, what? Eleven to go? Are you telling me he couldn't reach out and make something happen from behind bars?"

"I don't rule anything out," I admitted.

His eyes widened. "I certainly wouldn't. If Bobby Kennedy had gone on to be president, Jimmy Hoffa couldn't hope for *any* kind of mercy. But one of these days Nixon just might pardon him."

"Nixon hasn't done that yet."

Maheu lighted up a cigarette—a filtered Kool. "Closer to re-election time he might. A Teamsters endorsement would go a long, long way, next time 'round. But enough politics." He beamed at my date. "Say, Miss Romaine, I should apologize. The plan was, I would join you folks for supper but then I got tied up with the doggone Atomic Energy Commission."

"It was quite good," Nita said.

He let some smoke out. "I'm sure it was. But I've taken a few too many trips around that menu already." He patted his tummy.

"Why the Atomic Energy Commission," she said, "if you don't mind my asking?"

"Don't mind at all. It's a public concern, and especially a concern of my boss's. They stopped the aboveground testing but the underground testing continues, and it's very dangerous. A health conscious man like Howard Hughes takes notice of such things."

That last had just a hint of mockery in it. A hint.

"So, Nate," he said, "how is it *you* rate so high with my boss?"

I tossed a hand. "Mr. Hughes? I did a job for him once, years ago, and he was happy with the outcome."

Maheu leaned back into the booth, folded his arms, shook

his head, consigning his Kool to an ashtray. "Well, I've done some jobs for Mr. Hughes myself, y'know. This is kind of a cute story, Nita…is it all right if I call you 'Nita,' Miss Romaine?"

"Certainly."

"Is that short for Anita?"

"It is."

First I heard of it.

"Anyway," he said, sitting forward, folding his hands prayerfully on the white linen tablecloth, "when we made the move to Las Vegas, Mr. Hughes wanted to travel by night and arrive before dawn. I set up a decoy operation to have a fake Hughes seen leaving the Ritz in Los Angeles, taking the press along with him. But our train had brake problems and repairs meant we'd sit on the tracks for hours and arrive in Las Vegas possibly as late as the afternoon. In broad daylight. That would *not* do with Mr. Hughes. In the middle of the night, I arranged for another train to take us to Vegas at a cost of $18,000. It was an executive decision that I knew might cost me my job. But Mr. Hughes was thrilled with how I handled things."

"And that," I said, kidding on the square, "set the stage for you to buy all these casinos for him?"

A twitch of a self-satisfied smile. "Oh yes. The Desert Inn, of course. But also the Sands, the Castaways, the Frontier, the Silver Slipper…we still haven't closed the Stardust deal, but we bought the Landmark and, in Reno, Harold's Club. And of course, among other properties, we bought the CBS affiliate here, KLAS, because Mr. Hughes wanted to ensure that movies would air all night…and be titles of his choice."

"Mostly," I said, "movies he produced at RKO."

"Is it true," Nita asked, eyes narrowed, "that initially Hughes was just renting the Desert Inn penthouse, and before Christmas the management tried to kick him out to make room for the holiday high-rollers? And your boss said, 'Buy the hotel'?"

Maheu's smile was as big as it was friendly. "That one's a legend. Really, Mr. Hughes had a half-billion windfall on his TWA deal and needed to avoid suffering a huge tax bite. That's the only thing he fears more than germs, y'know—the taxman."

Nita laughed, then got serious. "How did Las Vegas feel about your boss rolling into town and taking over?"

"The town welcomed him! Vegas needed redemption from its gangster roots—from the beginning, local and state government here was infiltrated by mobsters." Maheu winked at me. "Of course, don't tell anyone I had meetings with Moe Dalitz and Johnny Roselli today, Nate."

Dalitz was the powerful mobster who my old buddy Eliot Ness ran out of Cleveland in the Thirties, and Roselli was Chicago's conduit to Vegas, likely getting a piece for them (and himself) out of every deal Maheu cut for Hughes.

Maheu's affable manner gave way to pride. "I've made Mr. Hughes the third-largest landowner in the state, right behind the federal government and the state power company." He pretended this was for Nita, but I was the real audience. "If he wants someone fired, I do the firing. If he wants something negotiated, I do the bargaining. If he has to be somewhere, I appear in his place."

Nita frowned. "He really *is* a recluse, then."

"He is. I go out into the world for my boss. I deal with congressmen, governors, bankers, Presidents, and, sure, the occasional mobster. I travel in a private jet, throw parties for two hundred people without a thought about what kind of germs they might carry. I can walk into any major hotel in this nation and let a stranger carry my bags and step onto an elevator with other strangers and go up to my comfortable suite without immediately taking a bath. And yet I've never met the man."

Nita's eyes popped. "What?"

Too casually, he said, "I've never met Howard Hughes. Oh, I have a direct line from my office at my home, and speak to him ten, fifteen, thirty times a day. We exchange lengthy hand-written notes, constantly. He sees only his doctors, cook, waiter, and one of his lawyers. And yet, Nate, he wants to see *you*."

"He does?"

Maheu nodded. "Mr. Hughes will see you tonight. In person. He's a night owl, you know. An insomniac of the first order. I like to think he doesn't meet with me because he doesn't want me to see what he looks like, plain and simple—how his germo-phobe ways have reduced him to something that doesn't go at all well with his still sharp mind and incisive business sense. Otherwise, it might hurt my feelings, Nate...that he wants to see you."

The curtain rose and the full orchestra, seated off to the right, began to play "What Kind of Fool Am I?"

Around midnight, I dropped Nita off at Caesar's Palace, sug-gesting she grab a nap while I was gone, if she wanted to go striptease-clubbing with me later.

She arched an eyebrow. "Like that's a mission I'd send you off on alone." She threw me a wink as she climbed out, no small feat in that form-fitting black evening dress.

The casino resort home of Howard Hughes just up the Strip combined cheapness with opulence, formed as it was out of cinder blocks but finished with sandstone. Guiding the Jag up the driveway, I passed under an old-fashioned ranch-style hori-zontal sign that said *Wilbur Clark's Desert Inn* in script against a cactus logo. After the excesses of Caesar's, the DI (as locals called the place) seemed almost restrained. Almost.

Its 300 guest rooms were behind the main building in wings

that surrounded a figure-eight swimming pool. I strolled through the lavish pink-and-green resort, its interiors redwood with flagstone flooring, past the ninety-foot-long Lady Luck bar that overlooked the casino, which was going full-throttle at the witching hour.

Maheu had said Hughes' security chief Hal Harper would be waiting for me at the southeast corner of the building by the elevators in back and he was—the tall, broad-shouldered, paunchy ex-cop was pacing and smoking like an expectant father. He wore a rumpled brown suit over a tan sport shirt and apparently hadn't been told that even Jack Webb wasn't wearing fedoras anymore. Must have been how Harper managed a pale complexion in this sunny clime.

He saw me coming, produced something meant to be a smile that came off a grimace, dropped his cigarette into the standing ashtray by the elevators (no smoking around Mr. Hughes), and grunted, "Heller."

"Good to see you, Hal," I said, which it wasn't.

Harper was a brutal thug who lost his job for beating up suspects years ago—as a rookie he'd specialized in Zoot Suiters back in the '40s and moved up in later years to black offenders (frankly, just being black was enough to offend Harper). We'd intersected but never tangled, though that was a small miracle.

"Gotta pat you down," he said.

"Fine. I'm heavy. You can take the gun if you give it back."

He nodded, slipped the nine millimeter Browning from my shoulder holster and shoved it in his belt, bandolero-style. Gave me a full frisk and, at no extra charge, a whiff of his multiple packs a day habit.

Bored with his life in general and me in particular, Harper pressed the elevator button and the door opened almost immediately, as if not wanting to offend him. I followed him onto the empty car and watched as he inserted a key into what would have been the ninth floor button if it hadn't been replaced with a keypad lock. He turned the key and we started up.

He said, "Mr. Hughes doesn't allow in many visitors."

"So I hear."

"Just be prepared. He's sick and you might be surprised by his, you know, condition. Don't say nothing. Make like he's normal."

I was making like Harper was normal, wasn't I?

I said, "Discretion is my middle name. Actually, that's just an expression. My middle name is Samuel."

He looked at me, squinting like he'd never encountered humor before. Or maybe a squint was all that deserved.

We stopped at the third floor. A young couple in casual clothes, laughing, started to get on and Harper held up a traffic-cop palm.

"Next car," he said with unnecessary menace.

They just looked at him like he'd splashed water in their faces and he hit the DOOR CLOSE button and they were shut out. We started up again.

"Say, Hal. You wouldn't happen to know a guy named Thane Cesar, would you? Thane Eugene Cesar? You might know him as Gene."

He looked at me slow. We were between the fifth and sixth floors. He pushed the STOP button—a cute little stop sign image that didn't go with the abruptness of our halt.

Harper gazed at me dead-eyed. "Gene does some work for the Hughes organization, time to time. Why do you ask?"

"I'm doing background research for a *Life* magazine article on the Robert Kennedy assassination. That's why I'm here. Cesar was a witness."

He sighed, then decided to say, "We bring him in for this and that. He's reliable. Anything else you want to know, Heller?"

"No. Thanks. That's helpful."

"We aim to please." He glanced upward. "Just so you know—there's security to go through."

"I thought you were the security."

He grinned. His teeth were large and yellow with crooked incisors. "Oh, I'm just the start of it."

Harper wasn't kidding. The elevator door opened onto a guard desk in a partitioned-off entryway with its own door behind the uniformed, armed sentry, a white-haired, barrel-chested individual who looked like Pat O'Brien in a bad mood. The desk had two phones and a logbook. That was it.

"I frisked him," Harper said. "He's wearing a shoulder rig but I got the gun. This is Nathan Heller. Mr. Hughes is expecting him."

Grouchy Pat O'Brien came around and gave me another frisk. Then he had me sign in—name, time of arrival, a space for time of departure. The other names on my page were delivery men or hotel workers, and they had each filled a box specifying what they delivered. Maheu wasn't among those who'd signed in, backing up his claim that he never dealt with Hughes in person.

Harper got back on the elevator and the door closed him in as the white-haired guard said, "You can enter Penthouse One now." He unlocked a door in the partition and the hotel hallway, what was left of it, was there with a door with a peephole.

I supposed the thing to do was knock, so I did. I got eyeballed through the peephole, then the door cracked open and I said, "Nathan Heller to see Mr. Hughes."

The door came open and a crew of four middle-aged men in white short-sleeve shirts and dark ties and slacks were bustling

around what had been a hotel bedroom before being transformed into an office with several desks, an IBM typewriter,
Xerox machine, telecopier, two four-drawer files, and a paper
shredder.

Without a word I was shown to a door by one of the middle-
aged men, who said to it, "Mr. Heller is here, sir."

"Send him in," came a gravelly but firm mid-range male
voice. It certainly did not sound like the voice of a reclusive
eccentric who avoided human contact.

The middle-aged man said softly, "Mr. Hughes doesn't shake
hands. Don't be offended."

"Do my best," I said.

He unlocked the door and I went in, the door closing tight
behind me, the medicinal smell almost overwhelming.

This was a bedroom without a bed, rather small—perhaps
fifteen by seventeen—with blackout curtains and the only light
a flickering television somewhere to my right, sound down. My
eyes took a few moments adjusting to the near darkness cut by
the TV's strobing effect, but soon I could make out my host.

In a well-worn black Naugahyde recliner with big wooden
TV trays on either side of him, Howard Hughes sprawled out
tall and naked and damn near as bony as a concentration camp
corpse. The male member that had once plunged proudly into
one beautiful starlet after another was now a withered relic
nestling helplessly against a skinny leg like a baby bird against
the side of its nest. His fingernails were as long as a Chinese
emperor's and his shoulder-length stringy gray hair and
matching beard would have challenged the grooming habits of
the most careless hippie.

"My apologies, Mr. Heller," he said, gruff but affable, "but
this is a necessary procedure for me."

The lanky, scrawny figure was in the process of rubbing his

exposed spotted flesh with a paper towel soaked in alcohol from a bottle; wadded-up discarded towels were on the floor around him like big grotesque snowflakes. On the TV tray to his right were various magnifying glasses, a telephone with an amplifier, and a stack of lined yellow pads with fresh pencils. The other TV tray had several neat stacks of filled yellow pads, a TV remote, a roll of paper towels, and a box of Kleenex. A paper bag on the floor near the chair brimmed with used tissues, and a silver bell resided on the tray, presumably to summon aides. A couple of air purifiers were going, also on the floor.

"You catch me at a bad moment," Hughes said, as he rubbed himself down, pausing only to apply alcohol to a fresh paper towel. "But, trust me—if you knew what I know about germs, you would take similar measures yourself."

An interesting point of view, considering everything in this place was covered with a layer of dust. Magazines and newspapers were stacked up along the walls and in the far corner were capped, stacked Mason jars of a yellow fluid. I didn't think it was apple juice.

"Please, Mr. Heller," Hughes said, gesturing with a bony hand at the end of a bony arm. "Have a seat. I've prepared one for you."

There was indeed an armchair, the seat and back draped with power towels. I sat.

"Be sure to speak up," he said. "I'm hard of hearing."

For all the grooves in that face, for all the loose flesh and those sunken eyes, the once handsome man he'd been could still be made out. He'd retained his mustache and, from time to time in our conversation, he would smile, as if to reassure me that within that husk was the man for whom I'd done a job, once upon a time.

"I seldom meet with people," he said, rubbing an elbow with

an alcohol-drenched paper towel, "but I was struck by your integrity, when we first did business."

I smiled. "My integrity doesn't come up all that often."

The sunken eyes managed to tighten in their sockets. "Well, I recognize it when I see it. You found the job I asked you to do distasteful, and by God it was. Maheu and his scurvy little private dicks picked up performing that kind of task for me. Did whatever I asked. And while I value Bob Maheu, I don't respect him. Best you not repeat that."

"That's between the two of you, sir."

He rubbed a shoulder with a soaked paper towel. "You wanted to talk to me about Bobby Kennedy. About his murder."

"I'm researching a piece about the assassination for *Life* magazine."

"Well, that's fine. That's good."

Not what I expected. "If I might ask, sir....Why do you feel that way?"

He grinned like a skull. "Well, half the *Life* staff is CIA and can, if necessary, be handled. But I'm not thrilled that the Kennedy boy was taken out. He was a cocky little punk, but at least he was on my side with this damned atomic testing out here. Nixon isn't, or Humphrey either!"

His voice was surprisingly strong.

"The Atomic Energy Commission," he said, "started in exploding nuclear devices near here back in '51, above ground, while assuring the public everything was hunky-dory."

I nodded grimly. "Who can say how many people died due to fallout from those 'safe' explosions?"

He nodded the same way; he'd forgotten all about rubbing himself with alcohol. "International treaty put a stop to it in '63, but the AEC bastards just moved the tests underground."

"I suppose that's better than up top."

A skinny arm gestured around him. "I'd barely moved in here, Nate, when those sons of bitches set off an atomic bomb beneath the Pahute Mesa, rocking buildings all over Las Vegas, including *this* one! Then they blasted a 4,000-foot trench in the desert floor, a month later. This shit is bad for tourism, and it's bad for my health!"

The latter, of course, being his major cause for concern.

He was saying, "My science people put a report together linking radiation leakage to mutations, leukemia, cancer, you fucking name it."

"And you went to Bobby Kennedy about this?"

He nodded emphatically and I wouldn't have been surprised if his skull fell off and rolled across the floor to me. "We did. And he took our $25,000 campaign contribution, all right. Of course, I gave $100,000 each to Nixon and Humphrey, too. You learn to hedge your bets in Vegas."

Right then I knew: If Hughes was being straight with me—and I thought he was—there was no percentage in him being part of a plot to assassinate Bobby Kennedy.

I asked, "Do you know a security guard named Thane Eugene Cesar? He's supposed to have done work for you out here. And he was standing right behind Bob Kennedy when the fatal shot was made...from behind."

He waved a parchment-skinned hand. "Cesar's some minor leg-breaker. One of Maheu's nasty little elves. We have need for that kind of thing, from time to time."

"Maheu's man?"

"Yes. He worked for Maheu's security firm in L.A. What's it called? Bel Air Patrol."

"I'll look into that."

He sat up slightly in the recliner; it was a skeleton rising from a tomb. "Nate, if the CIA's behind this, you won't get very far. We both know that. *If* they're behind it."

"*Somebody* funded it," I said. "Who do *you* think that could have been?"

He folded his hands above his exposed penis. "I could guess, but then so could you. Mobsters, spooks, right-wingers, military-industrial complex? Take your pick. Of course, *I* may have funded the thing."

"*What?* You…?"

His shrug damn near creaked. "Maheu's my man who deals with the CIA. If they wanted the Kennedy brat gone, he might well have facilitated it. I don't dirty myself with politics anymore, local *or* national. Too damn distasteful."

I didn't know what to say to that.

He reached for his TV remote with a gnarled hand. "Is there anything else, Nate? Good to see you again after so many years. But, uh…well, KLAS is airing *The Outlaw* in fifteen minutes."

Owning a TV station had its perks.

EIGHTEEN

In a cluttered stretch of the Strip between a coffee shop and motel, with rent-a-car and steakhouse signs shouldering in for attention, the most notorious dance club in Vegas nestled, its sign rising above all the others—the giant head of a cartoon black cat, black letters outlined in pink neon,

Pussycat
a'
GO-GO

against startling yellow, a marquee below promising

STARK NAKED AND THE CAR THIEVES

(a band, apparently) and

TOPLESS DANCERS.

Nita and I left the Jag in the parking lot behind the pink-and-gray vertical striped bunker that was the club and walked around front to go in under the black-and-white striped canopy.

In her sleeveless honeycomb dress with white hose and yellow low heels, Nita looked remarkably fresh for the long day we'd had; of course she'd grabbed a nap while I called on a nude old dude who saved his piss in jars, and that can be disconcerting. But I'd showered and shaved back at Caesar's before getting into my navy blazer (cut to conceal a hip holster with a .38), white turtleneck, gray slacks and slip-ons. Nita claimed I looked presentable and who was I to contradict her?

We were, after all, going out to an "in" place known for getting its second wind after the earlier tourist crowd was long gone. Around two A.M., Sin City's showgirls, musicians, dealers, and even headliners rolled in after work to party at the Pussycat. Though there was a race book attached, and a small casino area with half a dozen blackjack tables and a couple dozen slot machines, this was mostly a rock 'n' roll dance club, where topless go-go girls gyrated on stage, echoed by fully clad patrons on a packed, good-size dance floor.

Just inside, to the right, was a wall of framed photos depicting various bands that had played here. Again, thanks to my son, I recognized about a third of the names, among them Sly and the Family Stone, Gary Puckett and the Union Gap, and Paul Revere and the Raiders. Just beyond this were celebrity snapshots—Ike and Tina Turner giddily happy, Bobby Darin looking like a hippie, James Brown apparently bored and other famous faces, sometimes on the dance floor, other times laughing it up at the small pink-tableclothed tables. Right now out there, Johnny Carson was dancing, a trifle awkwardly, with a grateful, sexy Juliet Prowse.

The smoke in the room was a mix of tobacco and weed; as basically a non-smoker—I only revert under stress—it didn't appeal. We secured a table on the front edge of the dance floor, ordered drinks—Coke for me, ginger ale for Nita, as we were not here to party—and took in the entertainment.

Stark Naked and the Car Thieves were alternating their own compositions ("Can You Dig It," "Nice Legs, Shame About Her Face") with covers ("Don't Worry Baby," "Big Girls Don't Cry"). They wore matching brown pantsuits and orange-and-white scarfs, which I felt sure my son would have said was surprisingly corny for a band with such a cool name. Cool in his opinion.

The interior design of the place was given over to current psychedelic tastes—the bar that faced the stage was red padded faux leather and behind the bartenders, above the rows of bottles, a giant sparkly version of the club's black cat logo rode a sparkly red wall. A side wall was given over to black-light Fillmore posters, glowing under fluorescent blue, another was red-draped, one was a vast red-and-black checkerboard, the stage backed with an array of circular designs in every color not in the rainbow. A mirrored ball right out of a 1920s nightclub in Berlin reflected all this back at a crowd of bare-armed, wonderfully miniskirted young women and ridiculously oversize-collared and flare-trousered men of various ages.

I wondered if I could have felt more out of place. Johnny Carson didn't seem to be having any trouble fitting in. Of course he had his own clothing line.

Right now a single dancer was go-going centerstage under red lights and a strobe effect, the band positioned off to her left, stealing looks at her. Slender, curvy in a nicely narrow-waisted way, she seemed happy to be cavorting in her near alto-gether, shaking her long straight red hair, her firm pert breasts bouncing along, the gold lamé panties just barely sufficient to avoid arrest.

The band was playing an organ-dominated instrumental, the old bump-and-grind replaced by a more dreamy feel yet with an insistent beat. From behind red velvet curtains to the dancer's right emerged two more naked-but-for-panties dancers, already swinging their arms and hips, as if they'd come to work boogeying, a blonde just as lovely as the redhead, and a brunette who was larger breasted, her hair a shoulder-length bob of wings and curls. Perhaps a little older than the others, she had a lot of personality…and a pug nose.

I nodded to Nita, acknowledging this as Elaine Nye, aka Marguerite.

And it didn't take the topless dancer long to spot us—we were seated along one side of the dance floor and were only occasionally blocked by Johnny and Juliet and the other dancers. Miss Nye's expression, just for a flash, broke character and betrayed alarm. But I smiled at her and waved a piece of paper. A green horizontal piece of paper inscribed 100. Now she smiled, too.

Two more songs from Stark Naked and the Car Thieves ensued with the go-go girls going through a range of dances: hitchhiker, Watutsi, loco-motion, pony, mashed potato, frug. It all seemed very freeform but they were all doing the same dance, so there was a nice minimal sense of choreography.

When the girls left, the band added vocals to their mix and—in about fifteen minutes, wrapped in a sheer red robe and with a red bra on—Elaine Nye came regally out from backstage and found a chair to join us at our little table.

"This is my friend Nita," I told her. "Nita, this is Marguerite."

"Call me Elaine," she said with a frozen smile. "I'm only Marguerite at the Classic Cat in L.A. Listen, a couple of things."

Cheerily I said, "Yes?"

"First, I don't get off till five. Which means *we* don't get off till after that, if you catch my drift. And second, threesome costs more—even B.Y.O.B."

Nita asked, "Bring your own bottle?"

"Bring your own babe," the dancer said to her. Then to me: "And there's one more thing. Mister, I didn't drug you or anything. You passed out, must've been tying one on or something, and I helped get you to the doc's. He said he could get you back on your feet. That's all I know so don't bother going there. I did you a favor. That's between you and the doc and leave me the fuck out of it."

My right hand rested on the table, still kind of waving the hundred, clutched between the thumb and middle finger of my right hand. "No, that's not going to fly, Elaine."

An eyebrow went up. She was a pretty thing, a little hard,

but I even liked the pug nose, or maybe what it might represent. I handed her the C-note. When she had it, I clutched her wrist. Hard.

The other eyebrow joined the first one up near her hairline.

"You were party to a kidnapping," I said, softly, smiling a little. "And what's worse, it was mine."

"Listen, mister—"

"You listen. I will overlook that you slipped me a nail-polish Mickey Finn. We'll just let that slide by."

Her eyes flared. "What the hell do you want then?"

"I want you to accompany us to the FBI and share everything you know about Dr. Joseph W. Bryant."

Her features tightened. "What is it you think I know?"

I shrugged. "You tell me. But I figure you either have, or used to have, a polka-dot dress in your closet."

That chilled her. The blood drained from her face and she tried to talk but nothing came out. Nita and I were staring coldly at her and that couldn't have been fun.

"Do you know who I am?" I asked her.

"Some...some kind of investigator or something."

Apparently I'd finally found somebody from Hollywood who didn't see me as the Private Eye to the Stars.

"Elaine," I said, "the doc told you and your friend Susie, back at the Classic Cat, that he's the hypnotist who programmed Sirhan Sirhan."

She shook her head and all that brunette hair seemed to shiver. "He told us a lot of crazy things. He's a regular of ours. Digs threesomes. We see him together, all the time, and he brags about all sorts of—"

"No. You know it's more than talk. You helped him kidnap me, remember? You do know that kidnapping is a Class A felony? If I go to the FBI about that—"

Her hands came up, palms out, and it stopped me.

She leaned in, looked at me, looked at Nita and back to me. Her voice was very soft and had a tremor, like a poor radio transmission.

"All right," she said. "But I don't want to talk about anything else—no girl in the polka-dot dress shit. Get me? That night… you *know* what night I'm talking about…I did what I was asked to and had no fucking idea where it was going. *None.* I was high and thought I hallucinated it all for the longest time. Now I'm in it up to my ass and…I've kept my head down and now you're asking me to…I don't know. I don't know."

I kept my voice low and steady. "I have friends at the FBI. I have enemies at the LAPD and in the CIA, but I'm tight with the FBI. And if I give them *your* name with my belief about what all you've been involved in, they will come looking for you, and they will land hard. You'll be in that proverbial world of hurt, which is right where you don't want to be."

Her features wrinkled up like a crushed paper cup, and she glanced back toward the stage and then at me. "You don't understand. He's *here.* He's here *tonight.* Right now!"

"Who is here?"

Her words came in a rush. "The doc!" She leaned closer. "Look, like I said, I work till five. I'll go with you to the FBI. Just don't say anything to the doc. He'll be out of here before me. All he handles is the intermission, puts on his little show, and then he's gone. You need to crawl into some quiet corner where he can't see you."

And she got up and scurried backstage.

Nita and I looked at each other.

"What the hell?" I asked her, blinking.

"What the hell?" she asked me, blinking back.

But we took Elaine's advice and went back to the bar and

found the most out of the way spot over at one end and settled in, not knowing what to think.

That was when Dr. Joseph W. Bryant, in a red coat and yellow tie worthy of a ringmaster, came through the red backstage curtains as if he had brought them along with him. His flared pants were a bright floral print and he wore a corny gold sultan's turban. The audience laughed and a few whistled and one or two cheered and got a smiling bow out of him. The doc had clearly performed here before. With his Coke-bottle glasses magnifying his eyes, Bryant brought to mind Shemp in the Three Stooges playing a swami. I saw Carson at a table with a showgirl, amused, perhaps by the Carnac the Magnificent turban.

Standing at the top of the dance floor in his full six three and nearly four-hundred pounds—the stage behind him, the band on a break and the go-go girls, too—he said, "For those of you who don't know me, allow me to introduce myself—I am Dr. Charles W. Bryant, M.D., J.D., F.A.I.T.H., F.A.C.M.H. That's a lot of alphabet soup that spells out the world's most prominent hypnotherapist."

His pause and lifted chin, thrusting his Amish beard forward, prompted applause and more hooting and such. Nita and I had our backs to him, watching in the mirror behind the bar.

"But do not fear," Bryant said. "I also have a degree of sorts in show business—starting out as I did as Tommy Dorsey's drummer."

Chuckles.

"And tonight we're here at the Pussycat A Go-Go to have some fun." He began to pull chairs away from tables and made a row of four of them facing the audience, saying, "I am looking for four female volunteers! If you have participated in one of my demonstrations before, please do not raise your hand."

The doc filled the chairs with young women, all of whom

were fetching examples of the female gender, no surprise in a room filled with off-duty showgirls.

Soon the hypnotist was putting them under: "Your arms are limp as a rag doll. Your legs are limp as a rag doll. You are deeper and deeper relaxed. Deeper and deeper, deeper and deeper relaxed...."

He then put them through their paces, telling them to stand with their hands free, heels together. Then to look up at the ceiling, taking a deep breath. To close their eyes and start breathing normally and then count. Told them, when he touched each one on the shoulder, that he wanted them to visualize themselves as steel, and himself as a magnet, pulling them toward him—he did this with each lovely woman individually, and they would fall forward where Bryant would catch them.

"One way to cop a feel," I said to Nita, who smirked and nodded.

All of it was a pretty common hypnotist schtick. He told them their arms were made of stone and they were unable to force them down; he got them laughing as they watched a funny movie; had them cheering a racehorse on and then hiding the winnings; feeling pricked by a nonexistent pin and jumping accordingly; then thinking they were naked—two of the women didn't bother covering themselves with their hands.

"Showgirls," I said to Nita.

"Or strippers," she said.

Finally he told them they were now wearing bikinis and it was time to dance. They did, rivaling anything the go-go girls had to offer, albeit a clothed version. In the miniskirts it was still fairly racy.

As the four women, post-trance, returned to their tables, Bryant encouraged applause from the audience, who again hooted and hollered and clapped.

"That concludes the entertainment portion of our presentation," he said, in a more serious manner. Or as serious as a guy in a red coat and turban could be. "Now it's time for the commercial announcement."

That produced light laughter.

He spoke briefly of his clinic on the Sunset Strip and mentioned his other locations—San Diego and San Francisco—before announcing his seminar beginning tomorrow at the Flamingo: "The Bryant Method and Technique of Hypno-Analysis."

Very somber for a man in a stupid hat, he said, "This is a course for doctors of medicine, of osteopathy, and registered nurses, thirty of whom have signed up. I will be discussing treatment of Anxiety, Frigidity, Impotence, Homosexuality, Insomnia, Kleptomania and, of course, the Walking Zombie Syndrome."

"Of course," I said.

"Cotard's Syndrome," Nita said matter of factly. "People who think they are dead but are walking around."

"You might be too smart for me."

"I might."

Bryant was saying, "I am accepting six volunteers to participate in what I call Instant Therapy. Before your very eyes, I will take a case history, administer the Bryant Association Test, arrive at a diagnosis, and affect a cure, in any one of the afflictions I just mentioned. Follow-up may be needed at my Los Angeles location, but a basic cure is guaranteed, demonstrated for the medical professionals in attendance. You will pay the same amount as they—$175 for the course, including lunch and a cocktail party on the day you are scheduled."

This guy was the most dangerous kind of huckster—a knowledgeable con man.

"It's psycho-surgery," he said off-handedly. "Much like removing a bullet. You've got to find out what you're looking for—the bullet, that is, the traumatic incident, and sew up the wound with positive reinforcement."

He got his seminar participants, practically rushed by beauties, a few of whom he had to disappoint, two of which had been his subjects earlier. He wrote their information down.

I said to Nita, "That 'bullet' business hits a little too close to home."

"Your doc's a clown," she said thoughtfully, "but no laughing matter. Even after all that burlesque, I can believe he could've made a robot assassin out of Sirhan."

Bryant returned the chairs to the tables and slipped backstage. At the same time Elaine Nye in silver lamé panties and all that fetching skin came through the red velvet curtains onto the stage, bouncing out dancing to the band playing "Gloria."

Nita said, "Maybe we should slip out and come back for Elaine later. I wouldn't want us to be seen by Bryant."

"I'm afraid if Elaine doesn't see us sitting out here," I said, "she might just take off."

Nita nodded. "Young women like her can disappear awfully easily these days. A change of name, and poof."

I gave her a look. "They can disappear more ways than one. I have to make that clear to her."

Nita nodded again.

We found the most out-of-the-way table we could and settled there, ordering another round of soft drinks. Still, I made sure Elaine, on stage, noticed us; but generally I felt we were tucked away where Bryant wouldn't make us. Elaine had indicated he'd be out of here now that the intermission show was over.

That was when a massive presence loomed over us.

"Mind if I join you?" Dr. Joseph Bryant asked. He was out of the red jacket and in a more discreet herringbone leisure suit, apparently the work of Omar the Tentmaker.

"Please," I said. "Sit."

He did, making the chair disappear. "I hope you enjoyed my little presentation, Mr. Heller."

"It was a dandy. How do you hang on to your M.D. license, anyway? Instant Analysis? Jesus."

A pudgy paw waved that away. "The patient signs off on the session, and the document defines 'Instant Analysis' as simply a first session. No, I'm fine with the AMA. They approve of me and my work wholeheartedly."

I grunted. "So they approve of drugging and kidnapping? Even without a prescription?"

The smile between the big bug eyes behind the glasses and the Amish beard was thick-lipped and wet, no more disturbing than a bad X-ray. "That's why I wanted to speak to you, Mr. Heller. Why I'm interrupting your evening out. Would you mind introducing me to your charming friend?"

"Not at all. This is Nita Romaine. You may have seen her on television."

His smile widened. "I believe I have. *I Dream of Jeannie*?"

I should have known. A guy with a sultan's turban in his wardrobe was bound to watch that show.

Nita admitted, "I did several of those. I hope you enjoyed them."

"Oh, I did, dear. I did." He turned to me, serious. "Mr. Heller, your assumption that I had you narcotized in some fashion the other day, that's simply not the case. Marguerite called me to lend a hand, after you passed out. And I did."

"Yes, and I want to thank you…"

"No, that's quite all right."

"...for not giving me a post-hypnotic suggestion during your intermission spiel and start me clucking around the room like a chicken."

Nita smiled.

Bryant looked offended.

"My arm still hurts," I said, "where you gave me that shot of God knows what. Did you find out what you wanted to know? I'd hate for you to go to all that trouble for nothing."

He stood and the chair fell behind him, as if he'd made it faint under his weight. "I told you I gave you a sedative. You got violent. And I can see that you have a streak of violence in your nature, and it's a pity I don't have a slot left tomorrow in my seminar so that you might receive instant analysis. You could certainly use it."

He stormed out through a side exit.

Elaine on stage had noticed this. She was smiling and doing her go-go thing, but a tightening around the eyes gave her away. The other two dancers came back on and she slipped off through the red curtains.

She emerged from backstage perhaps five minutes later in a thrown-on-looking blue-striped blouse and denim shorts. She leaned a hand against our table and said, "I'm gonna talk to the manager. Tell him I'm sick or something. Okay? And we'll go see your pals at the FBI. Are they open at this hour?"

"It's Vegas," I said. "Everybody's open at this hour."

That got a tiny smile out of her and she went back to the bar, where the bald middle-aged manager was back talking to the bartenders. She was explaining animatedly and he was nodding, shrugging, obviously giving her the go-ahead. It was about four-thirty A.M. now and things were winding down.

I followed Nita and Elaine out that side door, and we walked around the parking lot at the rear of the building. Dawn wasn't far away but you'd never know it—night was a blackness alive with the fireflies that were the city's thousands of neons. I was unlocking the Jag when I got grabbed.

I heard Nita squeal and had a glimpse of her standing on the rider's side being held from behind by a guy who I recognized at once, even though I'd only seen him that one night, that key night: *the curly-haired fan who'd infiltrated the Royal Suite, and who'd later gotten an autograph from Bob on a poster tube in the Pantry.*

And there was Elaine, backing away, looking distressed but not scared, actually giving me a little "I'm sorry" shrug before fading away.

I'd been grabbed the same way as Nita, somebody clutching both my arms from behind. I thrust my elbows back, hard, got an "Ooooof!" out of it and the hands released me. I spun and lost half a second realizing this dope in the fedora was Hal Harper, the security guy who worked for the Hughes organization. He threw a punch that I ducked and I swung a fist into his balls and got a satisfying yelp out of him. Even more satisfying was how he went down on his knees and tried not to cry.

That was when somebody else to the left side of me knocked my ass out.

NINETEEN

Thwack, scoop, rattle, whump.

The sound, rhythmic but not musical, was not at once identifiable. A crunch, a raspy scooping of sand or maybe gravel or just any hard material, and then a rattling thud.

Not close, or at least not nearby. Or was it just something I was dreaming?

Thwack, scoop, rattle, whump.

I opened my eyes and was staring into a child's scorched face—no, not a child, a mannequin kid's disembodied head, a boy with almost feminine features, smiling a little, not at all concerned about being badly burned or separated from his body. I was on my side, head aching from the blow that knocked me out, hands tied behind me, secured—bound somehow, as were my ankles, by rope. Looked like lengths of clothesline. Behind me it would be the same.

Thwack, scoop, rattle, whump.

I was in last night's clothes, save for the blazer, missing in action somewhere, the empty .38 holster still on the belt of the gray slacks, which like my white turtleneck were smudged with dirt in random non-design. My shoes were gone, too, my socks on.

Thwack, scoop, rattle, whump.

I swung myself into a sitting position and found I was not alone. In my immediate field of vision was a family of mannequins—the rest of the boy was on its side over to the left, the apparent parents near toppled armchairs they'd been dumped from and flung halfway across a table, the man grinning and armless (his upper limbs scattered here and there in the featureless room), the woman in two pieces like the Black Dahlia, both husband and wife attired in burnt-black unidentifiable clothing. A few pieces of living room furniture were upended here and there. A window had no glass though the brick fireplace looked fine, and the walls were blank but for one askew framed portrait of Jesus—one of those idealized 1950s portraits of the son of God. At least the eyes didn't follow you.

Thwack, scoop, rattle, whump.

What the fuck *was* that?

I should know but I didn't. I craned my neck and realized I had company in addition to the J.C. Penney window dummies. Nita, pinned-up hair come undone and hanging, her honeycomb dress and white hose splotched with dirt, lay on her side, hands behind her, ankles bound like mine, unconscious but breathing. Beyond her was another figure, male, in a sport shirt and slacks, also on his side but facing away from us, his wrists secured by a length of clothesline, ankles, too. Shoes gone.

Thwack, scoop, rattle, whump.

Somehow I got my stockinged feet under me and stood and hopped like a fucking rabbit over to Nita. She was still very much out, but the man was moving, coming around. I hopped to the other side of him, and damn! It was Shep! Shep Shepherd, my CIA buddy. He had a contusion along one side of his face and looked generally roughed up.

Thwack, scoop, rattle, whump.

I leaned toward him as best I could. Speaking in a whisper came automatically: "What the fuck, Shep?"

He blinked a bunch of times, gathering the pieces of his consciousness together. He gave me an embarrassed gap-toothed smile.

"They....they grabbed me at my hotel." He was whispering,

too. "Parking lot. This bunch...they must work for the rogue Company faction, ones behind all this...."

"At least one of them was at the Ambassador. I think he may be the shooter. Hal Harper's another. Is there a woman with them? Young woman, good-looking?"

"N-no. Not even an ugly one."

"This one's no dog. Topless dancer, stripper from L.A.— she's the polka-dot dress girl."

"Hell you say."

"I was getting ready to take her in to the FBI and she seemed to be cooperating, but she must've got a phone call off to these pricks. How many?"

"Three that I saw."

Thwack, scoop, rattle, whump.

"I'm gonna get down there with you. See if you can untie me. I hope you were a fucking Boy Scout."

We got back to back, wrist to wrist. It was hot, not humid, but still hot enough that we hadn't been at it long at all before we were sweat soaked. He worked on the knotted rope binding me. It probably didn't take him more than three minutes, but it felt like forever.

Thwack, scoop, rattle, whump.

I sat up and untied my ankles. "I think I know what that sound is."

"So do I. They're digging holes."

"Just for shits and giggles, right? Not graves or anything."

"Yeah. Just for fun. Do you know where we are?"

I started untying Shep's wrists. The knots were tight and tough. "Atomic City, maybe? The little fake town the government built and dropped an H-bomb on, just to see what would be left?"

"You're close. This is Survival Town. Nothing much was left of Atomic City, so they built a second one, better."

"Survival Town."

Shep nodded. "Pride of Yucca Flats. We're an hour or so outside Vegas. They made it complete with cars, power lines, even people...well, bogus people. Concrete-block structures. Reinforced brick buildings. Reinforced masonry homes, like this one."

As I worked at his bonds, I was listening and not just to him. "They stopped digging."

"Taking a break maybe."

I heard footsteps in sandy earth, growing closer. I wasn't quite done with Shep's wrist ropes and just patted him on the leg, then went over where I'd been before and resumed my position. I made only one adjustment: I took the decapitated kid's head along.

I heard a voice outside call out: *"I'm getting my lighter! Think I left it in the kitchen! Be right back...."*

The shell of the kitchen was adjacent, no door separating us, so when he stepped inside the house through the doorless doorway, his footsteps on the disrupted floorboards were like cries of pain.

"Here it is," he muttered, to himself.

I could see him: the ex-cop, Harper. He was in a short-sleeve yellow shirt, brown slacks and that out-of-date fedora. He got a pack of smokes from his breast pocket—Chesterfields. A .38 was stuffed in his waistband, mine I thought. Lighting up with his recovered Zippo, he looked toward where we were and, apparently, decided to check on us.

He stepped into the living room and I flung the kid's head at him. It clocked him good, right in the forehead, but wasn't enough to put him on his back though it startled the hell out of him and he was off-balance, in the doorway, when I threw myself at him. I got him by the knees and took him down with a *whump* and then climbed up his prone body like a ladder and collected the .38 along the way.

His eyes were huge when my face was in his and his mouth came open as I shoved the barrel of the snub-nose Police Special into the flesh where his jaw met his throat and I could see the flame in his open mouth as the bullet traveled up through his brain and out his skull.

That had worked out just fine. The shot wasn't loud at all—between his fat neck and the journey through his head and out, it barely rivaled a cap gun.

Back in the living room, I didn't take the time to help Shep finish with his wrists, figuring he could finish that up himself and undo his ankles, too. Muffled though that shot had been, it still might have been loud enough to draw the others to us—two at least.

So I said to him, "Take care of Nita," who was starting to come around.

With my .38 in hand, I stepped over and around Harper's corpse in the doorway. I bent down and with my left hand took the lighter from his dead fingers, then lifted the pack of Chesterfields from his breast pocket. I shook out a smoke one-handed and fired it up. Did I mention since after the war I only smoked in combat situations?

I sucked some of the cigarette into my lungs and went over to peek out the non-existent kitchen door.

Survival Town had no streets anymore. No sense of organization at all—just a brick building here and a frame two-story there, a few spiny Joshua trees, some scattered yucca, clumps of mesquite, and two assholes digging graves in the middle of it all. One was a dyed-blond Hispanic, tall enough to be Sandy Serrano's guy in the gold sweater on the steps outside the Ambassador, though right now he was just in a t-shirt and jeans, splotched with occasional dirt and sweat stains from the hard work he was doing. He looked bushed. Poor baby.

The other was the dark-curly-haired fan who'd crashed the party back at the Royal Suite last June, and who in the Pantry had got the last autograph that Robert Kennedy ever gave. He was working on his own hole—one of three right in a row—the other grave in progress having been the late Harper's responsibility.

They were taking a beer break. They'd brought a cooler along to our murders. Well, why not be comfy no matter what the situation? Good to stay hydrated. Tired, the pair drank their beer and laughed and joked and leaned on the handles of their shovels with one hand and (between chugs) cradled cans of Blatz in the other. Me, I just smoked my confiscated Chesterfield and thought about my next move.

They were a good twenty feet from me and the range of a .38 like my spare piece was only reliable at around six, and I wasn't somebody who spent his spare time at a firing range, so I played it the best I could.

I burst out and thrust the gun toward them and yelled, "Get those fucking hands up, right now!"

The blond went for a gun in his waistband and the dark curly-haired one did the smart thing and just turned and ran off, putting more space between himself and my .38. The blond fired off a round that didn't come anywhere near me and I sent one back at him, which he caught in the belly, doubling him over. I would rather have got him in the head but body mass was my friend in this case.

He stumbled and fell and almost wound up in the grave he'd dug, but not quite. Maybe in the movie.

As for the fan, he was heading for shelter, going into a two-story frame house, which looked like something the Big Bad

Wolf could have blown down in one huff or anyway puff. Still, there had been a lot of desert wind out here since the founding of Survival Town and well over a decade since an H-bomb had been dropped nearby, so maybe the place was sturdier than you'd think. It was possible he'd assumed a window position to pick me off, so I ran low in serpentine fashion at the structure, which had either been unpainted at the time of the blast or the bomb or the wind had blown off every scrap of paint.

No gunshot came my way.

That didn't mean anything. I hadn't seen him pull a pistol and hadn't noted one in his waistband or in a holster either. He was in a dark blue t-shirt and jeans and it was possible at a distance that a weapon had blended in. It was possible he was unarmed. But probable he was carrying.

When I got to the doorless front door, I plastered myself to one side, my back to the outer wall, and listened. Listened. And listened some more.

No sound of footsteps, no heavy breathing. It was a two-story house and he may have run upstairs to lie in wait. Or he could have been more professional than I took him for and done any one of a number of smart things—he'd been part of a pretty goddamn skillful team to take Bob Kennedy out the way they'd done. A murder in a packed room, a programmed patsy, a security guard accomplice to hold the victim in place for his slaughter!

Not an amateur, then.

I went in low and fast and hit the deck. Found myself in a living room with a family greeting me with blank stares and friendly smiles—more mannequins, Mom and Dad sharing a couch, a boy on the floor with his upended train set, a girl with her legless, one-armed doll. Only the little girl was twisted impossibly at the waist and the little boy's arms were nowhere to be seen and Mom was on her side with a scorched, tattered

276 MAX ALLAN COLLINS

lamp shade next to her and Dad's head was turned toward the window, as if he'd seen the atomic blast coming.

On my feet again, I prowled, room by room, easing into each, pausing to listen for any sign of life, watching the floorboards to seek a path where I wouldn't make a sound or anyway much of one. Most rooms were empty, the walls bare and distressed and smeared with dirt. The apparent kitchen was just a counter and some cabinets. Ceilings were partially exposed to their wooden framework. A room toward the back had a mannequin man and woman under the covers of a double bed. They looked embarrassed, but none the worse for wear despite an H-bomb.

That left the second floor.

A paint-peeling white wooden staircase, enclosed on the right, rose with the occasional step missing like a sideways grin shy a few teeth. No way to head up there silently. But at least that side wall could be leaned against....

I started up doing just that and the wood beneath my stockinged feet whined as if that little boy had finally noticed his train set wasn't right. The open passageway at the top of the stairs could be filled at any moment with that curly-haired fan with a gun blasting away like Sirhan Sirhan in the Pantry, only this time it wouldn't be blanks.

Then finally I got to the top and only a hallway awaited, and it occurred to me that this was a typical American home of the Fifties but built on the cheap and had been turned by an atomic bomb into a kind of tenement. But I didn't have time to look for irony in the rubble of a mad doctor's experiment. Somewhere in the back of my combat-addled brain I knew that I shouldn't kill this curly-haired motherfucker.

No.

I needed him alive, to talk, to tell the whole story, to help me make a joke out of the inherently absurd Lone Gunman theory and expose, finally, finally, fucking finally, the conspiracy that had taken my friend from me and twisted my country's future into old hawks and young druggies.

He popped out of a doorway, at the far end of the hall, firing—*he did have a gun!*—and again I hit the deck but he was running right at me, desperate bullets flying just over my head and around me when the floorboard gave and like terrible teeth came up around him and the building swallowed him.

I was on my hands and knees and crept over to the ragged hole the floor had made in itself and there he was, on his back, with one of the floorboards he'd taken with him, sticking up through his chest in jagged bloody judgment like Christopher Lee on a bad day. He wasn't quite dead yet, and blood was pumping out of him, onto the wooden stake, joining the dripping red that the tip of the thing had taken with it and was now oozing back to him. The face under the dark curly nest of hair was contorting and his hands were reaching toward me, as if for help.

The only thing I could do for him was shoot him in the head, which I did. But to be honest with you, that was more for me than him.

Outside, I tossed my smoke and headed to my little home away from home where Shep was on the floor holding a shivering Nita to him. Hotter than hell though it was, she might have been freezing. I relieved him of her and handed the gun off to him as she folded herself to me and I held her.

"All three are dead," I said to him, "goddamnit."

Jesus looked reproachfully at me from his crooked frame for my language.

Shep sighed. Nodded. "We could have used that Michael Winn alive."

"That's the curly-haired one's name?"

"Yeah. The other one has a bunch of names, mostly Cuban. You all right?"

I nodded. "I'd like to get out of here. Can you have this mess cleaned up for us, or do we need to go official?"

"I'll take care of it," Shep said. "They must have had at least one car to haul the three of us out here. Let's see if we can commandeer it and find our way back to town."

Nita clung to me.

"Any town but Survival," I said.

TWENTY

That evening, after sleeping all day, we again went down to the Garden of the Gods pool for a swim. Mid-evening, when most couples were out gambling or dining or being entertained by showbiz royalty, we were among a handful of twosomes languorously lounging in water just cool enough to contrast with the desert warmth under a starry sky with moonlight making the surrounding Roman columns glow. The major difference between us and the other couples—I was not the only older male with a younger female, you understand—was that the dreamy atmosphere was compromised by our recent living nightmare.

We sat kicking a little on the edge of the pool where the dripping aftermath of swimming a few laps quickly evaporated. Sinatra was singing "Fly Me to the Moon" on the sound system. Nita was in her Peter Max-print bathing suit, hair up again, and I was in the green-and-black Tiki trunks. It was almost if this were the night before and we had blinked away the intervening events. Leaning her hands on cement, bent over toward me a bit, she said, "Should we talk about it?"

My hands were on my thighs. "About almost getting killed? Or what I had to do to stop it?"

Her smile was tiny. "I've been on so many TV shows, from *Maverick* to *Man from U.N.C.L.E.*, where the, uh, bullets were flying. Only once before in my life was I exposed to the real thing."

"The Pantry."

"The Pantry. And even that seemed unreal. But this morning…

just hearing the sounds of it, then seeing the aftermath. Two men you…"

"I killed three. You only saw two of the bodies. Yes. Like the Pantry. Do you think less of me?"

She clutched my arm. "No! No. You saved us. My God, you saved us. But I know now what…just how *serious* what I asked you to do really was."

"You mean looking into Bob's murder?"

"Yes. Yes."

"And now you want me to stop?"

Her eyes, in modified Cher makeup, popped. "Yes! No. I… I don't know." She let go of my arm. "It's just so fucking *real* now…."

"We use to call it battle fatigue. Or shell shock. There are other terms these days."

"For…?"

"For the stress and distress that follows combat."

Her eyes narrowed. "Is *that* what that was?"

I shrugged. "I don't know what else."

"Nathan!" She clutched my arm again. Whispered: "He's *here*."

"What? Who is?"

She bobbed her head just past me. "Your friend. From this morning…Shep."

I looked where she was looking. Shep, in Ray-Bans, a fresh Hawaiian shirt and Bermuda shorts, was sitting in a deck chair at a little metal table under an umbrella that was apparently protecting him from moon burn. Same little metal table as before. A foot in a sandal rested on a knee. He raised a hand in a motionless wave. Offered his gap-toothed smile.

"Checking up on us," I said.

"Because he's your friend," she said.

"Because he's my CIA handler. I'm an asset…unless I've become a liability after Survival Town."

Now she grabbed my hand and squeezed. "Oh, Nate. Tell me he's a friend."

"Sure. He's our friend. He gave us a ride back, didn't he, in that Chevy I hotwired? Better than the car trunks we got stuffed in going out there."

"I'm…afraid."

"Good. Just don't go to pieces on me." I nodded to a small adjacent pool from which steam rose. "Why don't you relax in the whirlpool a while. I'll see if he wants something."

She did that as I got out, fetched my towel and used it, then padded over to a waiting deck chair by Shep under the umbrella. I wrapped the towel around my shoulders. It was cooler tonight than last. Conversation echoed around us, unintelligible.

I said, "You look none the worse for wear."

Indeed his side-of-the-head contusion seemed already to have healed.

"I'm okay," he confirmed. "How are you two kids doing?"

"Well, this kid is over sixty and slept like a stone since I saw you last, just to stay afloat…as we say here at the Garden of the Gods."

"Stones don't float. But, yeah. That was rough this morning. I should have been more help."

"You kept Nita safe while I took care of business. That was enough."

He nodded. Searched for the right thing to say and came up with: "We need to talk."

I grinned. "The worst four strung-together words in the English language, though usually coming from a woman. Let me guess. I'm to drop this. All of it."

He nodded. "I'll take it from here. Now it's a matter of inner-agency house-cleaning."

"Better find a big broom. Taking Bob Kennedy down required a major covert operation, a team much larger than just that curly-haired kid and the tall Cuban in the gold sweater. Maybe start with the bartender in the makeshift bar downstairs who dispensed dosed drinks to Sirhan. I wouldn't be surprised if there wasn't a second girl in a polka-dot dress—that dress and its polka dots may have been a hypnotic trigger for Sirhan. Then there's somebody in a maroon coat watching the door onto Sandy Serrano's fire escape where the gold-sweater guy and the polka-dot-dress girl entered, accompanied by Michael Winn...or maybe that was the similarly curly-haired, programmed Sirhan himself. That door later became the exit for two of them. In the Pantry, of course, there was Thane Cesar, whose mission was to maintain his grip on Kennedy, and hold him in place while the gold sweater guy likely did the close-up shooting. Or perhaps Thane did some of that, but certainly not all five shots—he was just too exposed."

Shep took off the Ray-Bans and tossed them with a clunk onto the metal table; his dark-blue eyes fixed on me coldly.

I went on: "The assassin couldn't really fire into a crowd that included Cesar and other conspirators. That's why Sirhan was shooting blanks, creating the diversion of all diversions, meaning someone else fired into the crowd to make it look like Sirhan's bullets were real. After all, bystanders getting hit is what really sold it. Trajectory indicates this additional shooter was standing on that serving table with the Nye girl—the curly-haired Winn, right? Whose resemblance to Sirhan may have been part of a Plan B or C. Sirhan shooting like that created confusion, utter pandemonium, sending potential eyewitnesses to the floor, covering their heads, unsure of what they'd seen or even if they'd seen anything."

"Sounds," Shep said quietly, "like a pretty bold scheme."

"Oh, it was bold, all right—bolder than Dallas, which is saying something. And yet similar—a perfect patsy, multiple shooters, a public event ripped apart by gunfire. A hell of a finale to a decade of assassination."

A curvy blonde mini-toga-ed waitress delivered a Gibson and a rum and Coke. I hadn't even seen Shep order them. He signed for it, gave her a wink, and she was gone. He shoved my rum and Coke over to me and plucked the onion from the Gibson and popped it in his mouth. Chewed lazily.

He flipped a hand toward my drink. "Go ahead and refresh yourself, Nate. Nothing in that but Coca Cola and Bacardi, I promise. I'll even taste it, if you like."

"I'll take you at your word, Shep." I took a sip. They weren't scrimping on the Bacardi. "So let me guess. You want me to leave this to you. Let you clean house and cover up and then I don't have to worry about having an unexpected aneurysm or a fall from a height or maybe get a sudden urge to turn the Jag's motor on with the garage door down."

"I won't lie to you," Shep said. "I believe this to be a rogue CIA operation, in which case consider who the assets involved might be—the LAPD, right-wing assholes, Cubans, the Hughes organization, the mob, just to scratch the surface. You need to be satisfied with what you've got, Nate—that you removed from the face of the earth the scum who killed Bobby in that Pantry."

On the sound system Dino was singing, "Ain't That a Kick in the Head." Brittle laughter made a sophisticated laugh track.

"I won't lie to *you*, Shep. As President, Bob planned to over-haul the Company but good, and he meant to uncover his brother's assassins and the spooks and gangsters who sent them. So I don't think this necessarily *is* a 'rogue operation.'"

"You expect me to confirm that?"

I didn't bother answering. "Here's the thing, Shep—I'm not

convinced your presence in the Atomic desert this morning wasn't to guide me, and stage-manage me."

That seemed to amuse him. "Really? To what purpose?"

"As you said, to satisfy me. That I'd wiped out the literal killers of my friend. Who just happened to be some highly questionable assets of the Company's—cut-outs who could use cutting out. Two birds, one stone kinda thing. Besides...you've got the goods on me—I killed those three at Survival Town, and you hung onto the gun."

He twitched a smile. "With your fingerprints on it, yes."

I leaned on an elbow. "That's what got me thinking, Shep. Why as tired as I was I didn't get right to sleep, when we got back this morning. What *really* got me thinking. I handed you that .38 and somehow I never got it back."

He tossed his head, opened a hand. "Let's say you're right. You're *not* right, Nate. You are a trusted asset of mine and a valued friend, but...let's say you're right. What would you set out to do, at this juncture? Remove every player? Kill Thane Cesar and Elaine Nye and Bob Maheu and Dr. Hypno and Howard Fucking Hughes and whatever LAPD stooges and mobsters helped facilitate this plot you've cooked up in your imagination? How about CIA directors past and present? Allen Dulles is already dead, but you could settle up with Dick Helms. Where would it end?"

He sat forward suddenly.

Through his teeth, he answered his own question: "I will tell you where it would end. With you dead."

"Maybe I've lived long enough."

He smiled and it quickly turned into a sneer. "I don't think that's sincere, old chum. I think you enjoy your fame and your money and your Jag and your Beverly Hills bungalow and your *Playboy* pad back home and your precious coast-to-coast A-1

Agency. And I also think you value the lives of your son and maybe that little gal in the whirlpool over there...*Take it easy!*"

I was halfway out of my chair.

The dark-blue eyes narrowed at me. "Do you think I am personally threatening you, or am I merely letting you know what others might do? The things that might well happen beyond my control? All I can do is to advise you, as an old, dear friend, to be satisfied with what you have accomplished and move on with your life. Even Nate Heller can't kill them all."

"I could make a good start," I said, looking right at him.

An unconcerned shrug. "Yes, you could probably manage that. I am better looked after than most, but you could. And my wife Sheila and my two grown children, Bradley and Susan, who you have known for years, with whom you've broken bread, would be terribly sad to lose me. Just as those you love would be devastated by your tragic demise. But neither of us, Nate, are young men. As you pointed out, we've lived plenty of life."

I said nothing.

That gap-toothed grin returned. "What is the point, Nate? Do you know for a fact that Sirhan Sirhan was some kind of innocent victim in this, and is rotting unfairly away in his prison cell? Or is it just as likely he came on as a willing participant and any programming was designed to ensure his discretion and success? I mean, Jesus! This farce has already faded into history, Nate, not even a year later!"

He stood. Finished his Gibson. Put on his Ray-Bans.

"Let history be history, Nate," Shep said. "Don't go around rewriting it."

He slipped into the night and I joined Nita in the whirlpool. The air was cool enough that the warmth of the water felt good.

Nita asked, "What was that about?"

I told her.

She said nothing as I gave her an only slightly condensed, censored version of my conversation with Shep, her eyes widening and narrowing as was appropriate, and toward the end—when various possible deaths came up, including mine and hers—her eyes filled with tears. None rolled down her cheek, however—she was, as they say, made of sterner stuff.

"We've gone as far with this as we can," I said. "Sirhan Sirhan is on Death Row, whether he belongs there or not, and no matter how many people disappear in the desert, Bob Kennedy is gone forever."

She thought about that, then said, "So…what now?"

"Well, we're in Vegas," I said with a shrug and the best smile I had left in me. "Why don't we get married? I figure our odds are better in a wedding chapel than a casino."

She shrugged too, smiled a little.

"I'm game," she said.

Robert Kennedy had grown up hero-worshiping Herbert Hoover, was closer than any of his siblings to his ruthless business tycoon father, began his legal and political career supporting Joe McCarthy's anti-Commie witch hunt, urged victory over Communism in Vietnam in the early '60s, and participated in a plot called Operation Mongoose to assassinate Fidel Castro and overthrow the Cuban government.

Like Joe E. Brown said at the end of *Some Like It Hot*, nobody's perfect.

But my friend Bob evolved perfectly into a crusader for the poor and a Vietnam dove, embracing the anti-war protest movement of the Younger Generation. Someone once said that he "felt the deepest, cared the most, and fought the hardest for humanity—crying out against America's involvement in the Vietnam war, championing the causes of blacks, Hispanics, and

Mexican-Americans, and crusading against the suffering of children, the elderly and anyone else hurt or bypassed by social and economic programs."

And it got him killed.

Why were any of us surprised? He seemed to have been waiting for it to happen, daring Fate to repeat itself after the murder of his brother Jack.

But of course Fate didn't kill Jack or Bob—men did, and some made it happen while others allowed it and covered it up and in other ways aided and abetted. Shep Shepherd was right. I couldn't find and remove every co-conspirator in this evil morass any more than a surgeon, however skilled, could root out the cancer in a patient riddled with the stuff.

Over the years, from a distance, I kept track of many of those I'd encountered in my brief RFK murder inquiry. With a private investigative agency at my beck and call, it wasn't difficult.

Several in law enforcement who participated in the cover-up—Manny Hermano for one—were rewarded for their efforts, earning themselves better jobs and sometimes government contracts. Hermano left the LAPD (for the second time) and became a teacher and I suppose passed his wisdom on. He died in 2009 in Palm Desert, California.

In 1971 forensics expert and prosecution shill Wayne Wolf was promoted to head of the LAPD Crime Lab, in as fine an example of the Peter Principle as I've ever seen. Upon his retirement from the LAPD he became president of Ace Guard Services—the firm that had dispatched Thane Eugene Cesar to the Ambassador Hotel on June 4, 1968. He died in 2012 in North Hollywood. I never met him.

Sgt. Pete Shore, a cop who lived up to the idealized LAPD of Jack Webb's *Dragnet*, got pushed into early retirement and took a position as a small-town sheriff in Missouri. Former FBI man and criminalist Will Harris made no secret of his opinion that Sirhan Sirhan was not a lone shooter, giving many interviews on the subject; he died in 2007 after a distinguished teaching career.

Thomas Noguchi, "coroner to the stars," was reinstated on July 31, 1969. Over a long, attention-attracting career, he performed autopsies on Marilyn Monroe, Sharon Tate, Janis Joplin, David Janssen, Divine, William Holden, and John Belushi, among other show biz luminaries. These were some of the famous co-stars in his story but they only made one guest appearance each.

Grant Cooper, lead attorney in Sirhan Sirhan's defense, also enjoyed a celebrated career, but by the time of his death in 1990 his reputation had been tainted by rumors that he'd thrown his most famous case. Nor was his prestige enhanced by the Friars Club card cheating scandal, where his chief client was mobster Johnny Roselli.

Over the years, evidence continued to surface that undermined the notion of Sirhan as the lone assassin. Bullets recovered at the crime scene, for instance, could not be matched to Sirhan's gun. And then there was the ever-climbing number of bullets, which some had adding up as high as eighteen. An audio expert identified thirteen shots on a recording of the assassination.

"The gunshots," the audio expert said, "are established by virtue of my computer analysis of waveform patterns, which clearly distinguish gunshots from other phenomena. This would include sounds that to human hearing are often perceived as exploding firecrackers, popping camera flashbulbs or bursting balloons."

The thirteen shots captured on tape indicated some were fired too rapidly, at intervals too close together, to have come from Sirhan's weapon alone.

In 1977, Dr. Joseph W. Bryant was found dead in his room at the Riviera Hotel in Las Vegas shortly after being summoned to appear before the House Select Committee on Assassinations. Though no autopsy was performed, his death was ruled natural causes, although rumors persist that the doc died by gunshot. What's one bullet more or less at this point?

Bryant, it was learned after his demise, had been an associate of JFK-assassination suspect David Ferrie. He had taught hypnosis techniques to Ferrie, and they had both been members of the same obscure religious sect. Such odd coincidences (or "coincidences"?) seemed to turn up everywhere in this case. For example, Sirhan Sirhan had worked with the brother of Arthur Bremer, would-be George Wallace assassin, at the racing stables in Santa Anita.

Was it a coincidence that Thane Eugene Cesar worked for the Hughes organization at Lockheed? Or that Cesar had been employed by Hughes' man Maheu at the Bel Air Patrol security firm? Cesar dropped out of sight for a time, turning up in 1994 in the Philippines, his last known place of residence. He passed a lie detector test for a journalist who became his agent. (*EDITOR'S NOTE: Cesar died on September 11, 2019. His agent was asking $25,000 an interview.*)

Elaine Nye married Korean War veteran Jack Hart in Hollywood in 1973. Jack wrote several well-known rock songs and, as an agent, represented at various times Eddie Cochran, Rosemary Clooney, and Glenn Campbell. According to his son from his first marriage, Jack claimed to have worked for the CIA in mind-control experimentation. At some point in the '70s (according to Elaine's daughter from her first marriage), the couple was on the run from the FBI, hiding out in Missouri with relatives. Elaine liked to brag that she'd been the polka-dot-dress girl—she would wear the dress once a year just to piss her husband off. Once she had wanted to wear the dress to church and Jack, who was somewhat abusive, had forbidden it. They split up and she became a nurse, an alcoholic, and a fundamentalist Christian, not necessarily in that order. She died in 2013.

Robert Maheu was fired by Howard Hughes in 1970. He stayed in Vegas, establishing Robert A. Maheu and Associates and becoming, according to reliable sources, one of Las Vegas's leading citizens. Sketchier sources claim Maheu liked to take credit for masterminding the assassination of Robert F. Kennedy. The *Mission: Impossible* man died of congestive heart failure at Desert Springs Hospital in Las Vegas in 2008.

Jack Anderson took over Drew Pearson's *Washington Merry-Go-Round* column and over time became as well-known as his late mentor. His mob-centric theory on the assassination of John F. Kennedy brought him criticism from mainstream media, but experts on the subject find much to admire in his thinking and research. He never took on the Robert F. Kennedy assassination, although his work on the Watergate conspiracy got him targeted for assassination himself.

Film director John Frankenheimer—while he never again reached the heights of *The Manchurian Candidate* and *Seven Days in May*—remained a successful moviemaker till his death in 2002.

Shep Shepherd died in his sleep in Washington, D.C., in 1975.

After he left Las Vegas, Howard Hughes moved to the Intercontinental Hotel near Lake Managua in Nicaragua. An earthquake in December 1972 sent him to the Xanadu Princess Resort on Grand Bahama Island, where he lived his last four years. In 1972, Clifford Irving claimed he'd co-authored the reclusive Hughes' autobiography. Hughes denounced the writer in a teleconference; a postal investigation led to Irving's indictment and subsequent fraud conviction. Hughes died on April 5, 1976, onboard a Learjet.

In September 1969, Dr. Eduard Simson-Kallas was informed his examinations of Sirhan Sirhan must cease. An assistant warden wrote, "I am concerned that Dr. Simson appears to be making a career out of Sirhan." Simson-Kallas resigned in protest and went into successful private practice. He died in Monterey, California, in 1987.

In 1994, defense attorney F. Lee Bailey's client, Claude DuBoc, accused of drug dealing, agreed to forfeit his assets as part of the plea bargain. But Bailey had transferred nearly six million dollars of those assets into his own accounts. He was disbarred in Florida in 2001 and Massachusetts followed suit in 2003. Later appeals to be admitted to the bar in Maine were unsuccessful. *(EDITOR'S NOTE: Mr. Bailey died in 2021.)*

In the 1980s, Sandra Serrano—administering a child care center in East Los Angeles—stayed active in politics, successfully running the election campaign for a leading Latina politician. When she loaned the candidate living expenses, Sandra arranged to pay herself back from campaign funds. The state sniffed out irregularities in the campaign's finances and the Los Angeles D.A. charged Serrano with embezzlement. Forty thousand dollars of legal fees later, she entered a nolo contendere plea, accepting conviction but not admitting guilt.

Serrano hadn't spoken in public about the assassination since June 1968. But researchers had unearthed tapes of the nasty interrogation by Hermano, and a documentary filmmaker sought her out. Serrano was told by the authorities if she stayed silent about June 5, her felony conviction would be reduced to a misdemeanor.

For two decades she never spoke in public about the assassination night, nor did she reveal the names of those in government who bargained for her silence; but she has since reaffirmed her original story about the girl in the polka-dot dress.

Scott Enyart, a young high school student at the time, shot three rolls of photographs at the Ambassador the night of the assassination and was perfectly positioned in the Pantry to record the tragedy. On his way out, the police stopped him and confiscated his film; he was told they'd process it for use in the trial. None of the photos made a courtroom appearance. He fought for two decades to get the photos back. When they were finally being delivered to him, the courier's car was broken into and the photos stolen.

In 1972, when the death penalty was banned in California, Sirhan Sirhan's sentence was modified to life in prison. The Board of Parole Hearings found Sirhan suitable for parole in 1975, but rescinded his parole grant. The Board conducted fifteen subsequent hearings, in which they found Mr. Sirhan unsuitable for parole. (*EDITOR'S NOTE: On August 27, 2021, the Board conducted Mr. Sirhan's sixteenth hearing and found him suitable for parole. Governor Gavin Newsom rejected the recommendation.*)

The bullets fired in the Pantry killed not just Robert Kennedy but the once grand Ambassador Hotel itself, though the latter's death was a slow one. A misguided 1970s renovation spearheaded by Sammy Davis Jr. included shag carpet, disco ball and purple decor, the hotel finally closing its doors in 1989. Following a lengthy battle involving the L.A. school district and new owner Donald Trump, much of the hotel was torn down in late 2005 and early 2006. The educational complex rising on the site included remnants of the old hotel—the coffee shop now a teachers' break room, the Cocoanut Grove an auditorium, and the Embassy Ballroom a library named for Paul Schrade, who had been instrumental in securing the property to build what is now known as the Robert F. Kennedy Community Schools.

On the last day of his life, Bob Kennedy saved a boy from drowning. What about that boy, that Kennedy son, who I watched him drag to shore? David died of a drug overdose in 1984. In 1997, his brother Michael, accused of having an affair with the family's teenaged babysitter, died playing football on the Colorado ski slopes. Kathleen fared better, being elected lieutenant governor of Maryland, and Joe won his Uncle Jack's congressional seat.

My son Sam runs the A-1 now, out of the Chicago office. Nita and I spend a good deal of time in Boca Raton, which we call our second home—the first is in suburban Oak Brook, although we still sentimentally consider the Beverly Hills Hotel bungalow our *real* "first home."

For the first five years or so of our marriage, Nita stayed busy with the budding indie film industry in Florida, and of course we'd go back to Los Angeles for pilot season. She never landed a series but even now does occasional guest shots. Like me, she's almost famous.

Our house is on a waterway and we often sit with a cocktail and watch the boats go in this direction and then that. Pretty young things water-ski by and I give them wistful looks like most old men do, and Nita tolerates that. Mostly these days she types up these memoirs from the yellow pads I scrawl them on. Me, I take on a job now and then, and occasionally settle an old score.

So if you are one of the bastards who helped take Bob Kennedy down, don't get cocky. I might get around to you yet.

I OWE THEM ONE

Despite its extensive basis in history, this is a work of fiction; some liberties have been taken with the facts, and any blame for historical inaccuracies is my own, mitigated by the limitations of conflicting source material.

The first Nathan Heller novel, *True Detective*, was published in 1983 and dealt with political assassin Giuseppe Zangara, whose similarity to Sirhan Sirhan was not lost on me at the time. Dealing with the Robert F. Kennedy assassination in *Too Many Bullets* feels like a bookend to the Heller saga, although one never knows when Nate might come up with another memory or two to share.

I married Barbara Mull on June 1, 1968, and we honeymooned in Chicago. The trip was designed to be brief, just a few days, and at the tail end we were confronted with Bobby's death—we were literally packing to return when the TV informed us. We'd had a lovely time in Chicago, but the tragedy came home with us.

Like most people, I accepted that Sirhan Sirhan was the lone gunman, despite my opinion—only confirmed by extensive research for the Heller novels *Target Lancer* (2012) and *Ask Not* (2013)—that his brother Jack's assassination was the result of a conspiracy. I had intended to deal with the RFK investigation in about one hundred pages, as an envelope around an as yet unwritten Heller novel about Jimmy Hoffa. In fact, I sold the proposed novel to Hard Case Crime by way of a synopsis based on that notion.

And then I began researching.

I quickly discovered that—despite a general feeling among the population that goes back to the event itself—the "open-and-shut" nature of the Robert F. Kennedy assassination had nonetheless led to more books about RFK's death than his life. The obviousness of a probable conspiracy meant the idea of my handling the case in one hundred pages or so was not workable.

I am grateful to my editor Charles Ardai for his support in letting Heller and me pursue this story in its own direction.

My usual practice, in the Nathan Heller memoirs, is to use real names as much as possible. That remains generally true here, but I have employed composite characters in several instances, primarily to keep the size of the cast manageable. For example, Manny Hermano takes the place of two LAPD detectives on Special Unit Senator, Lt. Manuel Pena and Sgt. Enrique Hernandez. Will Harris combines FBI agent William Bailey and criminalist William Harper.

In other instances, to provide me latitude, a fictionalized character represents a real individual—for instance, Sgt. Pete Shore of the LAPD derives from Sgt. Paul Sharaga. Dr. Joseph W. Bryant is based on Dr. William J. Bryan. Ron Kiser represents journalist/investigator Robert Blair Kaiser. Shep Shepherd, a character appearing previously in the Heller memoirs, is largely based upon CIA director of security, Sheffield Edwards.

Nita Romaine is suggested by Nina Rhodes-Hughes, a television actress (Nina Roman) who worked as a volunteer fund-raiser for the RFK Presidential campaign.

Even characters who appear here under their true names must also be viewed as fictionalized. Available research on the various individuals ranges from voluminous to scant. Whenever possible, newspaper and magazine interviews, and transcripts of courtroom and hearing appearances, have been used as the basis of dialogue scenes, although creative license has been taken. Time compression has been employed, sparingly.

The following biographies of Robert F. Kennedy were consulted: *American Journey: The Times of Robert Kennedy* (1970), Jean Stein (interviewer) and George Plimpton (editor); *Bobby Kennedy: A Raging Spirit* (2017), Chris Matthews; *Bobby Kennedy: The Making of a Folk Hero* (1986), Lester David and Irene David; *Bobby Kennedy: The Making of a Liberal Legend* (2016), Larry Tye; *Perfect Villains, Imperfect Heroes: Robert F. Kennedy's War Against Organized Crime* (1995), Ronald Goldfarb; *Robert Kennedy: A Memoir* (1969), Jack Newfield; *Robert Kennedy: His Life* (2000), Evan Thomas; and *RFK: A Candid Biography of Robert F. Kennedy* (1998), C. David Heymann. The most useful of these for my purposes were by Chris Matthews and Evan Thomas.

The number of books exploring Sirhan Sirhan as a programmed assassin and/or the notion of a second gunman is extensive to say the least. Here is a list of what I used: *The Assassination of Robert F. Kennedy: Crime, Conspiracy and Cover-Up—A New Investigation* (2018, 2020), Tim Tate & Brad Johnson; *The Assassination of Robert F. Kennedy: The Conspiracy and Coverup* (1978, 1993), William Turner & John Christian; *The Assassinations: Probe Magazine on JFK, MLK, RFK and Malcolm X* (2003), James DiEugenio and Lisa Pease (editors); *The Forgotten Terrorist: Sirhan Sirhan and the Assassination of Robert F. Kennedy* (2007), Mel Ayton; *The Killing of Robert F. Kennedy* (1995), Dan Moldea; *A Lie Too Big to Fail: The Real History of the Assassination of Robert F. Kennedy* (2018), Lisa Pease; *The Polka Dot File: On the Robert F. Kennedy Killing* (2016), Fernando Faura; *"R.F.K. Must Die!": Chasing the Mystery of the Robert Kennedy Assassination* (1970, 2008), Robert Blair Kaiser; *The Robert F. Kennedy Assassination: New Revelations on the Conspiracy and Cover-Up* (1991), Philip H.

Melanson; *Shadow Play: The Unsolved Murder of Robert F. Kennedy* (1997, 2018), William Klaber and Philip Melanson; *Who Killed Bobby?: The Unsolved Murder of Robert F. Kennedy* (2018), Shane O'Sullivan; and *Who Killed Robert Kennedy?* (1993), Philip H. Melanson.

Lisa Pease's *A Lie Too Big to Fail* is (at this writing) the most up-to-date and comprehensive work, truly essential. But it suffers from scattershot organization and a weak index. More readable, and an outstanding contribution to RFK assassination literature, is Shane O'Sullivan's *Who Killed Bobby?* (in its expanded, revised edition). The late Philip Melanson's contributions are key, as well, including his helpful mini book, a virtual primer on the case, *Who Killed Robert Kennedy?* Also readable and accessible is Tate and Johnson's *The Assassination of Robert F. Kennedy,* although flawed by the lack of an index.

The LAPD's version of events is *Special Unit Senator: The Investigation of the Assassination of Senator Robert F. Kennedy* (1970), Robert A. Houghton with Theodore Taylor. Moldea is the chief defender of Thane Cesar, and Ayton is the major Sirhan Sirhan as "lone gunman" theorist.

Autobiographies consulted here include *Best That I Can Be* (1998), Rafer Johnson with Philip Goldberg; *Coroner* (1983), Thomas T. Noguchi, M.D; *The Defense Never Rests* (1971), F. Lee Bailey with Harvey Aronson; *Next to Hughes* (1992), Robert Maheu and Richard Hack; and *Rosey: The Gentle Giant* (1986), Roosevelt Grier. Books consulted on John Frankenheimer and his career include *The Films of John Frankenheimer* (1998), Gerald Pratley; *John Frankenheimer: Interviews, Essays, and Profiles* (2013), edited by Stephen B. Armstrong; and *A Little Solitaire: John Frankenheimer and American Film* (2011), edited by Murray Pomerance and R. Barton Palmer. Books consulted on Drew Pearson and Jack Anderson include *The Anderson*

Papers (1973), Jack Anderson with George Clifford; *Drew Pearson* (1973), Oliver Pilat; and *The Columnist* (2022), Donald A. Ritchie.

Books used in addition to the Maheu autobiography that pertain to Howard Hughes include *Age of Secrets* (2022, second edition), Gerald Bellet; *Howard Hughes: His Life and Madness* (1979), Donald L. Barlett & James B. Steele; *Howard Hughes: Power, Paranoia & Palace Intrigue* (2008), Geoff Schumacher; *Howard Hughes: The Hidden Years* (1976), James Phelan; and *Howard Hughes: The Untold Story* (1996), Peter Harry Brown & Pat H. Broeske.

Material on Los Angeles and California includes the WPA Guides to both as well as *Are the Stars Out Tonight? The Story of the Famous Ambassador & Cocoanut Grove* (1980), Margaret Tante Burk; *Great American Hotels: Luxury Palaces and Elegant Resorts* (1991), James Tackach (text), Alan Briere and Lynn Radeka (photographs); and *If These Walls Could Rock: 50 Years at the Legendary Sunset Marquis Hotel* (2013), Craig Allen Williams and Mark Alan Rosenthal.

Films referred to include *Bobby Kennedy for President* (2018), a four-part Netflix documentary directed by Dawn Porter; *Conspiracy?* (History Channel) (2004), "The Robert F. Kennedy Assassination"; *Evidence of Revision: The Assassination of America*, "Part 4: The RFK Assassination as Never Seen Before" (2006), produced by Sarah Miller; *RFK Must Die: The Assassination of Bobby Kennedy* (2007), directed by Shane O'Sullivan; *Second Dallas: Who Killed RFK?* (2009), directed by Massimo Mazzucco; and *The Second Gun* (1973), directed by Theodore Charach.

Online I looked at numerous articles, including (but not limited to) "The Assassination of Robert Kennedy, as told 50 Years Later," Colleen Shalby, *L.A. Times*; "New Evidence Implicates

CIA, LAPD, FBI and Mafia in Elaborate Plan to Prevent RFK From Ever Reaching the White House," Jeremy Kuzmarov, *Covert Action Magazine*; "The Robert Kennedy Assassination," Rex Bradford, Mary Ferrell Foundation; "Survivor of RFK Assassination Is Okay with Parole for Sirhan Sirhan—and He Still Questions What Happened," Loria Rozsa, *People*; "RFK assassination witness tells CNN: There was a second shooter," Michael Martinez and Brad Johnson, *CNN*; "Re-examining the RFK assassination," R. Emmett Tyrrell Jr., *Washington Times*; "Did L.A. police and prosecutors bungle the Bobby Kennedy assassination?", Tom Jackman, *Washington Post*; "Robert F. Kennedy thought JFK was killed because of him," Irish Central Staff, *Irish Central*; "Could Robert F. Kennedy's Assassin Have Been 'Hypno-Programmed'", Eli MacKinnon, *Live Science*; "Robert F Kennedy was assassinated by Thane Eugene Cesar, declares RFK Jr," Chris Spargo, UK *Daily Mail*; "Pete Hamill's Eyewitness Account of Robert Kennedy's Assassination," *Village Voice* Archives; "New Life in Sirhan Defense," John Hiscock, *L.A. Times*; and "William Joseph Bryan: Sirhan's Handler and Set-up Maestro Extraordinaire," Russ Winter, *Winter Watch*.

My thanks to the many websites from which I drew information about locations, including (but not limited to) thelosangelesbeat.com (restaurants); hollywoodhangover.com (Classic Cat); themobmuseum.org (Caesars Palace); vintagelasvegas.com (Pussycat a' Go-Go); and urbanist.com (Survival Town).

Also helpful was "My Sony the Doctor (William J. Bryan, M.D.)," David Slavitt, *Esquire*, October 1970. I also wish to credit the poem, *Robert Kennedy's Final Day, June 4, 1968*, by Ed Sanders. My longtime research associate, George Hagenauer, read the book and provided notes. Thanks to my buddy Paul Bishop, a real cop and true friend. My good friend (and comic legend) Dave Thomas, my collaborator on the novel *The Many Lives of Jimmy Leighton* (2021), provided information and support.

Thanks as always to my friend and agent, Dominick Abel, who in 1981 took me on as a client after reading *True Detective* in manuscript. The Titan Books staff—including but not limited to Vivian Cheung, Nick Landau, Laura Price, Paul Gill and Andrew Sumner—has been supportive throughout. Nate Heller and I thank you.

Barbara Collins—my wife, best friend and valued collaborator—read each chapter even while she was working on her draft of our next *Antiques* novel. She is as lovely today as she was on our 1968 Chicago honeymoon and that is not an exaggeration. But I couldn't have guessed then what a great sounding board and editor she would become—not to mention wonderful writer herself.